Other Titles By

Giselle Carmichael

Shundasia Darpe!

Arms of a Stranger

Giselle Carmichael

Parker Publishing, LLC

Noire Passion is an imprint of Parker Publishing, LLC.

Copyright © 2007 by DeAnn Austin

Published by Parker Publishing, LLC
12523 Limonite Avenue, Suite #440-438
Mira Loma, California 91752
www.parker-publishing.com

ISBN 978-1-60043-020-6

First Edition

Manufactured in the United States of America

Cover Design by Chance Designs

Dedication

Arms of a Stranger is dedicated to the numerous men and women who left their lives behind to volunteer in the rebuilding effort along the Mississippi Gulf Coast. We couldn't do it without you. Thank you and God Bless.

Chapter One

Throw another bundle of shingles up here," Simone Ladner yelled down from the roof she was working on. Hurricane Katrina had devastated the Biloxi neighborhood she had grown up in. Like everyone along the Coast, she was doing her part to rebuild the area, one house, one block, one neighborhood at a time. Six months after the life-altering storm, things were nearly as bad as the day the storm washed ashore, but with the influx of volunteers from all across the country, as well as internationally, progress was being made.

"Rather than throw them, how about I give you a hand here?" a deep voice replied.

Simone paused, because she didn't recognize the voice. If she had heard it before, she was sure she would have remembered the deep sonorous sound. Footsteps vibrating the ladder alerted her that the owner of the voice was indeed bringing up the roofing shingles. She sat back on her haunches to await the delivery.

The February temperature was mild, the sky sunny and bright, just the type of day the people of the Coast needed to clean up and rebuild their lives.

A blond head appeared just over the roof's edge. Two plastic wrapped bags of shingles rested across his broad shoulders. She was always awed by the display of physical strength in the workers. One bundle of asphalt shingles could weigh anywhere from 70 to 140 pounds. The scene was repeated from sun up to sun down all up and down the coastline. She considered herself a strong woman, had proven it to herself since returning home and getting involved in the rebuilding process. However, carrying stacks of roofing shingles on her shoulders and back the way these guys did was way beyond her capacity.

"Here, let me take one of those," she said, scooting toward the ladder and sliding one bundle off his shoulder onto the roof. Turning again to the new arrival, who was built like the retired football player, Howie Long, she grabbed the other bundle and heaved it beside her. Then as she looked at him to offer her thanks for the help, she found herself staring into the greenest eyes the Good Lord had ever created. Something deep inside her stirred to life as her stomach clenched with desire and the heat of sexual awareness rushed from her toes to the top of her head. She slid back along the tar paper to give the big man room as he climbed from the ladder to the roof.

He was really big, Simone thought as he sat beside her. Wide, heavily muscled shoulders bunched underneath his denim shirt. His forearms were equally muscled and tan from the Mississippi sun. His hands, large and strong, effortlessly ripped away the plastic wrap around the shingles. The thought of those hands on her body nearly caused her to forget where she was. Simone shook her head to clear away the thought. The roof was not the place to be wigging out.

The stranger introduced himself, holding out his large hand in greeting. "Hi, I'm Keithen Knight."

"Simone Ladner." She took his hand and watched as hers was swallowed whole.

Keithen studied the small hand within his with curiosity. Although small and definitely feminine, there was strength in the grasp. There was also something magnetic about it, because it took sheer willpower to release it. As he met the warm cocoa-colored eyes and friendly smile of the beautiful woman returning his questioning gaze, he was sure she'd felt something as well.

"Nice to meet you, Simone." He released her hand and sat back looking at her. She had delicate features set in a creamy dark chocolate face. "Where should I start?" Keithen watched, spellbound, as she removed the baseball cap she wore. A shoulder-length ponytail fell free, curling around her neck.

"You can take this end, I'll work over there," Simone replied, and crawled back to where she had stopped working the day before.

"So where are you from, Keithen?"

"I guess my accent gave me away."

Simone glanced at him and laughed. "More like the lack of one."

"I'm a Native Californian. Born and raised in San Francisco." He smiled at her with pride. "I live on Belvedere Island. Ever heard of it?"

"Can't say that I have."

"It's a beautiful island across the bay with hilltop views of the San Francisco and the Golden Gate Bridge."

"Sounds beautiful," she replied.

"And you?" His green eyes watched her efficient movements with admiration as she laid a course of shingles and nailed them in place. He followed her actions and got to work as well.

Laughing, Simone paused and looked over. "Don't be deceived by the East Coast brogue. I was born and raised right here, though I lived in New York for four years."

"The storm brought you home?" He swung the hammer.

"Yes, it did. When I arrived back in the neighborhood not one house was standing on the block. I couldn't believe it. I grew up here and yet I got disoriented traveling around town because so much was gone. Landmarks I took for granted were nowhere to be found."

"I had to come," Keithen told her. "After weeks of watching the destruction, I knew I had to get involved."

"Well, on behalf of the people of the Coast, thank you."

Keithen nodded. He was humbled by the people he had met. In the face of all they had lost and the daily difficulties they continued to face, they were kind, giving, and so very thankful for any assistance. He and Simone concentrated on the work before them, laying shingles and nailing them down. The rhythmic pounding filled the air like music.

On hands and knees the pair worked from one end to the other, until their half of the roof was completely covered. The work was exhausting and dirty, but doing it gave Simone and Keithen a sense of pride. The team on the other side was nearing the ridge, so while they waited, Simone climbed down the ladder and quickly returned with water for everyone. She tossed each man a bottle then straddled the ridge.

Keithen unscrewed the cap to his bottle of water and took a long, thirsty drink, his eyes looking over to where Simone sat. She was just as dirty and sweaty as he and the other guys on the roof, and yet he couldn't take his eyes off her. Long thick lashes framed almond shaped eyes.

Simone felt Keithen watching her and observed him with curiosity. "So what do you do for a living, Keithen?" She rolled the cold bottle under her neck to cool herself.

"I'm a developer," he responded without explanation. He felt no need to tell her he was a millionaire developer of some of the most exclusive residential neighborhoods in the country, from Malibu to West Palm Beach

"As in residential developments?"

"Exactly, so you see, I'm familiar with a hammer and nails.

"Your talents are definitely needed around here." She downed the last of her water, then tossed the bottle over the side and returned to work on the ridge. Another hour went by before Simone checked her watch. She had to get over to the church. "That's it for me today, guys," she yelled to the crew on the roof. "I'll see you all later."

Keithen watched as Simone gathered her tools and headed to the ladder. As she drew along beside him, he stopped her. "Leaving so soon?"

"I'm afraid so. Hope to see you again, Keithen Knight," Simone said continuing to the ladder.

"Likewise." Keithen watched as she disappeared from sight. He could hear her saying her good-byes down below. He watched as she climbed into a late model black Chevy Silverado and drove off.

Simone stopped at the corner stop sign and glanced back at the Tyler house. Keithen Knight's big form was easy to spot on the roof, looking in her direction. He was ruggedly handsome and something about the man appealed to her. Perhaps it was his easy warm smile, or those captivating green eyes that looked right at her. Or maybe it was the kindness radiating from him. She smiled, thinking how the storm had brought all types of people from different walks of life together.

She turned at the corner and drove what should have been the few blocks to the church. Instead she ran into a roadblock. Another debris removal crew was picking up the remains of someone's home.

She placed the truck into reverse and backed to the intersection, then selected an alternate route. Driving along, she couldn't help but notice the abundance of plastic clinging to the trees and fences that remained. She wondered for the hundredth time where it all came from. Turning at the next corner, she was astonished by the debris pushed to the edge of the street forming mountains on both sides of the road. The stench of rotting food and molding furniture permeated the air. She increased her speed, trying to outrun the encroaching depression and make up time for the detour. Her grandmother would be looking for her and she wasn't prepared to receive a lecture about being late from Ruth Ladner.

She pulled into the winding driveway of East Biloxi Baptist Church, drove around back and parked. She grabbed her duffle bag of fresh clothing, and headed over to the large tent that had been erected on the grounds as a kitchen to feed the volunteers and people in need. She spotted her grandmother on the serving line for the noon meal and waved.

"I'm headed to the kitchen to start dinner," she shouted to her grandmother.

"How did it go today?" Ruth asked.

"Good. We accomplished a great deal."

"Did you get the roof on at Lorna's place?" Standing at only five feet, the coffee-brown woman, weighing no more than one hundred and twenty pounds, possessed a powerful presence that demanded respect. "They were almost finished with the ridge when I left."

"Good. Then you and the crew can move inside." Her wise eyes set in a thin face blessed by the passage of time held her granddaughter's. A black hairnet held her gray curls in place.

"Yes ma'am," Simone responded, knowing an order when she heard one. "We'll have Miss Lorna back in her house just as fast as we can. I better get cleaned up and changed into fresh clothing, Grandma."

"See you later, baby." Ruth watched her beautiful granddaughter walk away. She was so very proud of her. A professional chef trained at the Culinary Institute of America, Simone had given up her dream of restaurant ownership to return home and pitch in with the rebuilding effort. She had arrived driving on old work truck, loaded down with building supplies and much needed cleaning items, never once asking for repayment. A generous expression of love like that would definitely be rewarded.

Entering the church, Simone headed directly to the small bathroom. Locking the door, she shed her clothes and stepped into the small shower. She thanked whoever had had the foresight to include it in the renovations. When she was clean and dressed in fresh clothing, she headed to the large kitchen to work her magic. Two other church members had volunteered to assist her with preparations for the Sunday evening meal. While the other women talked, Simone thought about Keithen Knight and wondered where he would be eating.

Like clockwork the workers began arriving just before dark. They were exhausted and hungry, and looking for a hot meal. The men and women who had been in the area for several weeks or months knew Simone would be cooking Sunday dinner, which equated to a feast.

The dinner hour was for more than just eating, it was a time for visiting as well. Friendships had been developed and as the volunteer workers progressed down the serving line, sociable bantering went on. Simone enjoyed talking to the men and women. It was her way of gauging the rebuilding progress in the various neighborhoods. As she dished up her special macaroni made with seven types of cheese, a thunderous voice reached her ears. Her heart fluttered as she glanced down the line of bodies and spotted Keithen Knight. He was looking right at her, and the world disappeared leaving only the two of them.

"Pulling double duty I see," Keithen said when he stood in front of Simone. To his surprise he was excited to see her again. She was lovely, although younger than he usually liked. He held his tray out to her while admiring her blemish free complexion. It looked soft and smooth, making him want to caress a finger down the line of her high cheekbones. Her nose was slightly long and flared at the nostrils. But it was the brilliant white smile that she returned that had his blood pumping.

"Sunday is my day to volunteer in the kitchen. My grandmother works the lunch hour and I replace her at dinner," she told him. Taking into account his size, she gave him a little extra of everything. "Did you finish the roof?"

"We sure did. Tomorrow the inside work can begin on the Tyler house."

"I know Miss Lorna will be happy to hear the news."

"Miss Lorna?"

"Lorna Tyler. It's a Southern thing," she explained with a smile.

"Will I see you tomorrow?" he asked returning the smile. He quickly took note of her height. He guessed she was about five foot seven. At six feet, he preferred a woman with a little height. He silently scolded himself for the thought. He had just met the woman. He was in Biloxi to work, not to notice beautiful women.

"Most definitely. I'm assigned to the Tyler house and I'll be working there until it's ready for Miss Lorna to move in."

"Guess I'll see you there then." Keithen smiled as he moved away from the serving line and went in search of a table. Spotting the crew that he had worked with that day, he joined the men.

Simone watched Keithen as he walked away. His stride was powerful and sexy. *Sexy, now where did that come from?* She quickly pushed the thought away. . She was there to do a job, not search for a man, although if she were looking, Keithen Knight would be one heck of a find.

The line finally slowed to a trickle. She was ordered by the other women on the line to grab a plate and eat. She hadn't stopped long enough to eat anything substantial since that morning and she was indeed starving. With her plate loaded, she turned, searching for somewhere to sit. The volunteers liked to linger after dinner, socializing, so seating was limited. She spotted one seat available at the corner table where Keithen was sitting. As though sensing her looking in his direction, he glanced up and waved her over.

Simone smiled as she made her way to the table. She greeted the other men of the crew as she sat across from Keithen. After bowing her head and saying grace, she looked up right into his mesmerizing eyes.

"The guys here tell me you're responsible for this delicious meal."

"It's nothing," she responded dismissively.

Keithen could tell she was a little embarrassed by the attention. "The guys tell me you're a chef?"

Simone blushed. "Yes I am, although what I've been serving here in the tent is a far cry from my usual cuisine. The work crews aren't interested in presentation and entrees they can't pronounce, or that fail to cover the plate. They're looking for delicious hearty food that fills the stomach as well as comforts the soul."

Keithen smiled and nodded. He understood exactly what she was saying. How many expensive meals had he paid for only to return home to make a sandwich? "Well, I definitely appreciate your style of cooking."

"Thank you. So, Keithen, how long have you been here on the Coast?" She got down to eating her own food. Hungry as she was, it took all her willpower not to shovel the cornbread topped beef stew with savory broth into her mouth. If there had been any other man sitting across from her, she probably would have, but something about Keithen made her keenly aware of being a woman and wanting to act ladylike.

"Three months, off and on. I was working with the urban developers initially." He enjoyed watching her eat. It had been a long time since he had been around a woman who wasn't afraid of gaining a pound, not that an additional pound or two would hurt Simone. For her height, she was slightly built.

Simone chuckled, but said nothing.

"What's so humorous?" Keithen arched a brow and continued to stare at her until she answered.

Putting down her fork, Simone sat back in her chair and looked at him. "I'm not unappreciative of the developers' efforts and intentions; it's just that I believe a lot of what has been offered is useless. People who had homes before the storm want homes now. They're not interested in grand designs of condos or lofts. We Southerners like our own piece of soil."

Keithen listened with great interest. He had heard this said repeatedly by the locals and yet many of the planners had ignored it. "What I hear you saying is that the people want houses."

"Yes. Affordable houses, to be specific. Not the expensive condos with all the bells and whistles, or houses priced out of this world."

"I tend to agree with you," Keithen replied, enjoying the conversation. "So, Simone, what was a Southern girl doing in the fast paced city of New York?" His eyes moved over her face to rest on her smiling lips.

"I attended culinary school there and ventured into the restaurant business with a friend from the Institute. I used money I inherited from my mother's parents to join him in the partnership. It took us about two solid years of researching and planning before we opened. We served that pretty to the eye cuisine."

"Was it a success?" He had no doubt that it was.

"Yes, business was good."

"Will you be returning?"

"No. I sold my half of the business to my partner, Mason." She picked up her fork and continued to eat while they talked.

"Why would you do that?" Keithen asked, dumbfounded.

Simone laughed at the expression on his face. Obviously, he thought she was crazy for giving up the restaurant. "I needed to be home, and I knew the money I made from the sale could purchase a great deal of supplies. And besides, I'm not a big city girl."

"That's the most selfless act that I've heard. You're an amazing woman."

Simone shrugged. "Look around you. People down here are doing far more than that, including you." She began to clean the area around her, brushing crumbs off the table and picking up discarded napkins.

"You don't take compliments very well, do you?" Keithen grinned.

Simone laughed as she stood and gathered her plate and utensils. She waited for Keithen to do the same. He fell in step beside her, and at the trash can they deposited their Styrofoam plates. "It's been great talking with you tonight, Keithen, but I've got to get the serving pans to the kitchen and help with the cleanup." She looked up at him. She had really enjoyed spending time with him tonight.

"How about I give you a hand with those pans?" Keithen offered. For reasons unknown, he wasn't ready to call it a night.

Assessing eyes settled on him. "Sure, I'd appreciate the assistance, although I can't imagine why you would want to hang around here with me."

Keithen released a robust laugh. "Are you kidding? A woman who can cook the way you do and swing a hammer is someone I'd like to know better."

Simone playfully punched him in the arm. Her small fist made contact with solid muscle. "Well, it's your evening." She returned to the serving line and began removing the stainless steel serving pans. Keithen followed her lead.

"So where are you bunking?"

"I pulled a trailer behind me this time when I came to the Coast. I learned the first time about the shortage of housing and hotel vacancies. It's parked around back," he answered, motioning in the direction of the volunteer trailer park on the grounds of the church. The constant rotation of volunteers pulling trailers was a scene repeated all over the Coast. Church grounds, city parks, and recreational facilities were all being used to house volunteers. "My crew and I have been moving around the city working different projects."

"I guess that explains why our paths never crossed."

"Well, now that they have, you'll definitely be seeing me."

Simone arrived home a little after nine. Entering the modest three bedroom home, she followed the path around boxes into the bedroom. More boxes lined the wall in there as well. She had purchased her home shortly after arriving in the city. In the skyrocketing and desperate housing market after Katrina, the older ranch style house had cost far more than it was worth, but she needed somewhere to lay her head and still have enough money for building supplies. Her parents had taken in her grandmother after her home had been washed from the foundation and destroyed, so space was limited there. She walked into the bathroom and turned on the water in the bathtub. Sprinkling in her favorite bubble bath, she inhaled the melon scent and felt herself start to relax. She brushed her teeth while the tub filled up. When it was sufficiently filled, she turned the water off, removed her clothes, and slid into the warm sudsy water, leaning back. A sigh of sheer pleasure escaped her lips as she stretched out. Each evening she came home exhausted from the hard physical labor, but no longer were her muscles sore and achy.

When she got out of the tub, she stood before the bathroom mirror admiring her new toned body. She suddenly wondered what Keithen would think. *What the devil are you thinking? The man could be married with a family back in California.* She grabbed her nightgown and slid it over her head. Turning out the bathroom light, she went to her bedroom, pausing only to set the alarm on her clock before climbing into bed. Then she switched the lamp off and lay in the dark thinking about her day.

Chapter Two

Simone arrived at the Tyler house the next morning with Miss Lorna and Grandma Ruth in tow. As she walked to the back of her truck to unload her tools, a large green pickup pulled up behind her. The California license plate on the front of the vehicle, hinted at the driver. A smile instantly spread across her face as she and Keithen made eye contact through the windshield. Three other men she hadn't seen before were in the truck with him. She continued to unload her tools as well as chairs for the two women.

"Who's that, baby?" Ruth stood with Lorna their heads together watching the tall blond man as he climbed out of the pickup.

"His name is Keithen Knight. He's a volunteer from California. I met him yesterday."

"He sure is a big one," Miss Lorna whispered to Ruth.

"Good morning, ladies," Keithen greeted the three women.

"Morning," Simone returned. "Miss Lorna, Grandma Ruth, I'd like for you to meet Keithen Knight." Simone shifted the heavy toolbox to her other hand.

"It's a pleasure to meet you ladies," he said, shaking both women's hands. He then reached for the toolbox Simone carried. "I'll take this." Their eyes connected as his hand brushed against hers. A sudden wave of heat unrelated to the weather rushed over her.

Simone didn'Babt relinquish the toolbox right away. "I'm quite capable of carrying my toolbox."

Keithen smiled sexily as he pried her fingers from around the handle. "I have no doubt you are capable of anything you set your mind to, but for right now, you don't have to carry this thing."

Simone finally released the handle. She felt like a schoolgirl having her books carried by the high school jock. The thought caused the corners of her mouth to turn up. She fell in step beside him, headed toward the house. Remembering her grandmother and Miss Lorna, she turned. "Set your chairs under the tree. I'll see you later."

"Sure, baby," Ruth responded. She and Lorna did exactly that, watching as she and Keithen disappeared into the house. "What do you make of that, Lorna?"

"Child, I think that big man has got something else on his mind besides my house."

"That's what I'm thinking, too."

Lorna voiced concern. "You think Simone can handle him?"

"I brought down big Leon Ladner," Ruth laughed.

As the day progressed, Keithen indeed had Simone on his mind. They worked in the same room installing drywall. He silently admired her ability to handle it like a professional. She measured, cut, nailed, taped, and mudded as if she had been doing it all her life. Other than her hair, which was protected by a New Orleans Saints cap, she was covered from head to toe in fine white dust. But she didn't complain. Instead, she moved to the next room and started the process all over again. He didn't know a single woman back home who would dare to be seen covered in dust, let alone sweat. He found her to not only be capable, but refreshing. He appreciated the way she handled herself around the guys as well. She joked and laughed with them, but maintained a demeanor that demanded respect. And the crew honored that demand. They were mindful of her presence when telling their raunchy jokes or swearing. They were also very protective of her as well. Keithen had caught several suspicious glances when he walked in with her that morning.

He knew why the men wanted to protect and do for her. Though she had proven herself as one of the crew, physically able of performing the work, one sensed a femininity that couldn't be hidden by the dust and sweat. Nor could a man ignore how incredibly beautiful she was. Her big brown eyes looked right at a person and made them feel like the most important person in the world. For a man that was important.

Keithen rushed from the room, giving himself a chance to clear his thoughts. He was thinking of Simone in terms of man and woman, not friend and friend, which was all there was between them. His life was in California and hers would remain in Biloxi. He had a multimillion dollar business to run. When the need for sex hit him, willing women were readily available. Never had he thought of a committed relationship. *Until now.* Her outgoing, get involved spirit, and giving nature appealed to him. Those qualities combined with her physical beauty could spell trouble. He slipped back into the room and returned to work.

He had watched his friends' loveless marriages stagger on solely because of money, even though they were completely miserable. He didn't want a life like that, and therefore had no intention of getting serious about anyone. His current involvement with Courtney Bounds had lasted too long already. What began as social escorting had evolved into a poor excuse of a relationship. They didn't agree on much. Hell, they didn't even talked any more and when they did the conversation was superficial. Courtney wasn't interested in his dreams or views on life, only her own wants and desires took precedence. His trip to the Coast had been cause for argument, as she didn't understand his reason for going. He had noticed signs of her thinking in the long term, using words like *us* and *we*. When he returned home, he would have to let her down easy, make her see they weren't right for each other and had no future.

However, as Simone glanced across the room at him, his heart responded with a jolt of excitement. The sight of her this morning had placed a smile on his face as big as the state of Texas. But he had made decisions about his life and a woman like Simone was nowhere in it. She valued family and would one day want one of her own. Through her actions, she demonstrated that she loved deeply. She was the type of woman a man pledged his life to.

"Hey, what's on your mind?" Simone asked, noticing the faraway look in his eyes. He had been staring at her, although she was sure he hadn't been aware of doing so.

Keithen snapped to attention. "I was admiring your abilities. Who taught you to hang drywall?"

"Carlos did." She motioned toward the Latino man in the next room. "He's a great teacher."

"I can tell by the quality of your work." He smiled at her and turned back to work on his own section of wall. He should have been finished awhile ago, but had allowed himself to become distracted by thoughts of her.

"Tell me about yourself," Simone requested as she also went back to work. She had enjoyed talking with him last night. This morning he had been rather quiet and contemplative. She wondered if he was missing home, or perhaps someone at home.

"Well, I told you that I was from the San Francisco area."

"I've always wanted to visit."

Keithen looked directly at her. "Then you should. I'd love to show you around."

"Perhaps I will. So tell me about your business." She plastered mud over the tape on the drywall, enjoying the sound of his deep voice.

"I develop exclusive neighborhoods across the country."

Simone paused to look at him. "Why exclusive neighborhoods?"

"It's what I know." Keithen kept working without looking at her. In the face of the destruction around them, his way of life seemed extravagant. Not one home had been left standing in this neighborhood. Some families were forced to live in tents on their property while waiting for assistance, and back home he had six thousand square feet for one person.

Simone turned over his words. "Is that your way of saying you're wealthy?"

Keithen continued to mud as he tried to decide how to answer. He liked Simone, responded to her like no woman before, and he would hate to see her change toward him because he had money.

"Yes, it is."

Simone waited for him to say more. There had to be more. "That's all you're going to say?"

"I tell you what. Let's finish in here and while we're eating lunch we can talk about it." Keithen needed time to decide how to explain what he was feeling, had been feeling for quite some time now. It had taken this massive storm and the havoc that it brought to make him take a long, hard look at his life. He had become spoiled and thoughtless, focused on making money and out witting his nemesis, Andy Haywood. The family values that he had been reared with were forgotten. He had chosen to live in the fast lane, surrounding himself with all that money could buy, friends and women included, and yet he wasn't happy. He didn't know exactly what was missing in his life, but knew something was. When he tried expressing his feelings to Courtney, she had laughed and turned the conversation back on herself. He hadn't mentioned it again. Then he had watched the news coverage of the hurricane, and of people sleeping in tents and others rummaging through mounds of donated clothing dumped in a parking lot. He had been ashamed. The purchase price of the painting over his fireplace could have paid for clothing and numerous new homes in the destroyed area. He had realized in that moment he had a civic responsibility to do something of importance with his wealth.

Simone sensed his discomfort. "Look, I was being nosey. You don't have to tell me anything. I'm simply glad for your help." She returned to work, throwing all of her energy into the mudding process.

Being back home had caused her to forget how private people from large cities could be. People along the Coast were open with their neighbors and friends. It wasn't much that didn't get discussed on a porch or in the grocery store. She had allowed herself to think of Keithen as a friend, but he wasn't. He was a stranger who had come to town to lend assistance. When he grew tired or bored, whichever came first, he would return to his wealthy lifestyle in Belvedere, never to think of her again. But she knew for a fact that she would think of him. The mere sight of him had awakened desire inside of her. His gentlemanly manners were sweet and refreshing. He was a hard worker, putting in numerous hours of back breaking work, now to know that he was a man of means who could have written a check instead, really impressed her. No, she wouldn't be forgetting him anytime soon.

A little after noon, Simone removed her gloves and stepped outside. She spotted her grandmother and Miss Lorna still under the tree with the cooler from her truck. They were eating the chicken salad sandwiches she had prepared for lunch. She removed her cap, swatting at her clothes with it to remove the fine white drywall dust. She cut a path across the yard toward her truck, where she carried a container of water for cleaning. Opening the nozzle, she caught the sun-warmed water in her hands and washed her face, then her hands. Turning the water off, she reached for the clean towel tied to the handle and rubbed it across her face. When she lowered the towel, Keithen was standing in front of her. They hadn't talked since their earlier conversation. She had finished her job in that room and moved to another.

She reminded herself that he was wealthy and probably had a different upbringing. Where she had been raised in a close knit community, with everybody knowing each other's business, Keithen's life had probably been more guarded. He definitely hadn't appreciated her prying questions.

"Can we grab a bite and talk?" Keithen asked. Her withdrawal had been obvious earlier and was even more apparent now.

"I'm going to sit with Grandma and Miss Lorna. I'm sure you want to sit with your friends." She tossed the towel in the back of the truck, preparing to leave, but Keithen reached out and stopped her from walking away. Simone's eyes rose to his.

"You're my friend and I'd really like to share lunch with you." He held her gaze, wishing she could see the truth. He very much wanted to share his personal discovery with her, because he knew she would understand.

She grabbed sandwiches from the cooler, tossing him two along with two large bottles of water. She led him to the property next door.

"Carlos told me this was your grandmother's home." He looked around, once again amazed that the only visible sign of a house ever being there was the foundation and the stairs leading to nowhere. They sat on those stairs to share lunch.

"Yes, it was. I spent many hours and summers sitting right here with my friends dreaming about my future. She taught me about the importance of a good education being the key to all my dreams, and then brought me back to earth by having me shell peas from her garden. It was also where my grandmother taught me about the Civil Rights Movement and responsibility to my community. Those were great times." She smiled with remembrance.

Keithen toyed with the cap on the bottle as he thought about the difference in their childhoods. He had grown up knowing he would join the family business, and attend his father's alma mater. He had felt no pressure to achieve, and although his parents tried to make him aware of the plight of others, he had ignored most of what they said. Instead he had become apart of the young social elite who thought of no one but themselves. "I didn't mean to shut down on you earlier, but my life is so far removed from here."

"I know you must find us boring and our lives simple." Simone suddenly felt very uncomfortable in his presence.

Keithen grabbed her hand and turned her to face him. "That's just it, I don't find the people here boring or the lifestyle simple. I find it sincere and loving. We volunteers are strangers to you, and you all treat us like old friends. You welcome us into your families."

"You volunteers have come to help us rebuild our lives making you a part of this community. None of you had to do it."

"Let me explain how the people in my circle would look upon volunteers coming to our aid if we needed help. We would think it was no less than what they were supposed to do. We have placed ourselves behind our gated communities, high above the average man, to live our perfect little lives. We're as fake as they come, from our personalities to our friends, body parts, and marriages. Money rules every aspect of our lives," he said cynically.

"So money can't buy happiness? Is that what you're telling me?" She studied the tiny frown lines around his mouth. Each word from his lips had been said as though it left a bad taste.

"That's what I'm telling you. I've enjoyed my weeks here in Biloxi, sleeping in a trailer, working from sunup to sundown, talking and getting to know people I never would have noticed before."

"Like me."

His eyes roamed the surface of her face. "Something tells me that I would have noticed you."

Simone blushed, before responding, "Your cynicism is unfounded because when you watched the news on our devastation, you noticed the pain and suffering, and came to help."

Keithen looked at her and laughed. "Are you trying to tell me that I'm not that shallow?" His amused eyes caressed her face. He found he enjoyed looking at her.

"I see something you obviously don't see. You left a perfect life to come to the aid of strangers, and that exemplifies humanity." She squeezed the hand that still held hers. "There's more to you than money, Keithen Knight. I see it in your eyes."

He locked gazes with her, hoping to see what she saw when she looked at him. "I like myself here, Simone. I've come to realize all that stuff back in California is simply stuff, and I can do without it. I've enjoyed meeting real people with down to earth values, and have them like me for me, not what I have or can give them. Our conversations have been meaningful and about something other than making money. The focus has been on others. I've even enjoyed getting my hands dirty." He smiled shyly. "I'm happier here in Biloxi than I have been in a long time."

"You sound like a man taking stock of his life." She noticed his thumb stroked hers intimately. The feel of his caress was nice, but stirred emotions inside her, she was sure he didn't intend. She removed her hand and placed it in her lap.

Keithen followed her movements and raised his eyes to meet hers. They were overly bright with an emotion that he wasn't sure he was reading correctly. Touching her had felt natural. The contrast in their skin tones had been an afterthought as his mind had been focused on the softness of her skin. He had wondered how her body would feel next to his.

"I have been taking stock, and I've decided changes are in order."

"Don't be hasty and don't allow our plight here to make you feel guilty about your lifestyle. You have a right to enjoy what you have accomplished." Simone looked down the street, very aware of the empty lots that stretched for blocks.

"What was life here like before the storm?" Keithen asked, wanting to see it through her eyes. He watched as a smile spread across her face and the years fell away.

"It was wonderful. Summers are hot and thick with humidity, and plenty of sunshine. Our winters are more like early spring than a real winter. People move slow around here, even with the casinos. Families are close and church is an important part of the community. Most people know each other or at least some of the same people, which I guess when you think about it, can be good and bad. Secrets don't last long, that's for sure."

"Water is an important part of our lives as well. Many of us make a living from it, and the rest of us enjoy its beauty and the activities around it. Fishing, jet skiing, parasailing, and boating are all popular here. What's really unique is our Christmas celebration. It's called Christmas on the Water!"

"What goes on?" Keithen asked, enjoying listening to her voice.

"The boats are all covered with Christmas lights and decorations for a parade on the water. Traditionally, Santa arrives on the last boat. Families line the beach to watch the procession. It's really a wonderful experience."

Keithen heard the joy in her voice and saw the childhood excitement in her eyes. "I'd like to see it someday." He wondered if he would ever come this way again, after his volunteer time was over. Then he looked at Simone, and knew he had a reason to return. No matter how much he told himself they were only new friends, he knew he lied, because she had touched him in a way no one had in quite a while.

Simone returned his gaze. "I hope you return someday after the city is back on its feet. Perhaps return for Mardi Gras or the Fourth of July."

"I know about Mardi Gras, although I've never attended, but what happens down here for the Fourth of July?"

"Concerts are held out on one of the barrier islands. Everyone enjoys the show from their boats or the beach of the island. Also, one of the local radio stations hosts a cookout at Jones Park. People pour out of the neighborhoods to celebrate together. Then at night the casinos put on a spectacular fireworks show that has everyone lined along the beach, staring into the night sky."

"I've noticed a theme of community and family in everything you've described. When I envision it, I see sunshine and lazy days of fun,"

Keithen told her with a wistful smile. "Last Fourth of July for me was another boring gathering of fake, self-centered people, gossiping about the latest affair or divorce."

Simone released a warm, feminine laugh drawing his attention to her smiling face. "Surely you know some down-to-earth people."

"Sure I do. Sonny and Rita, my groundskeeper and housekeeper. When I want the unvarnished truth, they give it to me."

Simone sighed as she gathered their lunch trash. She had spent some wonderful moments sharing with him and hated to see it end.

"Simone," a feminine voice called out.

Simone smiled before turning around. She would know that voice anywhere. She ran down the steps, then turned back to Keithen. "Come on, I want to introduce you to someone. Jasmine! Oh my God, it's good to see you." Simone hugged her best friend from high school.

"Mama told me you had come home," Jasmine Clark said. She noticed Keithen standing behind Simone and grew curious. He was looking at her friend with a deep yearning that made her wonder about their relationship.

Simone quickly made introductions and then launched into conversation about the devastation. "Your mother told me you weren't coming back."

Jasmine looked sad as her eyes filled with tears. "I was overwhelmed by the destruction. I didn't know if I had the strength to rebuild and risk another storm, but Bobby and I were both miserable living out of state. This is home. And when Mama told me you had left the big city to return home and help with the cleanup and reconstruction, I knew I could do no less."

Keithen enjoyed listening to and watching the two women. They smiled at each other with honest joy. Jasmine, a toffee-brown woman much shorter than Simone, was equally as beautiful. Her near black eyes held the sadness of one who had lost much, but her stiff spine indicated she was now geared up for a fight. She would no doubt start over right there in Biloxi.

He was amazed by the level of sincerity in their words. When Simone offered to lend her skills to Jasmine's reconstruction effort, he knew she genuinely meant it.

"I'll stick around and help as well, if that's all right with you," Keithen said, wanting to help honest working people.

"Is that all right? Honey, we welcome any help we can get," Jasmine said. "Well, I don't want to hold you guys up. I know Miss Lorna can't wait to get back into her house."

"We'll get together soon," Simone said, then gave her friend another hug.

"It was nice meeting you, Keithen," Jasmine said.

"You too and don't forget to let Simone know when you're ready for us."

"Thanks, I will." She turned and headed back down the sidewalk.

Simone and Keithen returned to work inside the house. They both had a great deal on their mind. For Simone it was the lost look she'd glimpsed in her friend's eyes that stayed on her mind. Jasmine was one of the most upbeat people she knew, and to see her down and nearly beaten was almost more than she could stand.

Keithen was thinking about his empty life. Since arriving in Biloxi, he hadn't missed his home or the long office hours he kept. What he had discovered was his desire to get back to the designing, planning, and implementing process of development. As he had toured the Coast during the course of his volunteering, plenty of ideas had come to him, but he didn't live here or work here. But did that mean he didn't have a responsibility to put his talents to work for the betterment of a community?

Chapter Three

Simone strolled through the mall in Mobile late Saturday evening. It had been a long time since she had taken a day off from her volunteer duties, but she really needed a break. The local mall had yet to open and so she had driven the forty-five minutes to Mobile. She browsed the racks, checking out the latest fashions. She had already made a few purchases, but without a job, she was more selective about her spending. However, as she came to the pretty blue dress hanging in the store display, responsible spending flew right out the window. The dress was beautiful. The wrap style and length would complement her body type. And already owning the perfect shoes to accompany it was the added push she needed to buy it. She left the store happy with her selection. She darted across the concourse to Victoria's Secrets and made several more purchases before leaving the store. Rounding the next corner, she collided with a man coming out another store.

"Oh, excuse me." Her package fell to the floor.

"Simone?" Keithen said, surprised. He reached out to steady her. His heart beat with happiness to see her. She had been on his mind for several days. He had deliberately left his trailer today to avoid sitting around thinking of her. His attraction for her grew each time they were together. Keithen stooped to collect the dropped bag the same time as Simone. His eyes settled on the lacy scraps of undergarments at his feet. An image of Simone standing before him wearing nothing but the delicate bra and thong struck him hard. His gut tightened with longing. Quickly sliding the thong into the overturned shopping bag, he passed the bag to her. Their eyes connected during the awkward exchange. Keithen was the first to remember where they were and stood. "I see we had the same idea." He raised his own shopping bag.

Simone stood, the heat of embarrassment rising to her face. As long as she lived, she would never forget the image of Keithen's large hand palming the blue thong. And the look of desire she'd just witnessed in his gaze had her thinking things she shouldn't. Her eyes zeroed in on the logo of his shopping bag. "I never thought of you as the craft type."

Keithen laughed. "I can't say that I am, but I needed a few supplies for a project I'm working on. Where are you headed?" He was searching for a reason to tag along with her.

"The bookstore. There's a new book I'm dying to read." He looked good in dark jeans. His hair was freshly cut and slightly lighter from the sun. "Care to join me? They sell the best coffee and desserts." She silently encouraged him to say yes.

"Actually that was my next stop. I'd love to join you." Keithen automatically reached for her purchases, adding them to his, and they fell in step together. As they passed a store window, he caught their reflection in the glass and liked what he saw.

"You realize you're always doing that?"

His eyes swung to hers. "Doing what?" He grabbed her by the waist, pulling her close, and out the way of rowdy teenagers. He regrettably dropped his hand once they were clear. Just because he was extremely attracted to Simone didn't mean the feelings were reciprocated. However, with each day that passed, he was hopeful.

"Carrying things for me. You took my toolbox the other day, and now my packages. Do you think I'm weak?"

Keithen released a sexy laugh as he looked at her. "No. I simply like doing things for you."

Simone had to force herself not to sigh with delight. She whispered a soft thank you as they entered the bookstore. They each went their separate way, then met at the register, and made their purchases. The bookstore café was their next stop. After placing their coffee orders along with cheesecake for Simone, they found an available table.

"I never pegged you as a romance reader," Keithen teased. He actually found it endearing.

"Go ahead and make all the jokes that you want. I've heard them before," she responded with a self conscious grin.

"I have none."

"Really? No advice like, 'You know they're not realistic'?"

Keithen shrugged his shoulders. "You're a grown woman. I'm sure you know the difference between fiction and the real thing."

"Do I? God, it's been so long since I've had a date I'm not sure that I do." She took a sip of her coffee.

"So there's no one special in your life?" Keithen asked curiously. He traced the rim of his cup with a finger. "The men of New York must be stupid."

Simone laughed. "Excuse me?"

"You're a beautiful woman with a kind heart, and a chef to boot. They must be stupid."

She giggled, spooning a bite of cheesecake. "What am I going to do with you?"

"There are a few things I can think of," Keithen said without thinking, then feared he might have offended her. "I didn't mean…"

"Didn't you?" Simone responded with raised brows. She enjoyed watching him squirm as he tried to remove his foot from his mouth.

"That depends on whether you're offended."

Simone smiled sexily. "I wasn't."

Her response pleased him more than he expected. It had been quite some time since he had been this attracted to a woman. The realization caused him to take stock of himself and the ramification of pursuing a relationship with her. But that was for later. Right now he was just going to enjoy her company.

"You know, I'm happy to see you taking a day for yourself. You really do work too hard." He reached for his coffee.

"You're probably right, but there is so much to do. When I'm sitting still, I feel like I should be doing something."

"I know what you mean, but you're no good to anyone if you get hurt or fall ill." He knew Simone didn't think of herself as delicate, but she was. Everything about her was feminine and slight.

"And what about you, rich boy? I haven't seen you slack off." She spooned more cheesecake into her mouth.

Keithen chuckled. "This time you're right." He leaned forward, taking her spoon. He scooped up more cheesecake, placing the spoon to her lips. He watched as they parted to receive what he offered. The sight had him thinking things he shouldn't. He shifted in his seat uncomfortably to ease the ache of his groin. When she slowly licked her lips clean, he quickly shoved the spoon into his mouth to prevent himself from groaning out loud. "We'll definitely have to do this again," he said, when they prepared to leave minutes later.

Keithen sat in his trailer working on an idea. He hadn't been this inspired in quite some time or motivated by something other than money. But as the idea began to take shape, he knew he was on to something. He was good at his business. Many had called him one of the best developers in the country. What he needed to do was take a ride out into the surrounding countryside. He needed someone who knew the area. One person instantly came to mind. It didn't take much these days to bring an image of Simone Ladner to the surface.

Everything about the woman appealed to him. He felt like a kid back in high school, mooning over a girl. But Simone wasn't a girl. She was a beautiful, desirable woman whom he had come to consider a friend. However, friendship wasn't the only thing that he wanted from her. He immediately pushed the thought away as he jumped up from his chair. He ran for the door, trying to escape his growing feelings for Simone.

He stepped outside, closed the door and inhaled deeply as he sat down on the wooden steps to collect his thoughts. What did he want from Simone? That was the question he had been wrestling with for the last several days and the very reason he had steered clear of her this last week. But he missed her.

He'd thought of her while he worked at another project. Tomorrow he would be returning to Miss Lorna's house to install the ceramic tile flooring she had chosen. Simone would be there to help him. Just thinking about being alone with her in that house caused his neck to tighten with tension. He needed a good run to ponder his thoughts.

Ten minutes later, dressed in running shorts, Keithen stretched his muscles, then started out. Soon he was in the zone where his mind was clear of clutter. As he passed slab after slab of what had once been someone's home, his future got clearer. He waved to complete strangers as he ran. He'd learned early on people didn't have to know a person to say hello. He tried to remember the last time that he had spoken to his neighbors back home. Thinking about it, he wasn't sure whether he had the same neighbors as when he first moved into his house.

That wasn't how he wanted to live his life. He wanted to speak to his neighbors and know their children. He wanted to go to the grocery store and hear the latest gossip. And he wanted to take the wealth he had been blessed with and use it to ease the suffering of good people. And he would. He turned at the next corner and retraced his steps back to the church. Now was the time to take a good hard look at his personal life.

Not that he had much to examine. There were empty relationships based on sex and money rather than deep emotion. The friendships he maintained were also hollow. The circle of people he socialized with wouldn't come to his aid if his home were destroyed. They wouldn't open their homes or, for that matter, feed him at their table. What they would do was talk about him, the way they had about others who had fallen on tough times. He pointed a finger right back at himself, because he had been equally as guilty. Then a storm named Katrina had struck and by some miracle, his humanity had been found and touched, filling his empty heart and life with something meaningful. He turned into the church parking lot and spotted just that something.

Simone saw Keithen as he jogged into the parking lot. She continued to unload the boxes of donated groceries, pretending not to see him. They had spent nearly all their available time together over the last three weeks, the attraction between them growing with each passing moment. She had caught him on several occasions looking at her with such intensity she thought she would go up in flames. He was protective of her and always the gentleman. Then, out the blue, things had changed. He had kept his distance from her this past week. He hadn't returned to Miss Lorna's house to work. She wondered if he would show tomorrow to lay the floors, but she wouldn't dare ask him. Heaven forbid the man should think she had missed him. If their friendship meant nothing to him, then so be it. Possibly what they had shared had all been in her mind.

She loaded another box onto the dolly while calling herself all kinds of fool. She had allowed herself to care far more for Keithen Knight than just as a friend. She appreciated his honesty about the type of life he had led. But most importantly, she admired the fact that he had left his cushy lifestyle to come to the aid of complete strangers. Now there was a word. *Strangers*. She and Keithen Knight were strangers. He was a wealthy man, and she a small town girl with an average life. Then of course there was the issue of race. Now what on earth allowed her to believe Keithen could see past the color of her skin to the woman inside? And what made a Mississippi girl who knew all the reasons why a relationship with him wouldn't work see the possibilities?

Keithen slowed to a walk and headed in Simone's direction. He felt good after his run. His mind was clear and focused on what he wanted. He was also clear about whom he wanted.

"Hi, let me get this stuff for you." He reached into the back of the truck.

"No thanks, I can handle it," Simone said, brushing him aside. She loaded the next box without looking his way. "I'm sure you're busy."

Keithen stood to the side scratching his head. *Now what the hell is going on?* "I'm not busy and I said that I would help," he stated a little more forcibly. He bumped Simone out of the way with his bigger body.

"Well, I'm sure you have better things to do." Her eyes glared at him. She stood with her hands on her hips. "I mean, you've obviously been too busy with whatever to help out at Miss Lorna's."

It suddenly dawned on Keithen what was eating at Simone. "Are you trying to tell me that you missed me?" He smiled roguishly at her.

Simone felt her anger rise. She stared at him, wanting to knock him upside the head. "You wish. I just thought you were a man of your word."

"I am a man of my word." He set the box back down and turned fully to face her. He leaned forward, placing both hands on the back of the truck, effectively trapping her within his arms. His eyes traveled over her face before resting on her lips. He recalled the way her lips had wrapped around the spoon in the café. He wanted to taste them so badly. Instead, he ran the back of his hand down her cheek. "I stayed away to do a little soul searching. I haven't been the nicest person. I've been blinded by my wealth and surrounded by self-centered people just like me. But I've changed since getting here. I like the person I am, and people like me for who I am, not the money." He smiled a little sadly. "I also like you, Simone." His eyes connected with hers.

"I like you too," she said softly, her eyes filling with understanding.

"Good, because I'd really like to spend some quality time with you, getting to know you."

Simone looked deeply into his eyes, searching for the truth. He didn't look away or blink his eyes as he waited for her response. "I don't do casual sex if that's what you're looking for."

"I've done casual. I'm looking for substance here; head, heart, body, and soul all involved."

Simone blew out a breath. The man had just said a mouthful, and her pulse was responding. "Let me see your wallet," she said suddenly.

"What?" Keithen replied, not sure that he had heard correctly.

She smiled at him. "Your wallet, please."

His eyes brightened, reflecting his curiosity. "It's in my trailer. You're welcome to come get it." He wiggled his brows.

Simone chewed on her bottom lip. She should have known he wasn't jogging with his wallet. Her eyes wandered down his hard body, stopping at the nylon shorts, which definitely didn't contain pockets. No, they contained incredibly long, muscular legs. Now she had talked herself into going to his private trailer. *Smart move.* She chewed her lip a little harder before saying, "Lead the way."

"Ah, don't you think we should finish unloading the truck?" Keithen asked with a big grin. It seemed the lady was a little distracted.

Simone dropped her head blushing as she remembered the items in the back of her truck. "Stop grinning and help me with this stuff."

Keithen laughed behind her as he grabbed the box that she slid forward. He couldn't believe the surge of happiness that he received from knowing that she was interested in him as well. There was no pretense with her, only sweetness and a sincere heart.

Simone stepped inside the small trailer and glanced in both directions before gathering her courage and moving further into the quarters. The efficiency of the small space was impressive. As she walked down the middle, she noticed that all the essentials were there, including a bed. She quickly backed up and collided with the solid wall of Keithen's chest. The size of the trailer suddenly diminished greatly. Turning around, her eyes rose sheepishly to his.

"Nice," she said weakly, holding his gaze. His body heat reached out to caress her.

"It has all the necessities." The corners of his mouth tipped up. He squeezed by her and walked to the sleeping area, returning quickly with wallet in hand. "I believe you wanted to see this."

"Yes, I did." Simone took the wallet, but didn't open it. She raised her eyes to his. "You expressed an interest in getting to know me better."

"I would love to."

She nodded, wanting the same thing. But she needed to ask a few questions. "I probably should have asked this before. Are you married?"

"No."

"Good. Are you involved with someone?" She watched his body language closely.

Keithen walked to the table attached to the wall on the right side of the trailer and sat down on the bench seat. As he tried to decide how to answer the question, he realized that the truth was the only way to go. "Not romantically."

Looking at him sharply, Simone eased down onto the bench seat across from him. "You're saying the relationship is strictly physical."

"More status, but strictly physical. I know that may sound harsh, but it's the truth. In my part of the world we tend to pick our affairs based on money and the advancement of our position in society."

"It does sound harsh. It also sounds extremely sad, because love is more valuable than money or social position."

Keithen was the one nodding this time. "Observing the people here on the Coast, I'm realizing that." He watched as Simone placed the wallet on the table. She flipped it open and searched through the individual pockets. "What are you looking for?"

She slid the wallet back in his direction. "Pictures. I was looking for a picture of a wife or girlfriend."

He leaned back against the bench and grinned. "You thought you would catch me in a lie."

"No, I was hoping I wouldn't, because I want to get to know you as well. However, I don't get involved with married men."

"Then there should be no problem with us spending that quality time together," Keithen said as he reached across the table and took her hand. "Say that you'll give us a chance."

Simone's stomach fluttered with nervousness. Her first instinct was to say yes, but she had to think with her head, not her heart. "Keithen, you're a man of means who has admitted to having loveless relationships. I'm not capable of that. Spending more time with you would lead to emotional ties. Are you sure that's what you're looking for?"

"That's exactly what I'm looking for," he told her honestly. "You've been all I really thought about these last several days. I realized I missed you. That has never happened to me before."

"Look, I'm not as worldly as you are, and I don't believe in sharing the man I'm seeing. So, if you're not planning on this relationship being monogamous…"

"I'm interested only in you."

Simone forced her mouth closed, halting her next words. She met his intense gaze, sensing his sincerity. Her eyes dropped to their hands, where their fingers were tangled together, and marveled at the sight. Complete opposites in every sense of the word, yet together none the less. "So what did you have in mind?"

Keithen released a sigh of relief. For a moment there he hadn't been sure she would agree to give them a chance. "Are you cooking today?"

"No. The men's group has decided to cook out today, which means I'm free."

"Good." He beamed at her. "Give me twenty minutes to shower and change. Then I want you to take me on a drive."

"A drive?" she asked, curious. "Haven't you seen enough devastation to last you a lifetime?"

"Actually, I'm interested in the countryside," he told her, heading into the bedroom area, removing his shirt.

Simone's next words went right out the window as her eyes roamed over his strong muscular back, and lower to where his shorts began. The man was well toned and a danger to her senses. She gave a sigh of relief when the bathroom door closed behind him. The sound of the shower had her conjuring up images of him wet and lathered. She glanced out the side window to focus on something other than the closed bathroom door, but as she listened to the shower, the stronger the images became.

She was getting incredibly hot. She slid from the bench, switched on the air conditioner and stood in front of the small window unit relishing the cool breeze on her sweltering flesh. She heard the shower turn off and did the same with the air conditioner. Then the sound of the blow dryer filled the trailer.

She was levelheaded, had always been levelheaded. She didn't have crushes or daydream about men, so why now? After several minutes of listening to the hum of the blow dryer it finally turned off and Keithen appeared in the doorway of the bedroom, and she had her answer. Six feet of male beauty encased in masculine hardness wearing a smile just for her. The maid in waiting didn't want to wait any more. She saw what she wanted and was going after it.

"Hope I didn't keep you waiting long," Keithen said in that booming voice of his. "Is it cool out here?"

Simone blushed. "No, it's perfect."

She drove north of Interstate 10, along two lane roads, narrating as they passed rural homes and new exclusive developments. The road curved left, then right. She took Keithen passed bayous fed by the Biloxi River, and homes that possessed a view of the water. Katrina's wrath was visible in every direction she looked. Then Simone turned onto a narrow side road that led to what would have been a new development. The remains of the storm surge up the bayou sat piled along the road's edge.

She slowly drove through the neighborhood, pointing out the things she liked about it. They continued on, finding pleasure in the drive, and each other. Simone relished the hushed, reverent tone of their conversation in the face of the destruction. They exchanged glances and touched, their attraction growing stronger. Simone made a couple of purposeful turns which drew Keithen's attention.

"Where are we going?"

Simone glanced at him and smiled. "I want to show you a favorite spot of mine. My dad would take us on long drives on the weekend when I was a little girl. One day we came to this spot, and I fell in love with it. I come here when I need to be alone to think."

Keithen envisioned a young Simone daydreaming. But as she pulled off the main road and parked the truck, he understood her passion for the spot. Despite the few downed trees, the slightly elevated land was still covered by towering trees. The tall grass and wildflowers were already in bloom due to their life cycle being thrown off by the storm. "It's beautiful."

"I know," she said, getting out of the truck. She closed the door and walked around to his side. "Come on. There's a little creek further inland that's simply perfect."

As they walked, Keithen reached for Simone's hand, threading his fingers through hers. He smiled at her, liking the fit. He also liked the land. It was perfect for his project.

"Let's head over there," he said, indicating a high point. He wanted a better look at the land. He stood at the designated spot with Simone beside him taking in the countryside Magnolia and Oak trees that were plentiful, and after time to recover from the storm would be spectacular. The magnolia blossoms would scent the air. He spotted the creek Simone spoke of and had to agree with her assessment. It snaked through the property giving off a relaxing gurgle. In another direction, the property was fairly level with an expanse of open land.

"So what do you think?" Simone asked quietly as she reacquainted herself with the area.

"I think you have an eye for beauty." Keithen looked down at her.

"I just know what I like," Simone responded, looking back at him. "I like you, Keithen Knight."

"Do you, Miss Ladner?" Keithen pulled Simone into his arms. "What will you do once things return to normal around here?" he asked, watching her closely. He found her eyes to be very expressive.

Simone glanced off into the distance. She had always seen herself running her own restaurant, and for a moment she had. However, life had thrown her a curve. "I'll probably apply for a position at one of the casinos," she replied, none too excited.

"You won't open another restaurant?" He trailed his fingers down her cheek.

"No. It requires too much capital and I put the majority of my money into purchasing building materials for my grandmother's home. She, like so many others, didn't have flood insurance and her homeowner's policy won't cover the damages."

"So, you're giving up your dream?" He caressed her back with long, tender strokes. He hated to think of her making someone else's dream come true at the expense of her own. "Come on, let's head back."

Still holding hands and talking softly, Keithen walked her back to the truck. As he opened the door for her, he spotted the for sale sign to the property, and mentally filed away the telephone number listed to be entered into his cell phone later. If things worked out the way he hoped, that number would come in handy.

Simone and Keithen arrived back at the church parking lot a little after sundown. They left the truck still feeling the closeness that they'd discovered on their drive. As they caught the scent of charcoal and tangy barbeque in the air, Keithen automatically reached for Simone's hand and strolled toward the grilling area. The men of the church were still serving and so they fell in line with the others.

Just as Simone accepted a plate, she spotted her grandmother and Miss Lorna sitting at a far table. Motioning for Keithen to follow her over, she sat down at the table beside her grandmother, and Keithen slid in beside her. His solid thigh brushed against hers as he settled onto the bench getting comfortable. The sensual friction caused flames of desire to blaze in her eyes. She shyly glanced at him and was rewarded with a flirtatious wink.

Simone felt the slow burn of attraction travel through her system. The feeling was so overwhelming she was afraid someone would notice, and when she caught her grandmother watching them, she tried to look innocent.

"I'm surprised to see you both still here," Simone said to her grandmother as a diversion.

"Deacon Brice was on the grill, and you know how well that man can cook," Ruth commented, waving a rib. Her perceptive gaze moved from one to the other before she signaled to Lorna that their speculation as to Simone's whereabouts had been right on the money.

Keithen half listened to the conversation. His thoughts were on the woman beside him, the complexities of her personality. On the one hand she was a strong, take charge type of woman. On the other, she was so femininely vulnerable that she inspired him to protect her even while she made him want her all the more. He glanced at her, realizing that what he was beginning to feel for her was strong and not going away anytime soon.

Chapter Four

Simone was having her doubts about Keithen. They had worked side by side over a week installing ceramic tile flooring in Miss Lorna's home. They had laughed together and shared stories of their lives, but each evening when the work was completed, they'd gone their separate way. She didn't understand what was going on with him. She was beginning to feel like a schoolgirl waiting around for the school hunk to notice her. But no longer. The rebuilding of her grandmother's home was to start today and she didn't have time to worry about a man.

She strapped on her tool belt and pulled on gloves. Marching over to the concrete slab of the home, she joined the crew in erecting the frame of the house. The smell of fresh timber permeated the warm air, a scent that Simone had become quite familiar with. It was the smell of progress.

By late morning, she and the crew were well into the framing of the house when Keithen arrived. She deliberately ignored him refusing to be distracted by a self-centered rich boy. She shot another nail into the two by four, disgusted with herself for wasting so much time on the man.

Keithen pulled on his gloves while watching Simone. He loved this physical side of her. She wasn't afraid of getting dirty, breaking a nail, or messing up her hair. Rather than running away from work, she jumped right in. A man would be lucky to have such a woman at his side.

He thought about the hours they had spent together working on Miss Lorna's home. It had been just the two of them in the house, and in between the tiling, they had managed to do a great deal of talking. In many instances their views were quite similar. And when they weren't, they enjoyed a spirited debate. A smile spread across his face as he approached her.

"I've been thinking about you." He fought the urge to press a kiss into the bend of her neck. He had missed her.

Simone cut a scathing glance in his direction, but didn't respond. Instead, she decided that a break was in order. If she stuck around any longer, those green eyes would soften her resolve. Turning off the nail gun and placing the safety on, she gently set it on the floor and left Keithen staring after her as she stomped a path to her truck, where she removed a bottle of water from the cooler. Tipping it back, she nearly spilled it down the front of her shirt when a strong arm hooked around her shoulders.

"You frightened me," Simone snapped angrily, squirming out of his grasp.

Keithen let her go, but zeroed in on her body language. He was surprised by her tone and the cold shoulder that he was receiving. He ran a hand through his hair. "What's going on with you?"

Dark, angry eyes glared at him. "I should be asking you that question."

"What are you talking about?" Keithen moved in closer, reaching for her.

Once again Simone dodged his grasp. "Don't. I'm not playing this game any more."

"I don't understand. What game are you talking about?" He forcefully pulled her into his arms. "My feelings for you are real, if that's what this is about.

"You have a funny way of showing it." She stared at him while pushing at his immovable chest. "Here today and gone tomorrow?"

Keithen smiled. He finally understood what had Simone so angry with him. He leaned forward and covered her mouth with his. Simone tried to avoid the kiss, but his large hand held the back of her head in place, preventing her escape. Pressing his mouth against hers, forcing her lips apart, he dipped his tongue into her mouth, rejoicing in the sweet taste of her. He allowed the kiss to express what he was beginning to feel for her in his heart. When he sensed her acquiescence, he lowered his hands to her waist, savoring the kiss. He finally pulled away to meet her eyes. His thumb swept back and forth across her lower lip. It was rosy and wet from his kiss.

"I'm not playing games with you, honey, and there's no one else, if that's what you're thinking."

"What I think is that you're spoiled and you expect people to be at your beck and call."

Keithen looked deeply into her eyes, slightly hurt by the accusation. "I've treated people like you say in the past, and thought nothing of it. But I haven't treated you in that manner."

"I'm sorry for saying that," Simone whispered, ashamed of herself. "But I feel like a teenage girl being yanked around by the jock."

Keithen smiled. "I'm not yanking you around. I've been working on something in the evenings, but I'm almost finished. How about dinner and a movie Friday?"

Simone placed a hand in the center of his chest and lightly pushed. "It's all right, you don't have to."

"Honey, I want to be with you. Have dinner with me." Keithen held her gaze while willing her to say yes.

Simone sighed. "All right I will."

Simone paced the living room floor waiting for Keithen, surprisingly nervous about their first official date. She had pampered her body and chosen to wear the new blue dress with him in mind. He had never seen her in anything but jeans and a baggy work shirt. Tonight she wanted the man to see not a member of the volunteer crew or his friend, but a desirable woman. She heard the sound of a car door closing and sucked in a nervous breath. After a quick dash to the mirror to check her hair and makeup, she ran to the door as the doorbell chimed. She counted to five before opening the door. She couldn't have the man believing she was anxious to see him.

Keithen stood under the porch light in complete shock. He had known Simone was pretty, beautiful even, but goodness, he'd had no idea the woman was this damn sexy. Her shapely little body and gorgeous legs were more than he could have hoped for. He finally managed to step across the threshold.

"Hi, you look incredible," Keithen said before kissing her lips. They stood awkwardly in the foyer.

Simone thought he looked pretty darn good as well. The denims had been replaced with expensive black slacks. "Thank you. I like your transformation, too." She retrieved her handbag from the entryway table. "Shall we?"

Dinner was at one of the few fine dining restaurants to survive the storm. The friendly hostess escorted the couple to a white linen draped table lit with soft candlelight. Keithen walked behind Simone, checking her out. He liked the navy blue dress she wore. Soft and classy, the cut was sexy on her slender figure. His eyes slid down her tight backside as he wondered if she wore the blue thong under the dress. At the table, he assisted Simone into her chair and waited for the hostess to leave them alone.

"I'm really glad that we got the chance to do this," he said.

"Me too," Simone responded, taking in her surroundings. As a former restaurant owner, she automatically noted all of the particulars, from the hostess's attire and demeanor to the presentation of the meal.

Keithen was keenly aware of Simone checking out the place. Obviously, she missed running a restaurant. Her eyes moved around the room, not missing much, he was sure. He smiled to himself when she cringed at the young waiter serving from the wrong side. Only someone who ran a top notch establishment would notice such a blunder.

"You miss the restaurant business, don't you?"

Simone returned her attention to Keithen, a thoughtful expression on her face. "I don't regret my decisions, but yes, I do miss the excitement of readying the staff for the evening rush. I miss the activity in the kitchen, and the regular customers who take pleasure in having you greet them by name or remembering their drink order."

Keithen took her hand. "Then why not open a new restaurant?"

"Like I told you, I don't have the capital, and a small business loan is out of the question."

"Why?" He didn't understand.

"Because," she responded, caressing the back of his hand with her thumb, "after I secure a job, I may need to take out a loan to help my grandmother complete the rebuilding of her home. The free labor is a lifesaver, stretching my dollars further, but prices on building materials are increasing each day."

"You're giving up your dream in order to help your grandmother." Keithen couldn't help but admire her desire to help. He didn't know a living soul back home who would go to such lengths for someone else. The people here put family and friends before self. It was really a beautiful way to live.

"Believe me, she's given up a great deal over the years for her family. My parents are providing her a place to live and my cousins are assisting other relatives, so the money I have will go to my grandmother."

The waitress arrived to take their orders. Simone was impressed with Keithen's knowledge of wines and concurred with his selection of a Merlot to accompany their meal. When the waitress was out of hearing distance, she turned the conversation onto him.

"So tell me about your development company. Do you build strictly in California?"

"No, Knight Development Corporation builds nationally as well as internationally. I have offices in six major international markets," he told her without making it sound as though he were bragging.

Simone instantly realized Keithen Knight wasn't just rich, but probably extremely worldly on top of it. His sophistication was smooth and subtle, but nonetheless noticeable. From the way he moved his large body to his studious green eyes and that boyish smile which caused her heart to speed up, the man was polished.

"Simone, what is it?" Keithen noted the moment she realized the magnitude of his wealth. He began to feel uneasy. It was just money. Didn't people realized it didn't buy happiness, or love? Or prevent a person from suffering like every other man. Oh, sure, he knew the pleasure money could buy, but also knew the pitfalls. He had stupidly surrounded himself with the very people he despised. He had forgotten he was a member of a larger world, and decent people would appreciate him for himself and not what he could do for them. He had found that here in Biloxi and liked it very much. He also liked the woman sharing his table. "Do I make you uncomfortable?"

Her smile was shy and so appealing to him. He wondered for the first time about making love with her, to her. Would it be as powerful an experience as he thought?

"That's just it. When we're together I forget about who you are and the world you come from. But when I'm reminded of it, I wonder how we can ever have a relationship."

"We can because we choose to have one, and my world, as you put it, is different from yours, but it hasn't hindered my desire to be with you. If anything, being with you has shown me how superficial my life is." His eyes settled onto her face. "I've realized that not only can I make money, but that I can make a difference with my money."

Simone read the sincerity in his eyes. She smiled at him. "What kind of difference?"

"I'm not ready to reveal what I'm working on just yet, but you'll be the first to know," he assured her.

The wine arrived. Simone critiqued the waiter's mastery in presenting the bottle. After a nod from Keithen, the waiter served them.

"How did he do?" Keithen asked as the young man walked away.

She laughed gaily, her eyes dancing with amusement. "He did exceptionally well and the wine was an excellent choice."

"Well, thank you, ma'am," he said with an imitation Southern accent.

"You're joking around, but that accent has a way of sticking with a person. Just imagine your friends' faces when you return home saying *y'all.*"

Keithen released a thunderous laugh. The hearty sound settled deep inside of her in that special place where he was starting to become important.

"That's nothing. Just wait until I tell Rita that I want grits for breakfast."

Simone choked on her wine before managing to swallow. She grabbed her napkin and laughed behind it. Tears formed in her eyes as she imaged the very sophisticated Keithen Knight eating a bowl of grits from fine bone china. "I'd pay to see that." She giggled some more.

"You don't have to pay. Simply come with me when I go home," Keithen surprised himself and saw the same look on Simone's face.

Their meals arrived. Simone used the moment to change the conversation. She admired the presentation of the meal, then began eating. She kept up a steady stream of conversation to keep her thoughts away from his intriguing invitation.

"You know about my family, now tell me about yours," she said to Keithen. "What do your parents do for a living?"

She was trying to distract him. Though his invitation had been unexpected, it was sincere. The more he thought about it, the more he liked the idea of Simone returning home with him. They got along great, and he knew she would love California. He would make sure of it.

"My father is an engineer. He runs the operation of the family's bridge building business. He turned over the residential and commercial development business to me a couple of years ago. My younger brother assists me in the daily operations of Knight Development.

"Your family builds bridges also? Wow, I'm impressed."

"It's an impressive operation, I have to admit." Keithen received great pleasure from her response.

"And your mother does what to fill the day?"

Keithen chuckled. "She does a great deal of volunteering with some really worthwhile causes."

"So they support your volunteering?" She ate her meal, enjoying the subtle blend of seasonings.

"My parents are actually proud of my involvement. It's my friends who don't understand my desire to help. Their answer is to simply write a check."

"Checks are good," Simone replied jokingly.

He chuckled. "Yes, they are, but this problem requires hands-on involvement.

"You're right." Simone placed her hand over his. "I'm glad you came to Biloxi."

Those words stayed with Keithen as he drove to Simone's home after the movie. There was the obvious meaning which he knew was sincere, but then there was the underlying meaning that set his pulse to racing with possibility. Influenced by the new Sanaa Lathan's interracial love story that he and Simone had viewed, he was more determined than ever to see where the relationship led."So what did you think of the restaurant?" he asked while Simone opened the door to her home. He followed her inside the single story house. The foyer led directly into the spacious living room overrun with boxes. Obviously, she hadn't taken the time to unpack her things and turn her house into a home.

"Oh, the restaurant was wonderful. And I loved the movie. Good choice," she said, walking into the kitchen. She quickly started the coffee maker. She returned to the living room and noticed him eyeing the boxes. "Please excuse the mess." She had forgotten about the boxes, so used to them, but the evening had been going so well that she hated to see it end. However, knowing what he was accustomed to, she was suddenly embarrassed. "This was a bad idea. My place looks like a warehouse."

Keithen zeroed in on her discomfort and grabbed her hand, drawing her to him. His eyes locked with hers. "Stop thinking about the money, and concentrate on the man." His right hand caressed her cheek. "I'm here with you and I couldn't be happier. If you want, I'll help you unpack."

Simone smiled because she knew he meant every word. "I'll get around to it eventually. I did manage to install the blinds."

He sat on the sofa and pulled her down beside him. "I'm not comparing our status or making judgments. I need you to just relax and be with me." His thumb trailed across her bottom lip.

"That's an easy request and I thank you for the offer, but tonight is about enjoying ourselves." Simone leaned forward and pressed a kiss to his lips. "I'll get the coffee. If you're bored, photo albums are under the coffee table," she said on her way out.

He watched her go, acknowledging how much he wanted her. He spotted the albums and pulled one out, then sat back to get a glimpse into Simone's life. The meticulous care with which the photographs had been cut out and each page decorated made it obvious to him she was interested in scrapbooking. "You and my mother share the same hobby," he yelled. "She does scrapbooking as well.

"Really?" Simone returned carrying a tray. She placed it on the table before joining him on the sofa. "I find it relaxing, plus photo albums look great when you decorate them. They're so much more personal."

"If you say so. I would think all that cutting out would be tedious." He accepted the cup of coffee.

"This from a man who designs and develops communities?" Simone laughed. She narrated the pages as he turned them, regaling him with stories. She showed him photographs of her cherished New York brownstone, pointing out all the work that had been done. Her love for the place was evident in her voice.

"It's beautiful. Did you do the work?"

"I did most of it, and what I didn't know how to do, I learned from lessons at the nearest building supply store."

"You're something, lady," Keithen said with admiration. "You have an eye for design."

"I know what I like."

Simone reached for the album of the restaurant. She wanted to share her pride and joy with him. As she opened the first several pages, a deep ache of longing came over her. She quickly excused herself to the kitchen.

Keithen continued to look through the album. He came across a newspaper clipping of the opening night review. It stated in bold type that *The Arbor* was a five star establishment. From the pictures of the occupied tables and smiling faces of the customers, it appeared to be quite lucrative. He turned another page and paused.

"Who's the guy in this picture?" Keithen studied the photograph closely. He noted the African-American man was handsome in a dark complexion. He also noticed the guy's hand was on Simone's hip and seeing the way that he was looking at her, he felt jealousy flare inside him.

Simone came in with slices of her lemon pound cake. She passed a plate to Keithen as she leaned over his shoulder examining the indicated photograph. "Oh, that's Mason."

"Is that supposed to be an answer?" The words came out a little terse. He looked at the next page and cringed on seeing Simone wrapped in Mason's muscular arms once more.

She heard the tone and wondered about it. "Mason is, was, my partner. I told you we've been friends for years."

"This Mason is in love with you." He turned jealous eyes onto her. Searching her face for a reaction, he found none.

"He loves me like a little sister."

Keithen unleashed a laugh and snapped the book closed. He tossed it on the table, and then turned to look at Simone. "Like hell. That man is looking at you like you're his favorite meal."

"You are so wrong," she said, laughing. "Mason has never shown the slightest interest in me."

"Doesn't change the fact. Trust me, I recognize the look of hunger in the man's eyes."

Simone heard the jealousy in his voice and was surprised. "Well, he never said anything, and as far as I'm concerned, we are only close friends."

"Good." He claimed her lips in a possessive kiss. "I'm rich and I'm spoiled. I don't like to share."

Chapter Five

Keithen put the finishing touches on his surprise for Simone. Stepping back, he assessed his project. It wasn't his usual professional design as he had utilized city models intended for railroad enthusiast. He had spent countless hours planning and designing. He had taken all the information available and poured his heart and soul into this venture. Now all he needed was one lovely lady's seal of approval. He tossed a sheet over the table before leaving the trailer to await her arrival. He had called her at her grandmother's property and asked her to come by the church before heading home. She had phoned ten minutes ago to say she was on her way, and when he spotted headlights coming down the street, his pulse quickened. He recognized the truck and waved as she maneuvered into a parking space.

"Hi." Simone accepted Keithen's assistance in getting out of the truck. The look in his eyes was one of excitement and the smile on his face, childlike. "What's going on?" she asked, discovering herself smiling.

"I have something I want to show you. Actually I'm hoping you approve of it." Keithen led her by the hand along the meandering walkway which led to the volunteer trailer park.

Simone noticed the curious glances in their direction as she followed him. She had learned that the volunteer camp was like a small town neighborhood where everyone talked, or rather gossiped, and from the looks she would guess that people were talking about them. With the small travel trailers crammed close together, and everyone sitting outside because of the close confines of the trailer, she knew there was no such thing as privacy.

"Why didn't you simply bring it with you?" she asked, trying to keep up with his longer stride. The man was practically running.

"I couldn't. You'll understand when you see what I have to show you." Keithen reached his travel trailer and flung the door open. "After you."

Simone stepped inside, glancing around. She zeroed in on the large sheet-draped item.

"What's this?" Simone moved in closer to the table and his surprise. She looked at it with anticipation as he made a grand gesture of removing the sheet.

"*Ta-da*," Keithen cried, imitating a trumpet flourish. He stood to the side as Simone leaned forward examining his design. His pulse raced in anticipation of her thoughts. But as time passed without a response, his spirits slowly took a nose dive. Something was wrong.

Simone easily recognized the design as a new subdivision. There were nice cul-de-sacs and plenty of open green spaces or parks incorporated into the design. Single and two story homes were integrated into the plan. She identified schools, churches, and shopping areas. A pond sat in the center of the development.

"Is that a walking track around the pond?"

"Yes, and it's lighted," Keithen responded and moved to stand beside her. "The track is a complete mile around. I know women like to walk while pushing strollers." He continued to point out small details while Simone looked on with interest.

"It's wonderful."

"You like it? I tried to think of everything. You know, make it convenient."

"What's not to like. I'm sure you've included every luxury money can buy."

"Not quite."

"Well, another gated community is just what the Coast needs." She stood back staring at the design. She thought she had gotten to know the man. After all the time they had spent together, surely he would see where the greater need was.

Keithen looked at her sharply before glancing back at his design. He heard the sarcasm in her voice and knew she had misunderstood.

"Please, tell me you didn't buy the land I showed you to build this on?" Simone waved an angry hand over the elaborate layout. Her tone was heated.

"I did and this isn't a gated community for the wealthy," Keithen informed her, getting annoyed himself. "Do you think I haven't been paying attention to conditions around here?" His eyes flashed with anger. "Come here," he said, grabbing her by the arm to pull her closer to the table. "I designed this development with you in mind. Hell, I even named it Simone Place."

"Simone Place? You did?" her voice came out low, tinged with emotion. "This development is affordable housing?" This time she really looked at the design. It dawned on her that he had provided everything necessary, for people who would have to relocate from their flood ruined neighborhoods, because they were now designated flood zones. The shopping area and schools would provide employment to those who had lost jobs as a result of the hurricane. Tears suddenly clouded her eyes.

"Yes, it is. I wanted to do something for the wonderful people I've met, and for you."

Simone threw herself into his arms. "Forgive me for being an idiot."

Keithen held her close as he ran his hands up and down her back. "As long as you know," he said jokingly and sat her back so that he was looking into her eyes. "I wanted to design a community I could really be proud of, and I think I've done that. But what I need from you are suggestions to make it better. Once we nail down a plan, then I can get my team to work on making it a reality."

"What can I add?" Simone squatted down to look at Simone Place once more. It really was wonderful.

"Well, I was thinking we could look at some of my home designs and select those you feel would be more fitting. For example, the rooms that would be the most important or the features that would be a bonus."

Simone nodded. She bubbled with excitement as Keithen went to the bedroom and returned with his laptop. "What are you doing?" She sat down at the table beside him.

"I'm going to the company website to access the design section." He typed away until he reached the desired information. He was keenly aware of Simone pressed in beside him, watching over his shoulder. Her warm thigh caressed his, and her womanly hip nestled close. He groaned under his breath as he inhaled her intoxicating fragrance.

"Are all of these your developments?" Simone asked, glued to the screen. The homes displayed were more like mansions. Instead of the typical three bedroom, two bath, all-American home, the designs were showplaces for the rich and famous. Through the designs she gained real insight into what the man was accustomed to. God, she couldn't imagine what he thought after being in her cracker box of a house. "These are fabulous. I can't envision living like this."

Keithen looked over at her. He could easily see her wandering through his home. "They're just houses, sweetheart."

"For you maybe, but to the rest of us, they're fantasies." She brushed up against him, smiling. "So show me what you have for us common folk."

He turned, looking at her. His hand came up to touch her face because he couldn't resist doing so. His eyes stared into hers. "There is nothing common about you. My sweet lady, you are a precious one of a kind jewel."

Simone blushed girlishly. She leaned over, kissing him on the lips. When Keithen deepened the kiss, she gave herself up to the pleasure, wrapping her arms around his neck. She allowed him to pull her close and shivered at the feel of his hand caressing low over her backside. They finally separated and sat back, staring into each other's eyes.

Keithen turned back to the computer. He opened the design window and isolated those housing plans he thought were good fits for his project. But while he did so, his thoughts were on Simone and how good she felt beside him. He daydreamed about what life would be like with her at his side.

"These are all beautiful, but Southerners congregate in the kitchen." She looked on as he called up a new design.

"That's a keeper."

"What about this one?" Keithen brought up another floor plan. The spacious kitchen opened into an equally spacious family room.

"Perfect." Simone rested her chin on his shoulder. "Bathrooms and screened porches are also important."

"How could I forget those blasted piranhas with wings."

Simone laughed. "They're sand gnats."

"That may be, but those things feel like piranhas when they bite." He raised a hand and ruffled her hair.

They sat together for several more hours. By the time they called it quits, they had chosen eight home designs and added a daycare center to the plan. They had also narrowed down the types of businesses to be included in the shopping area. When Simone's stomach rumbled, Keithen produced two take-out meals from the refrigerator, and popped them into the microwave. He gave Simone a crash course in development over dinner. He spoke of building codes and building products, all of which she found fascinating. But as the hour grew late, she drifted off to sleep on the narrow sofa. Her head rested on his shoulder with her hand casually slung across his thigh. However, as she shifted her position getting comfortable, that hand landed dead center of his crotch.

Keithen stared at the hand resting against his tightening zipper. Even in sleep the woman stirred his blood. He wondered not for the first time what making love with her would be like. He sensed a lack of experience but with the chemistry between them, he had no doubt their desire would be equally matched.

He carefully positioned Simone against the back cushion as he slid from the seat. He stood watching her sleep. She had been excited as they designed Simone Place. She had asked intelligent questions and made insightful suggestions he never would have thought of. They worked well together. He scooped her up into his arms and carried her back to the bedroom. He removed her shoes, and then placed her under the covers. Grabbing the extra pillow, he returned to the kitchen area, clearing away his model. He went back to the table and quickly converted the area into a sleeping berth. Turning out the light, he folded his tall body into the tight space and sighed with pleasure. Not for the comfort of the bed, but for the woman sleeping in his bed.

The next morning Simone rolled over and stretched. Pulling the covers closer around her, she inhaled deeply, taking the scent into her lungs. It was a moment before she realized the scent reaching her nose wasn't her fresh breeze fabric softener. The scent was familiar, but where had she come across it? Fighting her way through the haze of sleep, it came to her. Keithen. She was smelling Keithen's aftershave, but why?

Her eyes suddenly flew open as she came wide awake. This wasn't her bed, or her home, for that matter. She immediately recognized the interior of Keithen's trailer.

"Oh my God!" she whispered as she sat up, throwing her feet over the side of the bed. She glanced down, relieved to discover that she was fully clothed. As she massaged her scalp with her hands, memories of the previous night flooded her mind. She had fallen asleep. Keithen, no doubt, had placed her in his bed. She looked toward the bathroom and discovered him standing there watching her. Her heartbeat burned rubber as it sped up with excitement. The man stood shirtless with his unbuttoned jeans riding low on his hips. *Oh my God!* A dark blond trail disappeared into the waistband. A persistent pulse settled between her legs, bringing her fully awake.

Keithen was acutely aware of Simone checking him out. Everywhere her eyes traveled, a blaze of warmth followed. He fought the urge to join her in bed. She looked beautifully rumpled, just begging for a morning romp.

"Good morning." He stood with a towel around his neck, trying to ignore the hammering desire of his body. He had just finished shaving when he'd heard her stir. "Coffee's hot."

Simone blinked to clear away the fog. "What time is it?"

"Eight-thirty."

"Oh my God!" she repeated as she searched for her shoes. All the while her fingers raked through her hair in an attempt to comb it. "I can't be seen leaving your trailer at this time of morning." She slipped her feet into her shoes, and then looked for her purse.

"It's right here," Keithen said, standing behind her. He placed gentle hands on her shoulders. "Slow down. You're behaving like you've never spent the night at a man's house before."

Simone shook off his hands. She wanted to tell him that she *hadn't* spent the night at a man's home before, or made love, but she wouldn't.

Past experiences had taught her to remain silent, if she didn't want to send him running in the opposite direction. "Why didn't you wake me up last night? I can't believe this is happening." She pressed her fingers between her eyes where a headache was starting to form.

Keithen slid in front of her. "You fell asleep on the sofa last night. I thought you were exhausted and needed rest. I didn't see the point in waking you."

"No point," she wailed, looking up at him. "You would have saved me from being embarrassed. People are going to think we slept together," her voice rose.

"Who gives a damn what people think?"

"I do. This is my home and I have to live here after you're gone."

Keithen glared down at her. He didn't like what he was hearing. "What bothers you most, the fact that people will think that we slept together, or the fact that they'll think you slept with a white man?"

Simone stopped dead in her tracks to look at him. She couldn't believe what she was hearing. Were they having the same conversation? She didn't think so because this situation had absolutely nothing to do with race.

"I'm going to ignore that because you aren't from around here. Race has nothing to do with respect and reputation. Perhaps you and your California friends slink in and out of beds so much no one notices any more, but this is Mississippi, people notice and talk."

Keithen understood respect. He sighed with regret. "I'm sorry for jumping to conclusions. With the state's racial history I thought…"

"You thought wrong." Simone ran a hand through her hair again. "I must look a mess. May I use your bathroom?"

"Sure. I left fresh towels for you." He stepped aside so that she could pass. He heard the water running and moved back toward the living area, giving her privacy. He looked out of the window, noticing people starting to move around. There was no way for Simone to leave his trailer without being seen. It would be left up to him to get her out of there. He heard the bathroom door open and turned as she entered the room.

"Would you like that coffee now?" He stood there feeling a little awkward. He hadn't felt that uncomfortable after a night with a woman in years, if ever. But he was definitely feeling uneasy at the moment.

Simone also felt on shaky ground. Waking up in a man's place was something new for her. She bet Keithen would get a kick out of that tidbit of information. "No, thank you. I have to head home before going to my grandmother's place. They're putting on the roof today and I want to be there to help."

"I won't be able to make it today. I'll be meeting with the owner of the property," Keithen told her. He moved around the small area pulling out various items. "Now, let's get you ready."

With brows raised, Simone looked at the things placed on the counter. "What's all that? And get ready for what?"

Keithen looked over at her and grinned. "Your disguise. I can't have you becoming the subject of camp gossip."

"You're kidding, right?" She giggled as she rummaged through the items. She picked up a yellow hard hat. "What am I supposed to do with this?"

"A lot of the workers around here wear hard hats." He placed the yellow headgear on Simone's head. "Tuck your hair under it." He stood watching as she did as instructed. "Perfect. Now we need to pad you up."

"I hope you know this is the craziest thing I've ever done." Simone stared into the mirror surprised by the transformation. Dressed as she was with a towel flattening her breasts and padded by two of Keithen's T-shirts under another button down denim shirt which hung to her knees, her feminine curves were well hidden. "Hey, I'm only trying to prevent you from becoming the topic of gossip. When you walk out there, keep your shoulders squared, your head down, and whatever you do, keep those lovely hips of yours from swaying."

"My hips don't sway." Her eyes met his in the mirror for a long heated stare.

"Oh baby, they definitely sway. I should know, I've been watching them."

Heat rose to her cheeks. "Okay, here goes nothing," Simone said, leaving the bathroom and their conversation behind. She headed for the main door. With one final look in Keithen's direction, she opened the door and did as he instructed, walking passed several people without receiving a single glance.

Keithen left the attorney's office after meeting the owner of the land. He held the documents which made him the owner of the property. He couldn't wait to show them to Simone. He knew she would be as excited about the acquisition as he was. His excitement struck him as odd, considering he purchased land all over the world. But this land purchase was special. It was Simone's land and with it, he would be fulfilling a community need meaningful to them both. As he reached the truck, he pulled out his cell phone before unlocking the door. He wanted to get things rolling on the project just as soon as he could.

"Jay, I need a project team put together. I just bought a piece of property that needs developing," Keithen informed his younger brother with excitement.

"Great, I knew that spiel about volunteering was bunk. What are we building; condominiums, strip malls, or are we getting into the casino industry?"

Keithen pinched the bridge of his nose with frustration. His younger brother was more cynical than he'd realized. But that had been him before coming to the Coast and meeting such gracious people. "I want you to listen to me close, Jay. I'm planning on building a residential development. The need for housing down here is dire, and we can provide quality homes. I think Noah's team would be perfect for this project."

"Noah is a tightwad when it comes to the budget," Jay remarked nastily.

"Noah is conservative, and since I'm building affordable homes, he's the man for the job."

"Did you say affordable? What the hell is wrong you, Keith? We could make a killing down there building a condo and you want to build affordable?" Jay released several expletives into the receiver.

Keithen unlocked the door to his truck and climbed in. Leaving the windows up, he took command of the conversation with a few choice words of his own. "You should get your butt down here and see for yourself how your fellow Americans are living. These are hardworking people who aren't asking for a handout, just a chance to get back on their feet. It's really a wonderful city and its people are terrific. I've made some really good friends here."

"Who the hell cares about making friends? Knight Development is about making money, and what you're proposing is crazy. We're going to be tied up with this project while other developers move in to score the big deals."

Keithen had had enough. "Knight Development is technically mine. Dad turned the company over to me, and I say what projects we are doing."

"I'll have Noah assemble his team. I'll be in touch when they're ready to head out," Jay sighed.

"Thank you." Keithen smiled as he snapped his cell phone closed. His brother was extremely intelligent with a killer instinct. Together they made a fierce team. But Jay's immaturity hindered the work when he felt the need to question and challenge every decision he made. His father called him self-indulgent, acting without thought. Keithen's mission, as the older brother, was to mold Jay into a responsible businessman. Backing out of the parking lot, Keithen left thoughts of Jay behind. He was headed to a brown-eyed lady who would be excited by his news.

Chapter Six

Keithen parked in front of Ruth Ladner's home amazed at how fast the rebuilding process was going. Simone's grandmother would be back on her front porch in no time. He slammed the truck door and scanned the area for Simone. A loud flirtatious whistle that would make a construction worker proud caught his attention. Simone laughed as she came from the rear of the house. She stopped short to give Keithen a quick once-over.

"Don't you look pretty, Mr. Knight." She smiled teasingly. Around her waist she wore a tool belt that jangled with each step that she took. The sight of it swaying on her hips was like a beacon, drawing him close.

He returned her smile, thinking she was the pretty one. Her eyes twinkled with flirtation, but soon held expectation as they spotted the documents in his hand.

"Is it done? Is the land yours?" she asked with mounting excitement.

"All mine," he responded, waving the papers in the air.

"Yes!" Simone ran in his direction and launched herself into his waiting arms, laughing as he spun around, sharing her excitement. "So how does this work? How long will it take before you start building?" She stood back on her own two feet.

Keithen led Simone over to Miss Lorna's front porch. The family friend had moved into her home just last week. "It's a lengthy process. The home plans have to be finalized, materials budget established, and vendors contracted. Then there is the city government to which we present our development proposal. And of course there will be city council hearings with the local residents before approval will be granted."

"Wow, I didn't realize so much went into development." Her spirits suddenly took a nose dive. "There are so many people who need housing."

He reached out, turning her face to his. "Don't lose hope. It will happen. This is all standard procedure and once we get approval it's a go." He leaned forward, kissing her lightly. "I'm going to need an interior designer to select things like cabinets, flooring, appliances, lighting, and a lot of other items." He looked directly at her. "I'd like that person to be you."

Simone's eyes widened as she sat up straighter. "Are you serious? I don't have a background in interior design."

"I know, but from your photo album of your New York brownstone and restaurant, I can see you have an eye for design. I really want you to say yes." He took her hand and placed it on his thigh. "You can do this. Your sense of color and style is sophisticated without being cold. I want people to walk into these houses and instantly know they're home."

Her heart was beating fast with excitement at the prospect of working on this project. Although she didn't possess a degree in design, she did know what she liked and enjoyed decorating. "If I say yes, you have to promise to treat me like any other employee while on the job."

"In that case, you have to accept a salary."

"Keithen, I can't do that. It would mean you're legally my boss, and dating you would be unethical."

"Who cares?"

"I do. It would be an unprofessional relationship. Let me do it as my gift to the community."

"Sweetheart, you need the money." His eyes met hers. "You have to start thinking about yourself."

Simone squeezed his hand. He was right, she did need the money. As it was, the funds from the sale of her half of the restaurant were quickly dwindling. "All right, I'll do it."

"And accept a salary?"

"Yes." Simone kissed his lips. "Thank you, but I intend to earn my money."

"I never doubted it."

When the first week of June arrived, Keithen realized that his decision had been a wise one. He sat in Simone's living room listening while she presented him with a thorough, itemized breakdown of supplies and suppliers. Sample books of kitchen cabinetry, countertops, floorings, and appliances had all been assembled and waited the day home buyers would make their selections. Every aspect of the design process had been addressed. Keithen was indeed impressed with her work ethic.

"I think you're in the wrong profession," he told her, sitting beside her on the sofa. "You have got to be the most organized woman that I know."

Simone laughed, looking at the living room of boxes. "Some might disagree with you."

Keithen also looked around and suddenly jumped up. "I'll see you later."

"What? You're leaving?" She followed him to the front door where he turned, kissing her.

"I'll be back."

Simone stood in the door as Keithen jumped in his truck and drove away. She closed the door and returned to the living room, where she continued to work on assembling sample books. By the time the doorbell chimed an hour later, she was in the kitchen preparing a light meal. She rushed to the front door and stood back as Keithen entered carrying an assortment of painting paraphernalia.

"What's all this?"

"Paint for the living room. I tried to match the color to your New York apartment," he told her, excited. His eyes sparkled with joy. "I thought it was time we made this place a home."

Simone was speechless. "You did this for me? I can't believe it." She looked at him, surprised by his thoughtfulness.

Keithen deposited his purchases on the floor and pulled Simone into his arms. "You do so much for everyone else I wanted to do something for you."

"Well, at least let me help." She couldn't believe he had remembered the color of her New York home.

"Not a chance. This is my present to you." He picked up a bundle of dark clothing she hadn't noticed earlier.

"I have to do something."

He glanced around the room, searching for something to occupy her time. "While I change clothes, move the boxes to the center of the room."

"That's all?" Simone stood in the middle of the floor staring at his back as he headed to the bathroom to change. Shrugging her shoulders, she got down to moving the boxes. She reached the box labeled draperies. Ripping it open, she was suddenly excited at the prospect of actually having her living room decorated. She heard the bathroom door open. Glancing up, she nearly swallowed her tongue as Keithen returned wearing baggy shorts and a sleeveless T-shirt. Miles of hard muscles bulged and flexed with his every movement. "Are you sure I can't help?" Her eyes trailed down his shapely calves.

"I'm sure, but you can keep me company." He chuckled to himself as he got down to taping off the moldings. He had seen the desire blazing in her eyes as he returned to the living room. It was nice to know the woman found him desirable. They had been moving slow, getting to know each other. Outside of a few kisses and cuddling close, their relationship hadn't progressed to a physical affair. As he'd gotten to know Simone better, he'd questioned whether she had ever been with a man. So much about her hinted of innocence

"If you were to open a new restaurant, what would you name it?"

Simone sighed from the sofa now stationed in the middle of the floor. "I don't know."

"What about Simone's?"

"It has a nice ring to it." She stretched out on the sofa to lie on her belly. "But you know, to name a place after yourself means you have no imagination."

Keithen laughed. He looked over at her and groaned when he spotted her lying on the sofa. The woman had no idea how badly he wanted to stretch out beside her. "All right then, put that imagination of yours to work."

Simone lay there calling out names off the top of her head. Keithen responded by groaning when the suggestions were really bad. He tossed a few of his own out there and received a similar response. They laughed together while he got down to painting.

"Mason called me Monee."

"Definitely not," Keithen responded adamantly. He turned to face her. "You're more elegant than that."

She blushed. "When have you seen me looking elegant? I only wear jeans and dirt."

Robust laughter filled the room. "I recall a sexy blue dress."

"You thought I was sexy?" Simone turned onto her side to look at him.

Placing the paint roller into the tray, he walked over to the sofa and pushed Simone over. Stretching out so that they lay facing each other, he threaded his fingers into her soft hair. "I find you sexy, period. Wearing jeans, gloves, boots, and a little dirt, my pulse responds to you." He covered her mouth, his kiss expressing his feelings. He drew her body firmly against him as his tongue frolicked in the honeyed depths of her mouth. She felt good in his arms and he had to fight hard not to climb on top of her. But then he felt Simone tremble and recognized it as nervousness. He deepened the kiss briefly, and then tore his mouth away, breathing heavily. He pushed the hair away from her face so that he could see her eyes clearly. They were bright and slightly anxious. "I should get back to the painting."

Simone's heart beat so profoundly in her chest she had to mentally tell herself to calm down. When the man touched her, her body temperature soared. He was hard and invitingly warm to the touch. When he looked at her, she felt beautiful. She sat up and drew her legs under her as she watched him place the first swipe of paint on the wall. "The color is perfect."

"It's a good match." He liked the light peachy color. His eyes were soft and moody when they looked at her. "I don't think you've ever said how old you are."

"Where did that come from?"

"I don't know," he said with a shrug of his shoulder.

She grinned at him. "Afraid I'm too young for you?"

"The possibility crossed my mind."

"I'm quite legal, Mr. Knight."

"Perhaps, but you're inexperienced."

Simone squirmed uncomfortably under his intense scrutiny, suddenly embarrassed. What had she done to give herself away? "I know you're used to dating experienced women, so if being with a virgin isn't working for you, I understand." Her voice was soft and uncertain. She had been here before. When men realized she wasn't sexually experienced, they made a speedy exit. She sat there waiting for Keithen to do the same. But this time she knew she had allowed her heart to become engaged. When this man walked away, she would be deeply hurt.

Keithen dropped the roller, not caring whether it landed in the tray or not. He cut a quick path back to the sofa and squatted in front of Simone, who sat with her legs under her chin, and her arms wrapped protectively around herself. He gently placed his hands on her legs. Looking her squarely in the eyes, he saw her bracing herself to be cast aside.

"Sweetheart, you can't get rid of me that easily."

Simone didn't respond. She tried to figure out his angle. "You're trying to win the prize and be the first?" Her tone was accusing.

He ignored the tone because he knew many men would see her as a challenge to be conquered. "You're a prize all by yourself. I'm not going to lie and say I don't want you, or haven't thought about the two of us together. I do and I have. However, I believe you're worth the wait." He caressed her legs. "I just don't understand how you've remained untouched, that's all. I see the way the guys around here look at you, and I'm sure Mason wanted you."

"I want to mean something more to a man than a good time. I'd like to know we have a future together."

"As you should." He thought how different she was from the women in his life. They used sex to get what they wanted, and he took selfishly. He shouldn't be with her, and definitely shouldn't be thinking of getting closer. She was too damn good for the likes of him. But he couldn't walk away from the one woman he wanted so desperately.

"Are you sure that you can live without sex?" A smile tugged at her lips

"I think I'll be okay." He leaned forward kissing her. "What about you?"

"What about me?" Simone asked, confused.

"Can you live without sex? I saw the way you were checking me out when I came from the bathroom." His eyes glowed with humor, and when Simone's mouth fell open in shock, he shook with laughter.

Simone shoved against his chest, rising from the sofa. "I have no idea what you're talking about." She picked up a spare roller and began painting the other wall.

"You still haven't told me how old you are." Keithen let her off the hook and returned to painting.

"Twenty-six."

"I knew you were young, but your wisdom is mature."

"That's Ruth Ladner you're hearing." Simone giggled. "Grandma is always spouting her wisdom, whether you want to hear it or not."

"She's wonderful."

"Yeah, she is." She glanced at him. "You didn't say how old you are."

Keithen pursed his lips before looking at her. "Thirty-four."

"Mature, aren't you?"

His head snapped in her direction. "Are you calling me old?" Keithen held the paint roller in a threatening manner.

Simone laughed girlishly as she took a step backward. "No, of course not. I only meant that you're wise." She yelled as Keithen gave chase out of the living room and down the hallway. They tussled playfully before Keithen scored a hit with the paint roller. Simone continued to giggle like a child. "I can't believe you did that."

"You had it coming for calling me old," Keithen replied, laughing. He tugged on the front of her blouse pulling her into the bathroom. He removed a washcloth from the linen closet then set about cleaning her chin.

Simone waited patiently while Keithen removed the paint. She looked into his beautiful green eyes while he worked. They were smiling and full of life, like the first day they met. "Your eyes are very expressive."

Keithen met her eyes. "I think the same about yours. One look into them and I know your mood." He tossed the washcloth onto the vanity.

"What mood am I in now?"

His lips thinned into a cocky smile. "The same one I am." He lowered his mouth to hers, nibbling at her soft lips. He ran his tongue across the seam of her lips until she opened for him. He stroked and dipped his tongue in a mating fashion, tightening his hands in her hair as he fed from her mouth.

His body was hot and achy. The woman was driving him out of his mind with her innocent sensuality. He ran his large hands down her back and lower to her hips, lifting her onto the vanity and sliding her forward, so that he stood between her spread thighs. He sighed, loving the feel of her heat against him, but knew she wasn't ready for anything more. He slowly pulled his mouth away to place a kiss on her nose, her chin, down the length of her neck, and finally in the opening of her blouse.

Simone tried to pull in him back to her. "Don't stop."

"We can go slow, honey. There is no need to rush our relationship."

"I'm a twenty-six year old virgin, Keithen. I don't think anyone would accuse me of rushing anything." She crossed her arms, aggravated.

Laughter rumbled up from his chest to reverberate off the walls. Simone sat before him looking adorably frustrated. Her bottom lip was pushed out like an unhappy child. He pressed a kiss into her hair while contemplating her words. "Honey, you aren't ready for me to take you to bed."

Simone pulled away from him, coming to her feet. He was right. She still wanted to know that she was more than a good time. She leaned against the bathroom vanity. "You're hot, Keithen Knight, and I'm attracted to you."

Keithen grinned, boyishly. "I don't believe a woman has ever called me that."

"Believe me, they have. You just haven't been around to hear it." She reached out, taking his hand. "I want you Keithen, but…"

"But what, sweetheart?"

"I need to know there's more than sex between us." She caressed her thumb nervously across his knuckles. "I'm also frightened. I know the mechanics of it, but there the knowledge ends. I'm afraid you'll find me a disappointment."

Keithen was moved by her honesty. He glanced down at her small hands holding his. "Trust, respect, and...*I can't believe I'm saying this*...love, are the most important factors. When you can honestly tell me you trust me to respect you and your body, and trust me to love you like the lady you are, then you won't be frightened. As far as being a disappointment, you could never be that to me. Meeting you and getting to know someone as special as you is a gift. You're a beautiful woman and the knowledge you speak of will come from your heart." He brought her hand to his lips, kissing her small fingers one at a time. "I'm not looking for a single moment of pleasure with you."

Simone raised her chin while her heart began a nervous tap dance. "What do you want?"

"Definitely not another empty relationship."

Chapter Seven

Keithen thought on that statement for the next several weeks. Refusing Simone's sensual offer had been difficult, but the right thing to do. He had returned to painting the living room while Simone looked on, their conversation more meaningful as they were building a foundation. Today ringing Simone's doorbell, he was to pick her up for a cookout at Ruth Ladner's new home. The volunteers had completed the home a week ago, and moved her in at the beginning of the week. Now he and Simone were able to focus their complete attention on the development project. He smiled when she opened the front door of her home.

"Close your eyes," Simone said, taking Keithen's hand.

"What's going on?" He looked into her excited face.

"Just do it, please." When he finally complied, she led him across the threshold of her home and into the living room. "Okay, open them.

Keithen glanced around the cozy living room admiring Simone's decorating talents. The plush mocha sofa that had sat against the wall now rested on an angle, anchored by a beautiful Persian rug. Behind it, she used a sofa table as a bar. Stripeddraperies of mocha, gold, and peach were hung at the double windows overlooking the front yard. A large leather ottoman served as a coffee table. Two chairs of traditional style also sat on an angle facing the sofa. Silver frames containing family pictures were placed on the dark wood end tables. An array of lighthouses and magnolia collectables were on display around the room. The design was contemporary and relaxing. "This is beautiful."

"You inspired me to continue with the rest of the house. So I headed to the paint store and got down to spicing up this place. Come on." She led him through the house, showing off room after room. The boring white walls of the kitchen were now a dark cinnamon that accentuated the white appliances. In the small dining room, she had done an elegant striping in contrasting shades of sage green. The bathroom where she had expressed her desire for him was now painted a calming taupe.

"Why didn't you ask me to help you paint?"

"I wanted to do it myself. I love turning a cold space into a warm, inviting area." She led him down the hallway to the spare bedroom.

"We missed the master suite," Keithen pointed out.

"Yes, we did, now can we move on?"

"I want to see your room." His smile was now roguish.

"What I have for you is behind this door," she purred sexily.

Keithen's face lit up as his eyes swept her body suggestively. "What have you done?" He turned the knob and stepped into a well equipped home office. "Simone, this is spectacular!" His eyes moved around the soothing gray room. Warm cherry furnishings created a functional working space. He checked out the shelving and cabinet space. A spacious credenza sat just inside the door. His eyes settled on the project table. He trailed his fingers across the surface, deeply touched by the display of love in the room. "Where did you get all of this? You shouldn't have spent money on me."

"I didn't spend much. I found most of the furniture at a thrift store in Mobile. You needed more space than your trailer to work on the subdivision. I thought this could work until you're able to establish offices on the site. And then there's the added bonus of seeing you each evening."

Keithen was overcome with appreciation and...love. No one had ever done anything like this for him. The people in his life expected him to do all the giving. "Are you sure I'm not going to be in your way? I'm afraid I'm not as neat and organized as you are." He caressed the computer generated map of Simone Place.

"I can't wait to have you here working. And when you're finished, close the door and it all goes away."

"I love the dove gray walls." He turned, looking at her. "You have no idea what this means to me. And you're right, the trailer was getting cramped with all the research documents. Thank you." Keithen wrapped his arms around Simone and held her close to his heart. She was such a loving woman, always giving to others. He had never met anyone like her. He raised his hands to frame her face. Looking into her eyes, he saw his future right here with this woman. There was no surprise or question to the realization. Contentment settled over him as he lowered his mouth to hers. He deepened the kiss, allowing what he was feeling to be conveyed. With his mouth he cherished her, like the gift that she had become to him. His desire was evident in the sighs of pleasure which escaped his lips. And when Simone wrapped her arms around him and held on tight, his body let her know how she affected him.

Simone felt Keithen's arousal. She pressed closer, no longer afraid of what she felt or her lack of experience. She felt safe with him. Wanted and desired by him. She let her desire free and matched the seductive stroking of his tongue while fitting her hips to his.

Keithen groaned from the feel of her. The thin dress did little to shield her feminine heat. He eased a hand under the hem of her short sundress to caress the soft flesh of her thigh. He made long sweeping strokes, raising goose bumps on her sensitive flesh, and setting off tiny tremors.

Simone tore her mouth away, needing oxygen. She drew in a shuddering deep breath when his large palm slid down the back of her thigh and back up. Her lashes fluttered before her eyes locked with his, followed by a shy smile.

"We probably should stop if we're going to make it to your grandmother's cookout."

"The cookout? Oh my God, you touch me and I forget everything." Simone stepped back, pushing her dress into place. She ran into the bathroom to reapply her lipstick. "Grandma will want to know why we're late."

"So what will you tell her?" Keithen grinned, thinking about the feisty Ruth Ladner. He had come to adore the older woman.

"I won't tell her anything. You'll tell her that you were late picking me up, and then apologize profusely."

"Simone, you would have me lie to your sweet grandmother?" He chuckled as he tried to get the words out.

"It's lie or tell her what you were really doing with her granddaughter." Simone walked out the front door, giggling as Keithen decided lying wasn't so bad.

Ruth Ladner spotted the couple slipping into the backyard. She noticed the conspiratorial glances flying between them as they parted and tried to blend in with the other guests. She had been watching her granddaughter over the last several months aware that she and Keithen had become romantically involved. She didn't know how far the relationship had evolved, but one look into Simone's eyes and she knew her granddaughter was falling in love. She wove her way over to the grill. Keithen was standing there talking to several of the volunteers who had worked on her home. He appeared to be a nice young man. The volunteers all liked him, and his crew members from California spoke highly of him. There were rumors circulating that the man was wealthy. She hadn't asked Simone because at the time, she hadn't felt it was her business. But if this man was spending time with her granddaughter, they had better get a few things straight.

"Having a good time?"

Keithen turned at the sound of Ruth Ladner's voice. The woman barely reached him mid chest, but he knew better than to cross her. "Yes ma'am. How are you enjoying being back in your home?"

"I'm blessed, child, thanks to you and all the other volunteers." She slipped her arm through his, and led him to a pair of vacant chairs. "You haven't been around much. Are you and Simone getting along all right?"

Keithen smiled. "Yes, we are. As for my absence around here, I've been working on a project for the community."

"Does Simone know about this project?"

"Yes, she does. I've actually asked her to work for me."

Curious brown eyes watched him closely. "Work for you? Exactly what do you do?" She accepted the chair he held for her.

Keithen looked her in the eyes. "I develop residential and commercial property. I've purchased some land here and with the city's approval, I'll be building affordable housing."

"*Your* affordable and our affordable may be two different things."

Keithen laughed to himself because Ruth Ladner didn't mince words. "I'm very aware people in the area are financially strapped. I'll be building homes to fit today's family and I assure you they'll be reasonably priced. Your granddaughter has accepted the designer position."

"Finally, someone who understands the situation. I'm so fed up with all these people rushing in here building condominiums at out of this world prices and calling it affordable."

"Simone helped me to see what was needed."

"She's a wonderful girl," Ruth said affectionately, looking at Keithen. "I know she lived in New York and ran her own business, but she's a small town girl at heart."

Keithen begged to differ. "Simone is no girl. She's a woman. A woman capable of great things."

Ruth's left brow rose as she settled a dark gaze on him. "You're interested in my granddaughter, aren't you?"

"Yes, I am."

The five-foot woman rose from her chair to demand his attention. "Keithen, I'm not one for beating around the bush, so I'm going to speak freely here. Your intentions toward my Simone had better be honorable. She doesn't need a fast talking big city fellow trying to talk her out of her clothes."

Keithen squirmed in his chair. The woman was direct. "Miss Ruth, I care about Simone. I know how special she is and I have no intention of taking advantage. I like who I am with her. She's taught me about compassion and a love of community."

"But you're a man with needs and desires."

"I'm a patient man. I'm not about to pressure Simone into doing anything she doesn't want." He reached out taking the older woman's hands. His eyes held hers. "I'm attracted to your granddaughter. I want your granddaughter. But I've also come to realize I'm falling in love with her."

Ruth didn't know how to respond. She had suspected Keithen was beginning to care about Simone, but she hadn't been prepared to hear words of love. "I like you, Keithen, but be very sure of your feelings."

"Hey, what are you two talking about?" Simone called, heading in their direction. She perched on the arm of Keithen's chair.

"Just getting to know each other better." Ruth observed the young couple. They seemed very comfortable with each other, and when Simone smiled down at Keithen, she knew her granddaughter was falling in love as well. She said a silent prayer for their happiness because she knew the world could be cruel.

"Did you tell Grandma about Simone Place?"

Keithen caressed Simone's hand on his arm. Her excitement about the project could be heard in her voice. "I did, but I have a better idea. Why don't we take her to see the property tomorrow, and then back to your place to look at the design."

"I'd like that," Ruth chimed in. She glanced at Keithen. "You didn't tell me the development was named after Simone?"

"It's how I think of the property, since she was the one who showed it to me." Keithen glanced at Simone.

Ruth loved what she was witnessing. Movement at the back door caught her attention. "Your parents have arrived," she said to her granddaughter.

Simone glanced toward the back door, and then looked at Keithen. "I'm glad they're here. I want you to meet them."

Keithen watched the Ladners and instantly sensed their kindness. Mr. Ladner was nearly the same height as Keithen and his wife an inch or two taller than her daughter. Both wore friendly expressions as they joined them.

"Don't you look pretty?" Delores admired her daughter's appearance, liking the sleeveless dress Simone wore and the gold hoop earrings. It had been quite some time since Simone had looked so lady-like. She noticed the man beside her daughter admiring her appearance as well. Her interest in him mounted.

"Thank you, Mom. You look great, as always."

"I try, baby." Delores looked directly at Keithen.

Simone took the hint and made introductions. "Mom and Dad, I'd like you to meet Keithen Knight. Keithen, my parents, Delores and Gary Ladner

Keithen stuck out his hand in greeting and was pleased with the firm handshake given by Mr. Ladner. He was surprised when Mrs. Ladner hugged him. He cut a surprised glance in Simone's direction. He wasn't accustomed to such a familiar act.

"Thank you," Gary said, "for all that you've done, Mr. Knight. You've made my mother's dream come true."

"I was only one of many. All of us have gained so much by helping out." His eyes landed on Simone and softened. He knew she understood how he felt.

Delores noticed the exchange between the handsome man and her daughter. She had heard her mother-in-law and Lorna whispering about Simone and a man, but she hadn't realized he was white. She half listened as Gary engaged Keithen and Simone in conversation. She noticed that Keithen was good-looking, big and tall with the deepest of green eyes. She understood her daughter's attraction, but questioned her judgement. Her eyes sought Ruth, who nodded, confirming her suspicion that the two were falling in love. Well, she had best get to know this Keithen Knight better, if he was going to be in her daughter's life.

"Keithen, I'm told you're from California," Delores said.

"Yes, the San Francisco Bay area."

"I imagine you must find Biloxi rather slow and boring."

"No ma'am, I don't." He looked at Simone. "There's a great deal to appreciate here."

Simone blushed.

"You're enjoying what the city has to offer?" Delores inquired with a stern expression. She watched the man sweat, pleased that he understood her clearly. Simone was her only child and she wasn't going to allow this man to casually play with her daughter's affections.

Keithen raised his chin as he locked gazes with Simone's mother. She too wanted clarification of his feelings. "Enjoy would be the incorrect word. I've come to treasure the beauty of the area, and its people."

A raised brow was Delores's only response.

Simone glanced from one to the other, thinking she was missing something. Had there been a deeper meaning in her mother's seemingly innocent question? She noticed her father and grandmother's keen interest. "Are you two discussing the landscape or are you talking about me?"

"We are definitely talking about you," Delores didn't hesitate to say. She was concerned about the man's motives. "I need to know the man's intentions."

"Mom, I'm not a child."

"But you're my child and I won't have this man taking advantage of you, and then returning to California." Delores shot Keithen a warning glare.

So much for the friendly hug. Keithen prepared for battle. "Would we be having this conversation if I were black?" he asked.

Delores's head snapped back in stunned surprise. She hadn't been expecting the man to be so direct. "No, we probably wouldn't." Delores thought on that for a moment. The race factor was her concern; she had been prepared for that. However, she would hope Keithen's parents would accept her daughter for who she was and not what box on the census she checked. "I consider myself a fair person, Keithen, and I'm willing to judge you by your actions."

"That's all that I ask."

"I had a really good time this evening." Keithen lay on the sofa with Simone cradled in his arms.

"My father didn't talk your ear off?" She laughed against his chest. "I love him, but the man can talk."

Keithen joined her in laughter, and then pressed a kiss into her hair. "He's quite knowledgeable about the politics of the city. He recommended a local attorney to assist me in meeting the city council about the development."

"I'm glad he could be of help. Mom was pretty quiet."

"Is that out of character?"

"No, not really," she replied with a shake of her head. "It's only that I expected her to pry more. Now that's her nature."

Keithen grinned. "I think she was in observation mode. Didn't you sense her watching us?"

"You think she still disapproves of the two of us?" She raised her head to look at him.

"I'm not saying your mother disapproves." He ran his fingers through her hair while gathering his thoughts. "Maybe she was sizing me up. Determining whether I'm worthy of her daughter." He winked, to lighten the moment.

"I'm trying to decide that myself," Simone teased, and yelped when she was flipped onto her back.

"Well, allow me to help you with that decision." Keithen kissed her. As he deepened the kiss, the cell phone on his hip rang. He signed with frustration as he rolled into a sitting position. "Hello."

"Hi Keith, it's me."

"Jay. What's going on?"

"I received your email and the plans are being drawn up for the project. The team is contacting local vendors for building supplies, and Kate will fly out to handle the interior design purchases."

"Kate isn't required," Keithen informed his brother. "I've found a wonderful designer here."

"You have?" Jay chuckled lasciviously. "She's a looker, I bet."

"Is that all you had to tell me?" Keithen's tone was sharp.

It caught Simone's attention. She ran a hand up and down his arm soothingly. "Is everything all right?" she asked softly.

"Damn," Jay said, "she's with you now, isn't she? No wonder you're trying to get me off the telephone. I'll be in touch. Enjoy your evening."

Keithen snapped his telephone shut. He closed his eyes, angry with himself because his past behavior was the reason for his brother's assumptions. He really had lived the life of a bastard. Turning his head to look at Simone beside him, he was forced to ask what he had done to deserve a woman so fine.

"Why are you looking at me like that?"

"You're a beautiful person. I don't deserve you." He caressed her lips with his thumb.

She looked at him with loving eyes as her fingers combed through his hair. "You're too hard on yourself. I wish you could see yourself the way I do."

"Believe me honey, I don't deserve you."

"Evidently you do, because I'm here." She leaned forward and kissed him. "Now where were we?"

Keithen returned to the trailer with thoughts of Simone on his mind. He pulled the refrigerator open and grabbed a beer. He continued on into the bedroom where he removed his shirt and climbed onto the bed. Reaching for his beer, he unscrewed the cap, taking a long swallow. He looked around the sparse room and realized he was happier now than he had been in quite some time. The new project was a labor of love that was truly needed by the community.

He laughed into the empty room because he was starting to think of Biloxi as home. The slow Southern charm was addictive and inviting. The community was gracious, embracing all the volunteers like family. The men he lived and worked beside were people he looked forward to seeing every day, and men he called friends. He'd also come to care about Miss Ruth and Lorna. He looked forward to their wisdom giving stories. And then, of course, there was Simone. Spiritually beautiful and loving, she had a way of making him feel worthy of the new relationships he had forged in Biloxi. He couldn't imagine a day without her. To see her face and to hear her voice completed his day. He downed his beer and reached for the telephone, dialed and waited.

"Hello," Simone answered.

"I hope I didn't wake you."

"No. Are you okay?

"I'm better than okay. I'm falling in love with you."

Chapter Eight

Those words stayed with Simone through the next week. Each time she thought of the late phone call, she smiled. The next morning when she answered the doorbell, Keithen had been waiting with flowers and a heart-stopping kiss.

She glanced toward the front table in the council chamber, spotting the man of her thoughts. Keithen looked handsome in a designer taupe suit and sage green shirt. He was all business as he presented his design plans for Simone Place and gave a portfolio to the council for further study. He provided the necessary financial papers to show that the project was fully funded. Simone could clearly see why he was a successful developer after observing him in his natural element. When the vote finally came, it was unanimous in favor of the development. The meeting was adjourned.

"Congratulations," Simone said, approaching the table. She easily slipped into Keithen's arms.

"Thanks, babe. Now it's time to get down to work."

"So you're the Simone behind the development name."

Simone and Keithen turned in the direction of the male voice. Simone beamed with happiness, recognizing her childhood friend.

"Hey Jimmy," Simone said, embracing the handsome man. Tall, dark, and with gorgeous dimples, he had been her first crush. "No one told me that you were on the city council."

"No one told me you were having developments named after you." He turned to Keithen. "James Archer, childhood friend of Simone's."

Keithen readily accepted the handshake. There was something about the man that made him like him. "I really appreciate the votes."

James dismissed his words with a wave of his free hand. "Man, we're grateful to you for this project. We have approved numerous condominiums and exclusive communities, but your project is the first to be planned with the common man in mind."

"Simone deserves the credit. She took the time to make me understand the need. The land the project will be built on was property selected by her." Keithen looked at her and winked. "She's equally invested in this project."

Simone's eyes softened as she looked at him. "These houses are going to be wonderful. Keithen has designed them with families and Southern living in mind. I can't wait for people to see them."

"The woman's proud of you," Jimmy joked with Keithen. He was happy to see his friend beaming with love. If anyone deserved happiness, it was Simone. "If I can be of assistance, let me know." Jimmy extended his hand in parting.

"I will." Keithen accepted his hand and watched as he kissed Simone's cheek. He waited until they were alone to speak. "He seems like a good guy."

"He is. I used to have a crush on him."

That got Keithen's full attention. He pulled her into his arms. "And how old were you when you had this crush?"

"Probably about eight. Jimmy beat up Todd Milford for pushing me down on the playground." She grinned at him. "Gave him two black eyes."

"I knew I liked the guy." He kissed her quickly before reaching for his cell phone.

"Calling Jay?"

"Yeah. I need to let him know the project is a go."

Simone sat at the table while he talked and listened as the brothers laid out the next stage of the project. She smiled to herself, thinking about how her life had changed since the hurricane, the biggest change being the man talking on the telephone. *The man she loved.* She walked over to the window overlooking the busy street below. Her heart was racing with excitement and a little fear as well. Thoughts ran rampant through her head, colliding and converging.

She walked to the other side of the room asking herself what she was doing falling in love with Keithen Knight. She would never be his equal, and now that she had accepted a salary from Knight Development, she was not only his girlfriend, she was his employee. But God help her, she had fallen in love with the man. She had to admire his kind and generous nature. Simone Place was an example of his generosity to her and the community that had accepted him as a member. Then there was his undeniable patience with her. He didn't try to force her into his bed. Each evening he kissed her good night and went home. And each night he did, she fell deeper in love with him.

"Ready to go?" Keithen asked.

Silence.

"Simone?"

"Huh?"

"What were you thinking about?" Keithen held out his hand for her to take, and led them out of the building.

"How proud I am of you," she lied. "Where to now?"

"The public works building. Water has to be run to the site, as well as electricity and cable."

"This is all so exciting."

Keithen smiled, enjoying Simone's enthusiasm for the development project. They left the building and turned right. Their pace was leisurely due to the high humidity and warm temperature. At the corner the light changed, forcing them to wait. An attractive red head pulled alongside Keithen, giving him a hungry once-over.

"Hi," the woman greeted in an exaggerated, seductive slow drawl. Her big baby blues fluttered flirtatiously. "This heat and humidity is a killer. My clothes are sticking to me already," she said, tugging at the form-fitting blouse squeezing her enhanced breasts.

Standing between the woman and Simone, Keithen merely nodded because he could feel Simone's eyes burning into the side of his head.

"A cold shower usually helps," Simone quipped as she threaded her fingers through Keithen's and crossed the street when the light changed. She glanced back at the gawking woman and winked. She knew the busty red head had never given a thought to the possibility that she and Keithen might be together.

Surprised laughter erupted from Keithen as they reached the other corner. "She was only being friendly." His eyes were bright with humor.

"And I was only giving her a good piece of advice." Simone smiled as he laughed harder. "Stop it."

Keithen opened the glass door to the public works building for Simone. He placed a kiss onto her cheek as she passed by. Inside, he took care of the necessary details. When he completed his business, they returned to Simone's home office exhausted, yet exhilarated to finally have the project underway. Keithen went right to work going down the checklist of things to be done. He got on the telephone with one of the local casinos. Because of limited housing in the area, the casinos were one of the few places to house his staff. By the end of the telephone call, he had successfully secured five suites.

"I heard you ask for five suites. Does that mean that you're leaving the trailer?"

He glanced across the room to Simone curled up in the comfy corner chair. She wore a pretty pink sundress which was draped over her legs. The vibrant color made her skin tone radiant. She had twisted her hair up off her neck during the evening heat and looked soft and feminine.

"Yes and no. Since I really won't be volunteering any more, I'll have my trailer moved to the property. I can use it as an onsite office." He rose from the desk chair to kneel in front of her corner chair. "I was thinking you would probably feel more comfortable visiting me in a hotel suite as opposed to a busy volunteer camp."

"No prying eyes and loose lips," she added.

"Exactly." He made himself comfortable on the floor. "Simone, I want you to think about something for me."

Dark eyes probed curiously. "What is it?"

He looked up at her as he covered her feet with his hands. "I want you to consider opening a new restaurant. Hear me out," he said when she started to protest. "You're a chef, a fine one who should be back in the kitchen of her own restaurant. Besides, I have the money to make your dreams come true."

Simone suddenly rose from the sofa, placing distance between them. She stood in the middle of the floor glaring at him. "You're paying me a salary already. Do you realize how difficult that is for me to accept from you? I don't need you to pay for my dreams as well. Leave me with a little pride, please." The words came out bitter.

Keithen was hurt and a bit confused. "I wasn't trying to step on your pride. I was trying to do something nice for the woman I care about." His voice escalated with anger.

Simone took a deep breath because she was acting like an ungrateful fool. The man was kind and generous, and not once had he deliberately made her feel less than an equal. She was doing that all to herself. She looked at him sitting on the floor looking perplexed and took the few steps to where he sat and joined him on the floor. "I apologize for being silly. My feeling out of your league isn't your problem."

He looked at her with a cutting stare. "I've never once treated you as beneath me. I personally believe you're too damn good for me, but I want you anyway. And I want to do nice things for you because I believe you deserve them. The money isn't going away, Simone, so you need to decide whether you can live with it." He rose quickly from the floor and headed toward the office door.

"Where are you going?" She jumped up behind him.

"I'm leaving. I think it best if we give each other a little space."

"Don't go," she whispered, taking his hand. "It's my problem."

"Yes, it is and you need to deal with it. I'm going to be honest here." His eyes were piercing with intensity. "I'm hurt you would accuse me of stomping on your pride." He shook his head from side to side, gathering his thoughts. "I believe in you. I want to see you succeed. Damn it, I want you to be happy doing what you love. I want you to be happy with *me*."

Simone heard the anguish in his words. How could she have said those things to him, when she knew they weren't really true? "Keithen, I am happy with you. I haven't been this happy or felt so cared for before. And watching you in the council chambers was so impressive. I'm proud of you."

"That all may be true, but you've admitted you're uncomfortable with my financial status. Why? I can give you the world if you let me." He looked at her, wounded. He watched as Simone collapsed back down to the floor.

"I don't feel like an equal partner in this relationship. Since accepting the interior design position, I've become your employee on top of everything else. I can't shower you with gifts. I haven't even offered you my body," she whispered, looking up at him with tears in her eyes.

Keithen dropped to the floor beside her. He stroked her hair. "You're wrong. You give me so much. This office was set up just for me. That's a gift. I'm completely happy and content with myself since meeting you. You've given me the ability to dream again, and see the good inside myself. I know I'm more than my bank account. You showed me that." He kissed her forehead. "I have a sense of community now, with new friends who really care about me. And although you haven't shared your body, as you put it, you've shared the most important thing, your heart. That single action is more valuable to me than money."

"You mean that, don't you?" Simone heard the sincerity in his voice and saw it in his eyes.

"Of course I do. Look at this room. You've given me a space in your home. That tells me you enjoy having me around." He took her hands in his. "I want you to feel as special."

Simone was truly humbled. She cupped his face with her hands and brought his mouth to hers. The kiss was tender and filled with the love that she felt. When she pulled her mouth away, she slipped her arms around his neck. "I'll consider your offer, but you don't have to buy me things to make me feel special."

"Okay, I hear you. But you have to understand I enjoy sharing what I have with you." He rubbed her back. "If you're uncomfortable working for me, I'll let you out of the design position."

Simone pulled back to meet his eyes. "I want to do it, but not for a salary. It'll be a labor of love."

"Would that be love for the community or love for me?" Keithen asked with a big stupid grin on his face.

Simone returned the smile. "I believe you know the answer."

Chapter Nine

All right, Simone, I know you well enough to know something is on your mind," Jasmine commented, watching her friend. It was two days later and Simone had met her best friend for lunch at a local diner.

Simone smiled because she knew there was no hiding from Jasmine. The two had shared secrets since they were little girls. "I did something I'm ashamed of, and although Keithen has forgiven me, I'm sure he hasn't forgotten."

Jasmine could see the little worry lines between her friend's eyes. "I'm sure it's not that bad."

"It is. I accused him of using his money to step on my pride."

"Yeah, that was pretty bad," Jasmine replied honestly.

"Gee, thanks."

Jasmine laughed. "I'm your friend. It's my job to tell you the truth."

"I'll remember that the next time you ask me if it looks like you've gained weight."

"You're wrong for that," Jasmine said, giggling. "I can imagine it's a little different dating someone who doesn't have to worry about money."

"Not really. I know I must sound foolish, but this really is my problem." She moved the food around on her plate with the fork. "I think I'm afraid he's passing time with me until he returns home to his real life. What do I have to offer a man with millions?"

"Love."

"Keithen said something similar."

Jasmine's face lit up. "He's told you he loves you?"

Simone smiled, remembering that her friend was a hopeless romantic. Her dark eyes were already wide and eager for the response. "He's told me he's falling in love."

"That's good. How do you feel about him?"

Simone glanced around the diner. The lunch crowd had thinned, so they were free to sit and simply talk. "I'm crazy about the man. He's nice and caring. This project is a generous gift to the community. He's going to offer the homes well below today's market, because he knows the need for affordable housing is so great."

"That is generous, considering how the price of housing rose after the storm. But how does he make you feel as a woman?"

The look in Simone's eyes changed to a soft warm glow. A smile tugged at her lips. She looked across the table and answered from the heart. "He makes me feel special. He believes I can do anything I set my mind to. He painted my living room so I could turn my house into a home."

"Thoughtful."

"You have no idea," Simone said, looking at her. "The man wants to finance a new restaurant for me."

"Get out of here!" Jasmine exclaimed, drawing attention to their table. She covered her mouth with a hand, looking embarrassed. "Sorry about that."

"No problem. It is shocking."

"It's extremely generous, Simone. The man must really care about you." Jasmine smiled happily.

"The offer was what brought on the accusation."

Jasmine sat there for a moment eyeing her friend. "This is about your cousin, Marty. Oh, Simone, you can't compare the two." She grabbed her friend's hand, trying to get her point across. "Keithen and Marty's husband are different people."

Simone nodded as she took a breath. "I know you're right, but you saw how quickly things changed. I never imagined Marty in such a situation."

"I know, I didn't either, but you can't punish Keithen because of what happened. You don't believe he's capable of the kind of behavior as Marty's husband, do you?"

Did she? Simone immediately knew the answer. "No, I don't."

"What does Miss Ruth think about you two? She's a good judge of character."

"She really likes him."

"And how does she feel about the other issue here? You know she's lived through some troubled days."

The waitress picked that moment to retrieve their dishes, and leave a dessert menu. When the woman walked away, Simone picked up their conversation. "That's code for racism, isn't it?"

"You and I both grew up here and have heard the stories. You know some people have strong feelings about interracial dating. I was just wondering whether she has expressed any concern."

Simone knew the stories of the Civil Rights protests and marches. Her grandmother had been right in the center of the action on the Coast and national level, but was a believer in judging a man by his deeds. "No, she hasn't. You know, Grandma said people of all races marched, and therefore every man deserves a chance." Simone paused. "But Mom had a problem with our dating. However after Keithen called her on her prejudice, she decided to give him a chance."

"So are you giving Keithen a chance as well?" Jasmine wiggled her brows teasingly. She laughed when Simone threw a napkin at her.

Simone laughed with her. "Until that man gives me a reason to change my opinion about him, yes."

"Well, I'm happy for you, girl. The guy seems really nice and this development with reasonably priced homes is a blessing. Hey, why don't we get the guys together? They need to meet each other."

"Good idea. Why don't you and Bobby come over to my place for dinner?"

"We'll be there. Make that blueberry thing for dessert."

Simone placed the floral centerpiece on the table and stood back admiring her handiwork. It had been ages since she had hosted a dinner party. The centerpiece was a beautiful arrangement provided by Keithen. She had used her fine china and crystal. The menu tonight consisted of her best dishes, plus the blueberry thing Jasmine had requested. She returned to the kitchen, moving from counter to stove as she checked on the meal. She smiled to herself as she felt strong hands slide along her waist. She leaned back against Keithen's strong chest, snuggling closer. These days she was feeling more secure in their relationship. That's why tonight's dinner was so important to her. She wanted Jasmine and Bobby to get to know the man she had fallen for.

"You're going to be exhausted before they get here," Keithen said, turning her around in his arms. He dipped his nose to her neck inhaling. "God, you smell good."

"Thanks," she giggled, caressing his cheek. "It's a new fragrance."

"I think I'll buy every bottle there is for you." His eyes were seductive and intimate.

"Well, you do have the money." Her smile was teasing.

Keithen returned the smile. He ran his hand over her hair as he brushed his lips across hers. "It's good to see you can joke about the money."

"Your beautiful words the other night helped me to feel confident about our relationship." She looked up at him. "The money isn't going away and neither am I."

"That's what I want to hear."

The doorbell chimed, calling a halt to the private moment. Simone jumped with excitement, pulling out of his arms. She threaded her fingers through his as she pulled him along to the door.

"Welcome to my home." Simone stepped aside for her guests to enter. Closing the door behind them, she made quick work of the introductions.

"Wow, girl, I love this room. The color is beautiful," Jasmine commented, wandering around the living room.

"Thank you, but I can't take credit for it." Simone turned loving eyes on Keithen. "He did all the painting. It was a wonderful surprise that made my house a home."

"That was really sweet." Jasmine winked at Keithen. The simple act went a long way in helping him to feel accepted.

"It's a great thing you're doing for the city," Bobby Clark said, shaking Keithen's hand. Standing about the same height, his body build was muscular but slender. His hazel eyes turned back to Simone. "Jasmine told me you were cooking and you know I couldn't miss that."

Simone laughed, wrapping her arms around her old friend. He and Jasmine had been an item since grade school. Their love an example of the way it was meant to be.

"I remember a time when we should have missed her cooking," Jasmine commented from behind Bobby. "Do you both remember the time she tried to duplicate her grandmother's secret brownies?"

Simone laughed uncontrollably as she tried to shut her friend up. "No one wants to hear this."

Bobby howled with laughter as the memory came flooding back. "I stayed in the bathroom for two days."

"That's what you get for being so greedy." Jasmine wiped tears from her eyes. "Simone and I took one, but no, you grabbed three." She shook with laughter.

Keithen stood on the sideline watching the three share a special moment. He appreciated their obvious love for one another, but was a little jealous as well. He and Jay had been this close once, but with Jay's repeated bouts of trouble and his own inheritance of the business, their relationship had become strained. His younger brother fought every decision he made and resented him more and more each day. They hadn't shared a moment like this in a long time.

"What did you put into the brownies?" Keithen asked Simone. He hooked his arm around her neck.

She turned to him with tears running down her cheeks. "You have to understand I was about eight, and my grandmother had taken an antihistamine and fallen asleep on the porch. We had asked her to make some of her special brownies. She said she would make them Sunday after church, but as I remember it, these two didn't want to wait. They said we could make them."

"Excuse me, but *you* said that you could make them," Bobby interjected. He smiled at his wife. "Didn't she?"

"You did say that."

"Of course you would agree with your husband," Simone snapped.

"You're stalling, honey," Keithen said to Simone. He bumped her hip with his. "What did you put in the brownies?"

Simone rolled her eyes before answering. "I had helped my grandmother make the brownies before. She would always go into the top cabinet and remove a bottle with golden- brown liquid. So I did the same thing."

Keithen's shoulders began to shake as he realized where this story was headed. "You put booze into the mix," he finished.

"Rum actually. It was my grandmother's secret ingredient, and she always poured some into the batter. But maybe not quite as much as I did." Simone looked at him innocently. "Alcohol burns off, but when you lick the bowl, spatula, and mixing beaters, then gorge on rum-soaked brownies, you're bound to feel it."

Keithen's robust laughter added more humor to the moment. By the time Simone told him about the spanking she received for not only making her friends sick, but for using the stove as well, he was doubled over with laughter.

"When Ms. Ruth woke up and caught us, we were all giggling and could barely walk. She banned us from the house for a week," Jasmine added. "But Simone couldn't sit for a week."

"My poor baby." Keithen kissed her head playfully.

"Stop it, you two." Simone waved them all into the living room where Keithen prepared drinks. She went into the kitchen for the appetizers.

Bobby and Jasmine followed Keithen over to the bar area. Bobby had heard about Keithen and Simone's relationship. He had also been following the progress of the planned development in the newspaper and on the evening news. He was quite impressed with the man's business savvy. "I hope we didn't bore you with our story."

"Are you kidding? I envy the relationship the three of you have." Keithen passed Bobby his drink, then handed Jasmine a glass of wine.

"We are close. She's a good woman." Jasmine excused herself to join Simone in the kitchen.

Keithen watched Jasmine make her exit. His lips thinned. "Why do I get the feeling I'm being warned?"

"Perhaps because you are. Simone's like a sister to me and I want to see her happy." Bobby sipped his drink. His dark, assessing eyes demanded that Keithen state his intentions.

Keithen read the command and his eyes connected with Bobby's, never wavering. "I'm not playing games here, or killing time until I return to California. I'm actually thinking about putting down roots here."

Bobby chuckled. "Oh, man, I know what that means."

Keithen's smile broadened. "I've fallen in love with the lady. I wasn't expecting it. A couple of short months, and the woman was under my skin." He moved around the room talking to this complete stranger because he needed to talk to someone. "I haven't told her I'm in love with her, just that I was falling in love. It's a little sudden, and there are so many issues to be resolved that I've chosen not to tell her the truth."

"I may be overstepping here, but what issues require resolving? You love her and I can see in her eyes that she loves you."

Keithen beamed with the happiness those words inspired. "Yeah, but she's a little uncomfortable with my…" He paused, not sure of how much to reveal.

"Look man, everyone who has a television in this city know that you're loaded. So you're saying Simone is uncomfortable with your wealth?"

Laughter filled the room as Keithen relaxed and came to the decision that he liked Bobby. "I offered to bankroll a new restaurant for her, and she got angry. She accused me of stripping her of her pride."

"That's Simone, man. Don't take it personally. The girl believes she has to do everything on her own. She'll give her very last dime to everyone else, but she doesn't know how to accept help."

"That's her." Keithen returned to the chair. "Why won't she accept my help?"

"I don't know for sure, but I think she believes people will see her as weak if she asks for help."

"Weak?" Keithen scoffed. "That woman works harder than any man I know, and emotionally, she's tough. She's taken on the responsibility of rebuilding her grandmother's home. I have the money. Is it so wrong to help the woman I love?"

"Not at all. I'd do anything to get my beautiful wife back in our home," Bobby remarked sadly. "We were blessed to qualify for the grant money, but I can't find a contractor to do the work now. They're all tied up with other jobs and it could be months before they start construction on our house."

"I have a crew ready to go, if you're interested."

Bobby glanced at him. "Are you serious? I mean, I know you and Simone have been helping out."

"Yes, we have and I told Jasmine I would love to help. The site is nowhere near ready for our skills, so we'll be available to work on your place."

"How much are you charging?" Bobby asked hopefully. With Keithen's crew and the state's grant money, he just might have his family in a home by fall.

"You buy the building supplies and I'll supply the labor free of charge, unless you're too proud to accept help from a friend."

"Pride won't put a roof over my family's head. Thank you, friend." Bobby stood and walked over to Keithen, extending his hand. His smile was one of gratitude and relief. "I really appreciate the help."

The women returned to the living room engaged in conversation. Simone carried a beautiful tray of delicious-looking appetizers. She deposited the tray on the coffee table, and moved over to the chair where Keithen sat. She perched on the arm, covering his hand with hers. From the kitchen she and Jasmine had been aware of the guys talking, but had been unable to detect their mood. However, entering the room, they had been quite pleased to see them sharing a smile and conversation. She focused on Bobby.

"Jaz tells me that you were able to salvage the bricks from your home. Will you be reusing them on the new house?"

"You better believe it. Reusing those bricks will save a great deal of money, plus it will help to make it feel like home."

"Who's doing the bricklaying?" Keithen asked with great interest. "I ask because I'll be looking for a good crew to work on the development."

"Actually, my guys and I are doing the work," Bobby told him with pride. "I've been laying bricks all my life. I'd appreciate the opportunity to bid on the job."

"I'd love the opportunity to work with you." Keithen removed his wallet and passed Bobby his card. "Fax your bid to this number. I'll notify my brother to be looking for it."

"Great." Bobby was enthusiastic about the opportunity to work on a large subdivision.

Simone announced that dinner was served and ushered everyone to the table. With skill and grace, she presented the meal in true culinary fashion. First to the table was her scrumptious Crawfish and Corn Bisque followed by crisp garden greens. For the entrée she presented tender prime rib, served with roasted potatoes, and asparagus with hollandaise. A Sonoma Merlot complemented the meal and enhanced the flavors of the food. By the time she brought out the blueberry cobbler with a scoop of homemade vanilla ice cream, everyone was salivating. The lively conversation was reduced to moans and groans of pleasure as they partook of the dessert.

"Bobby, you're going to have to roll me home." Jasmine sighed heavily as she collapsed onto the sofa. "Girl, that meal was wonderful."

"I'm glad that you enjoyed it." Simone went about serving coffee in the living room. Taking a seat beside Keithen, she smiled as the compliments kept coming.

"You could be serving meals like that in your own place," Keithen whispered close to her ear.

Simone glanced over at him with a faint smile on her lips. Her eyes were soft and loving because she knew he meant well.

"You two are going to have to stop looking at each other like that, or Bobby and I are going to have to excuse ourselves."

Simone blushed. "Well when you go, don't forget the kids' dessert."

"Sweetheart, was that an invitation to leave?" Bobby joked.

Keithen laughed heartily. "Simone tells me you have three children."

"Two boys and a girl," the couple replied in unison.

Simone and Keithen looked at each other and laughed. Keithen could see they were proud parents who adored their children.

"Do you want children, Keithen?" Jasmine asked pointedly, ignoring Simone's warning glare. "Simone loves children."

The woman has no shame. Simone wanted to crawl under the sofa with embarrassment. "Ignore her."

"No, I have nothing to hide." Keithen stroked Simone's cheek with the back of his hand. "I had never given children a thought because I didn't see myself getting married." His green eyes moved over Simone's face, thoughtful. "Lately, I've been doing a great deal of rethinking about the future."

Simone stole a glance in his direction. She didn't dare probe further, and didn't allow Jasmine to either. But as they closed the door to their guests, she couldn't stop thinking about his reevaluation of his life. It gave her great pleasure to know his desire for her had him thinking of the possibilities. She knew she wanted children. She also knew that she wanted a life with Keithen.

In the kitchen, Simone added the tray of dirty cups to the dishwasher. She found herself daydreaming about a life with Keithen and children. The kitchen would no doubt be the center of activity. They would share meals together as a family with Keithen at one end of the table and her at the other. He would look at her with love in his eyes, and watch his children with fatherly pride. As she added the detergent and switched the dishwasher on, she smiled at the dream.

"What are you thinking about?"

Simone startled as Keithen's voice penetrated her thoughts. She turned facing him and leaned against the counter. Her eyes traveled from his Italian leathers to his blond head. Did she dare tell him where her thoughts had been? "I was thinking about the evening."

Keithen chuckled and walked toward her. His eyes noted her guarded expression. He stood in front of her and crossed his arms over his chest. "You were thinking about what I said."

"No, I wasn't."

"Simone. This is me, darling. I've learned to read you pretty well."

"Obviously not." She moved to escape the conversation, but was halted by Keithen's outstretched arm.

"We don't have to avoid the conversation."

"Are you sure? I mean, Jasmine really put you on the spot."

He took her hand in his and led the way back to the living room. He took a seat in the chair and placed Simone on his lap. He looked at her for several minutes, appreciating her beauty and spirit. "When I left California, I knew who I was and what I wanted out of life. I knew I had no intention of ever getting married, and I sure as hell hadn't planned on children. But since I've been here, I've grown. I've seen a new way of life and I want it. I want the wife and kids. I want the house with a big yard and neighbors who gather on the porch."

"Oh, man, we've brainwashed you." Simone grinned. "We have you hanging out on the porch.

"Laugh if you want, but I want this life." He turned her face to his and placed a kiss onto her lips. "I've been dreaming about that life with you."

"I was daydreaming about a life with you and children," she whispered, embarrassed. "It's ridiculous and we're both getting way ahead of ourselves."

"Perhaps, but I don't think so." He kissed her once more. "What we feel for each other isn't going away. I think you and I both know that. So you have to become comfortable with the money."

"I told you I'll try." She smiled guiltily.

"Bobby told me you've always been the giver, never the one to accept help from others."

"To some extent that's true, but my refusal to allow you to finance a restaurant has to do with something else." She scooted off his lap to place distance between them. "Actually it has to do with *someone*."

"A man?"

"Yes, but not how you think." She walked over to the sofa and sat down. "My cousin Martine married a professional athlete who threw his money around, showering her with gifts. She quit her job to make herself available to him. She would fly to whichever city was in. He bought her cars, clothes, a home, and even her own upscale salon. He became her whole world."

Keithen had seen this happen before and knew this wouldn't be a 'feel good' story. He pushed Simone to continue when she drew quiet. "What happened?"

"For a while all was great. But then she began making excuses not to call and visit family. I grew concerned because she cut herself off from everyone."

"He isolated her." Keithen knew the type well. "He used his money to control her."

Sad chocolate eyes stared at him. In them, Keithen could see pain and fear and it tugged at his heart. "Tell me the rest."

"One day I received a phone call in New York from Marty. She told me everything. She said she felt like a prisoner. You could hear the desperation in her voice. I told her to leave him, but she refused, saying that if she left that she would have nothing."

"He had her dependent upon him." His jaw tightened with anger and disgust.

Simone watched the movement of the flexing muscle, knowing that Keithen was appalled. His whole body was tight with tension.

"Yes, he did, and she didn't understand she could start over. She had family who loved her. I tried to convince her to come to New York and stay with me."

"People have to want to leave. Only they can break the cycle. Was there any physical abuse?"

"No one really knows because the family didn't see her. But the last thing she told me was to stay in control of my life."

"The last thing?" He scowled at her, realizing the conclusion of the story. He moved to the sofa and swept a hand over her hair.

Watery eyes met his. "Marty committed suicide in her beautiful home, surrounded by all the material possessions she couldn't walk away from."

Keithen's mind raced with the information as he finally realized why Simone was so opposed to his backing her restaurant. He gripped her forearms with alarm, turning her to face him. "Dear God, Simone, you don't believe I would treat you so despicably, do you? Please say you don't." His voice was heavy with hurt. His eyes were eagle sharp, searching for any sign of doubt. Surely she knew his true nature by now. "From the moment I saw you on top of that roof, sweaty and capable, I understood why I was drawn here."

"You came to assist with the storm."

"And to find you."

Simone smiled bashfully.

"Do you not trust me to allow you to be your own person? Don't you know it was your unselfish, take charge personality that caused me to fall in love with you? I don't want to change that."

Simone's eyes flew to his on hearing those words. "You're in love with me?"

Keithen released her arms to frame her face. Love as bright as a million stars in the sky blazed in his eyes. "I know things move slowly in the South, but from the moment I saw you…"

"All sweaty and capable."

He released that thundering laugh that she had come to cherish. "Yes, all sweaty and capable. You were all I thought about.

Her eyes went glassy with unshed tears. She retook her place on his lap. Looping her arms around his neck, she leaned in close, with her lips next to his. "I've been told slow is good, depending upon what you're doing." She opened her mouth over his, demonstrating with an unhurried nerve wracking caress of her tongue against his. The slow strokes were sensually drugging. Each sweep into his mouth heightened their desire. Her hardened nipples pressed into his chest, and he groaned from the contact. Simone leaned back toward the sofa and pulled Keithen down with her. She made a place for him between her parted thighs as he adjusted his position. She withdrew her mouth to look into his eyes. "No, Keithen, I don't believe you would use your wealth to control me. I've come to know the man you are and I like him a great deal." She slid her hands down the wall of his chest as her lips sought his once more.

"Thank you, baby." He kissed her hard and quick, tangling his tongue with hers, then against the protest of his body, he pushed up from the sofa and headed directly for the door, pulling it open.

Stunned and feeling abandoned Simone scrambled into an upright position. "Where are you going?" Her body was hot and pulsing with desire. She had waited long enough and found the man she could trust with her body. She wanted him, needed him, to make the craving go away.

"Home." Hungry eyes slid along her inviting body, recalling the feel of every soft inch. "You and I aren't doing casual. When I take you to bed, you'll be there to stay."

Chapter Ten

Simone pondered Keithen's words. What exactly had they meant? What had he been suggesting? He had said he loved her and that they weren't doing casual. Did it mean he wanted something more permanent from their relationship? Did she?

Things were good between them. The man had been up front and unbelievably honest about who he was and she was more comfortable with his wealth. He had also been sincere in his desire to live a better life. She witnessed that sincerity each day he worked on destroyed properties for nothing more than the joy of helping others. And the new development project was all about giving others a new start in life. He was a good man, and she had fallen in love with him. Each moment they were together only reinforced her feelings for him.

She hummed happily to herself as she climbed the wooden steps to the onsite office. The trailer had recently been moved to the property, and the land was in the process of being cleared and leveled for the installation of utilities. The Knight construction team had arrived yesterday. Keithen had phoned and asked she come down to the site to meet everyone. But she was a little nervous. These people were friends and co-workers of his. Would they approve or disapprove of their relationship? Taking a deep breath, she grabbed the door knob and pushed the door open. The transformation of the travel trailer into office space stopped her in her tracks. The living and kitchen area now served as work space housing desks, files, and office equipment. Only the refrigerator remained as a reminder the trailer had once served as a living space.

"There you are." Keithen pushed away from the desk and walked toward her with a huge smile on his face. Her heart fluttered from the sight of him dressed in business attire.

"Hi. I see you've been busy."

"Took a crew one complete day to transform things." He kissed her quickly. "Come on in to my office, everyone's here." He admired her professional look. The soft yellow pant suit was beautiful. He also liked the way her hair was swept up in a cool style. He beamed with pride. He couldn't wait for the team to meet her, but as he reached for her hand, he noticed the anxious expression on her face. "Are you all right?" he said quietly.

Simone smiled, trying to cover her uneasiness. "I'm a little nervous about meeting your staff. What do they know about me?"

"They know you're a talented local designer that I've asked to join the team." The corners of his mouth tugged up. "Of course when I introduce you, they'll all know where the name of the development came from. No doubt they will begin to speculate about our relationship."

"Great." Simone rolled her eyes. "They'll think that I slept my way into this job."

"I'm not paying you, remember. There is no conflict here. You're a beautiful woman whom I've gotten to know and fallen in love with."

"Let's do this." She fell into step beside him as they entered his private office. She quickly scanned the room. Two men leaned over a desk looking at plans. A woman with dark brown, short hair sat in a side chair, reading over documents. As she and Keithen approached, all heads turned in their direction.

"All right team I'd like to introduce you all to Simone Ladner, the newest member of Knight Development," Keithen said.

Curious eyes settled on her, followed by welcoming smiles as they one by one came forward to greet her.

"Hi Simone, I'm Noah Lowe, project budget guy," the salt and pepper-haired man, introduced himself. He adjusted his thick glasses and stuck out his hand.

"Welcome to Biloxi, Noah." Simone shook the extended hand. She sensed a kind nature and astute business man.

The other man introduced himself as Colin Norton, construction foreman. About the same height as Keithen, he was of a thinner build, but his firm handshake indicated his strength. Lastly Simone greeted the woman, Jodi Frazier. The woman's brown eyes were friendly like her smile, but held a feminine curiosity. Keithen suggested everyone take a seat as they got down to business.

The experience was exciting for Simone. She learned so much about the home building business. She also learned Keithen got a high from the planning, negotiating, and scheduling of construction. She could watch him all day as his eyes danced with the thrill of the process. He talked of geological reports, supplier's pricing, manpower numbers, and financial budgets. He was involved in every aspect of the job, and yet it was obvious he valued the people around him. He listened to their input and graciously accepted their expert advice, which was obviously appreciated. By the time the meeting broke up, she was looking forward to working on the project with this group of talented people.

"I'm going to walk the team over the property." Keithen came over to Simone. "Do you mind covering the phones while we're out?"

"Of course not." She dodged his kiss. "What are you doing? There are other people in here," she whispered, pointing over her shoulder.

Keithen rolled his eyes heavenward. "All right, Simone, have it your way. But I'm sure they've put two and two together."

Simone suppressed a giggle as Keithen rounded up everyone and left the trailer. She went to the window to watch their departure, her eyes zeroing in on his tall figure. She smiled when he donned the yellow hard hat that had been a part of her disguise a few months back when she had feared being discovered leaving his trailer. Nowadays, she feared never being invited to his bed. She moved forward, leaning her head against the warm glass. She had never had such strong feelings for a man before, nor had she so wanted to act upon the feelings. Each time that she was with Keithen, her desire for him rose, and although he repeatedly put a halt to their sexual activity, she knew that he wanted her as well. Her thoughts returned to those words from a few days ago. Was it possible he was contemplating marriage? The sound of the telephone broke into her musings.

"Knight Development," Simone answered. She reached for a message pad.

"This is Jay Knight. I'd like to speak with my brother." His tone was impersonal and direct.

"Mr. Knight is out of the office. I'll have him return your call."

"Do that, ah…"

"Simone Ladner," she supplied.

There was a long pause. "Did you say Simone?"

"Yes, I did."

"As in Simone Place."

"Yes." Simone listened as bawdy laughter filled her ear. She took an instant dislike to Jay Knight.

"Interesting. Have my brother call me."

Simone stood with the telephone receiver in hand. She didn't know what to make of his remark. Replacing the receiver into its cradle, she returned to the window and spotted Keithen. He was showing the three her favorite spot. The idea of someone living there was a bit depressing. However, being realistic, she knew she wasn't financially able to purchase the property. She had nearly exhausted all of her funds rebuilding her grandmother's home. Monday morning she had an interview with a five star restaurant located in one of the casinos. With any luck she would be gainfully employed once more.

She returned to her chair experiencing a little self pity. She had lost her restaurant and special place. When she heard footsteps on the wooden steps, however, she was reminded that she had gained something as well.

Keithen returned to the office by himself, having sent the others home for the evening. He stood in the doorway sensing Simone's change in mood. Removing the hard hat, he placed it on the desk and approached her. "What happened? You look sad."

She was ashamed of herself for whining about what she didn't have. People were out there who had lost everything, including loved ones, and here she sat with this wonderful man who loved her.

"How can I be sad when I have you?" She forced a smile in an effort to feel better.

Keithen knew she was faking it. Something had taken away her happy spirit and replaced it with sadness. "I only want to make you happy."

"You do make me happy. I'll be all right." She reached for his hand and brought it to her lips. "I love you."

"I love you too, baby."

"Oh, your brother called while you were out. He wants you to return his call."

"What did he say to you? Is he responsible for this change in your mood?" Keithen knew what Jay was like and could imagine him saying something distasteful to Simone.

"He took a great interest in my name."

Keithen understood what she was telling him. His jaws tightened.

"He didn't know about me." She rose from the chair and stood in front of him, her arms folded across her chest defensively.

Keithen slid an arm around her waist. The movement forced her arms to open. "He knew there was a woman in my life. He just didn't know her name."

"Oh." Simone frowned. "He does now, and from the disgusting little laugh he gave me, he believes I'm another one of your *women*." Her eyes connected with his.

He tightened his grip around her waist and his smile became flirtatious. "Well, technically you are, but…"

"But what?" She gave him a stern look.

"But, you happen to be the woman I'm in love with."

Simone slipped her arms around his neck. She hugged him for several minutes without speaking. She just wanted to hold him close. To feel his heartbeat next to hers.

"What are you thinking?" He could feel the tension in her body.

"What do you think he's going to do with the information?"

Keithen released a laugh. "Oh, I'm sure he's told the old man that hard nosed Keithen has lost his mind to a woman."

Simone looked into his smiling face and trailed loving fingers down his jaw line. A smile played on her lips. "Have you lost your mind to me?"

"My mind and my heart."

"Good answer, Mr. Knight." She gave him a peck on the lips. "Walk me to my truck. I'm headed over to Jasmine and Bobby's. The building materials for their home were supposed to be delivered today, and I need to make sure everything is there before I start rounding people up."

"As soon as you know, give me a call, so I can let the crew know where we're working." Keithen took her hand and left the trailer. The gravel of the makeshift drive crunched under their feet.

"Don't you think you're stretching yourself thin?" Simone asked, concerned.

Emerald eyes looked down at her. "Worried about me?"

"Of course."

"Who works more than you?" he challenged her. "By day you're working on homes. In the evenings, you're working on this project, and Sunday, you're in the kitchen at the volunteer camp."

Simone rolled her eyes, annoyed. "Well, you'll be glad to know I may be cutting my activities back. I have an interview at one of the casino restaurants on Monday.

Keithen stood there for several minutes saying nothing. Simone knew how he felt about her working for someone else, but knowing about Marty, he understood her need for independence. "I'm sure you'll get the job." He pulled the truck door open for her.

"Thank you." Simone deposited a lingering kiss onto his lips. His words of support meant a great deal to her. "I'll talk with you later."

He stood back watching as her truck disappeared around the bend in the road. He had no doubt she would get the job. Every day eating at her table was a culinary delight.

He returned to the office and immediately called Jay. He was prepared to take a ribbing from his brother about Simone, but that was okay because she was worth Jay's wisecracks. He sat waiting for his brother to come to the telephone. While he did, he looked out the window to Simone's special place. The beautiful piece of land deserved a special house to complement its beauty.

"I'm glad to see you could tear yourself away from Simone," Jay said, coming on to the line. "What the hell is going on with you?"

"I've met a special lady."

"Special lady? You mean great sex."

Keithen sighed heavily. He could definitely understand why his brother was being so cynical. He had lived a 'love 'em and leave 'em' life. "Why did you call me?" He didn't bother to correct Jay's assumption because it wasn't any of his business that he and Simone hadn't made love. His brother probably wouldn't believe him anyway. So why was now different? He knew Jay would want to know. The only answer he could give him was that Simone was worth waiting for. He didn't want one night of passion with her. He wanted a lifetime of loving her and being loved by her. *God, I sound like a greeting card.*

"Now that Noah and the team are in place, when are you coming home?"

That was a reasonable question, Keithen admitted. He had taken care of all the city and legal dealings. Noah had headed construction for him on numerous occasions, but this was different. Simone Place was a labor of love. "I'm staying. Actually I'm thinking about opening an office here."

Jay swore. "She must be damn talented to have you jeopardizing our business."

"You don't know anything about Simone and me."

"*Simone and me.* Will you listen to yourself? The woman is a plaything."

"Shut your damn mouth!" Keithen shouted with anger.

In the San Francisco office, Jay stared at the telephone, wondering who the man on the other end of the line was. "Look, enjoy the lady for a few more days, but you have to get back here and take care of *your* business. I have some partying to do." His mind was racing with curiosity. Who the hell was this woman who had turned his brother inside out?

"I can conduct business from here." Keithen had no intention of leaving Simone. "I've mapped out a breakdown of responsibilities. An office in this part of the country could be quite profitable."

"Keithen, this isn't like you. We already have offices that are overflowing with business. California is your home."

Keithen glanced back out the window, ignoring the storm-damaged forest and seeing it for what it would be again, lush with pines, magnolias, and oaks. "I know you don't understand any of this, Jay, but I feel more at home here than I have in California for a long time. I have real friends who care about me, and a community that needs the homes I'm building."

"You're right. I don't understand throwing away a profitable business and way of living for a piece of..."

"Don't you dare refer to Simone in that manner."

"Okay, I'm sorry, but who the hell wants to live in Mississippi?"

"I do."

Jay swore once more. This wasn't like Keithen. That damn woman was responsible for his foolishness. "You listen to me, Keithen. You can't be serious about staying in Mississippi and opening an office there. Who ever heard of an international developer having an office in Biloxi? This company may not be mine, but I refuse to allow you to neglect the family business because some woman has you all tied up. Take her to bed for a week, but get your butt back here in time for Mr. Wong's visit."

"Jay, there are several companies here. Biloxi is centrally located to major cities and ports with a great deal of growth going on."

"You don't want to leave that woman. What the hell outside of a bed do you and some country woman have in common?

Jay was insulting and showing his ignorance, just asking to have his ass kicked. Keithen didn't care that he was young and spoiled. "You're welcome to quit anytime you like."

Silence.

Keithen pinched the bridge of his nose and took a calming breath. "Forget what I said. Look, you're not as worldly as you think. You really should get out more and experience what the world has to offer. Then you would know the beauty of the South and its people."

"The hell with its people. Will you be here for the meeting?"

"Yes. Make sure everything is in order," Keithen responded tersely.

Jay bristled. He didn't appreciate being called ignorant. Keithen didn't speak to him like this. Sure they disagreed on his lifestyle and exchanged words, but never had his brother suggested he leave the family business. Jay threw the telephone across the room with rage. This business was as much his as it was Keithen's. And the gated community for the Chinese businessman and his employees was a project worth millions. He had plans for his cut of the deal, and had no intention of allowing his lovesick brother to mess it up for him. Storming around the office, he finally came to a halt. He needed a plan to get Keithen back in California and away from that woman. But how?

"Mr. Knight, Ms. Bounds is here to see you."

Jay smiled broadly to himself as the answer to his question knocked on the office door. His green eyes, so like his brother's, danced with excitement as his devious mind went into overdrive.

Chapter Eleven

They were three days into the work at the Clark house. Simone and Keithen, along with his crew of volunteers, worked in harmony to get the home rebuilt. Bobby and Jasmine's excitement at seeing their home take shape was contagious.

Today the roof was going on. Simome sat perched on top, laying shingles, pretty much like the first day she and Keithen met. Their eyes connected over the ridge vent as both were reminded of that day. Keithen winked at her and was rewarded with one of her bright smiles. He was happy. Happier than he could ever remember being. His life had true meaning these days, and the woman smiling at him gave him true love. He allowed his mind to roam as he worked. For several days he had been turning over an idea. He hadn't reached a decision, but the idea wasn't going away. If anything, each day it intensified. He stole a glance at Simone once more.

Simone was aware of Keithen watching her. She didn't know what he was up to, but something was definitely on his mind. He wore a little smile as he worked, apparently having a silent conversation with himself. She smiled a lot these days as well. Her life was back on track with a new job. In two months, when the casino was ready to reopen, she would be the head chef at a five star establishment. She couldn't wait to get back into the professional kitchen. She had missed the smells and sounds.

Stealing a glance at the blazing sun, she wiped the perspiration from her forehead. Goodness, it was hot today, and it was only July. August was usually the hottest month, but with temperatures already in the high nineties, she wasn't looking forward to the next month. She looked around her noticing that everyone looked parched. Now was a good time for a water break. She worked her way over to the ladder and climbed down heading toward the front of the house to her truck. Her gray T-shirt was soaking wet, and her hair fell from its twisted knot, stuck to her sweaty neck. She walked across the lawn, listening to the sound of progress. As she reached her truck, a cab pulled in front of the house and stopped.

"Excuse me," the woman in the back of the cab called.

"May I help you?" Simone approached the back door.

"I hope so because I don't have any idea where I'm going," the woman responded, flustered.

Simone noted her lack of an accent. "Who are you looking for?"

"The Clark residence."

Simone stared at the woman, surprised. "Well, you've found it." She stood back as the door was suddenly thrown open. The woman, tall and willowy, unfolded from the back seat wearing a stunning white linen dress. Her long blond hair was freshly styled around her shoulders in an array of curls. Her makeup was flawless, at least for the time being.

"God, I don't know how you people live here with this humidity."

The snobbish tone piqued Simone's curiosity even more. "Since it's obvious you're not from here, do you mind telling me why you're here?"

Deep blue eyes gave Simone a lengthy once-over. She looked up and down the destroyed neighborhood, her revulsion quite evident on her pretty face. "I was told my fiancé was here, but I'm sure there's some mistake. Keithen wouldn't be caught dead in a place like this."

Simone's head came up with a snap, her eyes large with shock. Her heart beat heavily within her chest, almost painfully. "Did you say Keithen?" she barely managed to say.

"Yes. You know him?"

"The developer from California?"

"That's him." The woman began searching the grounds. "Keithen has a strong appetite, if you know what I mean. I came to satisfy it." She winked over at Simone.

The image of Keithen and this woman together nearly caused her to be sick. She looked away quickly, fighting back tears. God, he had lied to her. All this time, he'd had her believing he loved her, wanting him to take her to bed. He had said that he was bastard. Why hadn't she believed him and kept her distance?

Glancing back at the woman, she called herself all kinds of stupid. Why would Keithen want her, when he had this Barbie doll waiting for him in California? Her own hair was usually in a ponytail, or twisted on top her head haphazardly. She rarely wore makeup unless she was going out, and her hands were tough and callused from swinging a hammer. No way could she compete with a woman like this.

"Mr. Knight is around back up on the roof." Simone didn't watch the woman walk away. She ran around to the driver's side of her truck and climbed in. In a few minutes everyone would know she had been the man's fool. Embarrassment burned in her face. His deceit burned in her heart. She drove away at breakneck speed, hoping to be long gone before the woman found her man.

Tears streamed down her face as she hit the bridge leading to her home. The man was good. He had her believing he wanted to change, that being there in Biloxi with her, helping people, had given him new meaning in his life. She turned at the next corner thinking how he must have laughed at her all those times she had tried to entice him into making love with her, and he had walked away. Love was obviously a game to him. See how far the stupid little small town girl would go. What a pathetic joke she was. She drove into her driveway and threw the truck into park. Turning off the ignition, she sat for several minutes and had herself a long cry. She guessed she should be grateful he hadn't taken her to bed. She dragged herself out of the truck and into the house. Everywhere she looked in her home, she saw signs of him. The very living room, painted by him was a painful reminder of his deceit. She stormed into the office. At least he was going through with the subdivision.

Why had he lied to her? She had asked him point blank whether there was someone in his life, and he had said no. She closed the door to the office. She couldn't stand the sight of the room a second longer. It would have to be dismantled. Possibly she would turn it into a guest bedroom.

The trill of the telephone sounded as she stepped back into the hallway. Returning to the living room, she located the phone, mindful to check caller identification before answering. She didn't want to hear any more of Keithen Knight's lies. Not that he would call. The man didn't give a damn about her, she sadly admitted.

"Hi, Mason," she answered, trying to hide her heartache.

"What's the matter? I know something is wrong, Simone. I can hear it in your voice," Mason Herbert said anxiously.

"You know me too well, but I don't want to talk about it."

"That means a man."

Simone didn't bite. "What's going on?" She sat in the corner of the sofa. She recalled the many nights that she'd sat there in Keithen's arms, foolishly thinking the man loved her.

"I need a big favor. I have to have a little outpatient surgery."

"Nothing serious, I hope?" She forgot about her problems and concentrated on her friend's.

"No. I'll be up and around within a couple of days. However, the surgery has to be performed Friday."

"So what do you need me to do?"

"Can you come to New York? I have a large wedding reception scheduled for Saturday, and I don't trust anyone but you to make it happen."

New York would be perfect. She wouldn't have to face all those pitiful smiles and words of wisdom. She would lick her wounds in the safety of a friend's home, and be back in the restaurant that she'd helped to create. "I'll do it."

"Great! Look, I've made arrangements for tonight. I was hoping you could come two days early so we would have a chance to go over every-thing."

"Tonight is fine." She listened as Mason gave her all the particulars. Hanging up the telephone, she ran to her room and quickly packed her luggage. She threw it in the back of the truck and headed to the airport, making one stop. She would have a two hour wait, but at least she wouldn't be home when Jasmine came looking for her. She knew her friend would mean well, but at the moment, she wanted to forget Keithen Knight existed.

⸎

Keithen reached the ridge vent with his row of shingles expecting to see Simone. He searched the area below, but didn't see her. Checking in front of the house, he noticed her truck was gone. Perhaps she had gone to take care of an errand. As he waited for the crew on the other side to reach the top, a familiar voice drew his attention. He glanced toward the back of the yard and froze. What the hell was Courtney doing in Biloxi? His eyes locked with hers. He stomped over to the ladder and practically ran down it. All he needed was for Simone to see Courtney and get the wrong impression. But as he touched ground, the work crew glanced from him to Courtney with interest, and then he spotted Jasmine standing off to the right, with her arms folded and her gaze menacing. He swore under his breath.

"What are you doing here?" Keithen kept his voice low because they had an audience. He felt as though everyone was condemning him to hell. He grabbed Courtney by the arm and dragged her to the front of the property.

"Will you stop manhandling me?" She pulled her arm free. "Where are your manners or have you lost them down here in this backwoods town?"

Keithen's gaze hardened on the woman who had been so much a part of his self-indulgent life. He was disgusted with himself for the life he had led. Sex without love and complications. "No, I haven't lost them, but I'm about to lose my patience if you don't start talking."

The woman turned on her feminine charm, moving in closer. She ran her hand up his chest, quickly pulling it away with a frown when she encountered his sweaty shirt. "You smell," she said, covering her nose.

"It's called sweat, Courtney. Honest to goodness sweat," he snapped, annoyed. "What do you want?"

"I came to bring you something." She batted her baby blues flirtatiously. "I know your appetite and thought you could use a little pick-me-up."

Keithen's eyes slid down the woman's body. She was stunningly beautiful, and yet she did nothing for him. He looked around and realized people continued to watch them. Jasmine was headed in their direction.

"Where's Simone?" She glanced at the woman with contempt. "Who's this?"

"I'm Courtney Bounds, Keithen's fiancée."

"His what?" Jasmine practically shouted.

"No, you're not," Keithen snapped.

Jasmine's gaze swung from one to the other. "Well, one of you is lying. But I saw this woman talking to Simone earlier and now she's gone."

Keithen's heart skipped a beat. "What?" He turned around to Courtney. "What did you say to Simone? Did you tell her that lie about being my fiancée? I don't know why you wear that damn ring on your left hand anyway?"

"I wear it so other women will stay away from you." Courtney glared at him, then smirked, proud of herself. "That grubby little girl was Simone? The woman Jay was so concerned about?" She released a smug laugh. "He had me believing I was in competition with a real woman."

Keithen grabbed Courtney by both arms. "There is no competition because I'm in love with Simone. That 'grubby little girl,' as you call her, is more woman than you'll ever be. Look around you, Courtney. For goodness sakes, get your nose out of the air and see how your fellow man is living. Did you even notice the destruction on your way here? Simone has been breaking her back to help her neighbors reclaim their lives. Do you even know a hurricane swept through here?"

"Of course I do. I wrote a check to some charity," Courtney answered, offended.

"Well, that's something, isn't it?"

"You can't be serious about that woman. I've given you two years of my life."

"Come on, Courtney, you and I both knew we were just killing time. Look, I've changed since I've been here. I don't want to hurt you, but I like who I am. I've seen another way of living and I like it. I'm also in love with Simone."

Courtney looked at Keithen with new eyes. "You mean that, don't you?"

"Yes, I do."

"You don't belong here. Look around, you come from better than this."

"You're being a snob. I belong wherever Simone is."

"You're a fool, Keithen Knight. She will never fit into your life. Everyone says we're the perfect couple. I know how you like to be touched." She moved in close. "Damn it, think about what you're doing. Your business is in San Francisco. Where will you live with her?" she said, desperate to hang on to her way of life. "Everyone will call you a fool."

"That's okay, because I've been calling myself one for days now. I can't believe I've wasted my life living so unconscionably. Go home, Courtney. Make a good life for yourself, and tell that brother of mine to mind his own business." Keithen was anxious to get to Simone. "Jasmine, can you take her to the airport?"

"Sure." Jasmine knew Keithen was afraid of losing Simone. And for a moment there she'd had her doubts about him, but one look into the man's anguished eyes, and she knew what misery he was in. "Go find Simone."

"Thank you, Jaz." He kissed her cheek on the run. He had to get to Simone. She had to know she was the only woman that he loved.

He started the truck, and reached for his cell phone. Punching in Simone's number, he willed her to answer, but when the answering machine picked up, he swore with frustration. This couldn't be happening to him. He had waited all his life to find true love and just when it was in his grasp, Jay had struck, destroying it.

He sped into Simone's driveway, barely stopping to turn off his ignition. Her truck wasn't in the driveway. She had a garage, but the older house wouldn't contain a large truck. He knocked on the door anyway. After several minutes passed and she didn't answer, he knew he was wasting time. Where would she go?

Simone sat staring out the airplane window. Her soul was as battered as the Coastal landscape below. She had given her heart only to be deceived. But no matter how badly she hurt, she couldn't help wondering where Keithen was, whether he was with that woman. She swiped at a tear that threatened to fall. There would be no more crying. The man had made a fool of her, but that, too, would pass.

However, as the airplane finally leveled off, she found herself wondering why he'd done it. Was he really that cruel? She wanted to say yes. She wanted to hate him. But for the life of her she couldn't. She thought of the evening when he'd painted her living room. It had been such a generous act, and they'd had a great deal of fun in the process. Then there was Simone Place. She speculated on whether he would keep the name. She closed her eyes in an attempt to turn off her thoughts. The man didn't want her. How hard was that to comprehend?"

Keithen stood on Miss Ruth's doorstep. His heart thumped hard inside his chest. He needed to see Simone so that he could clear the air. She had to know that he loved her. What they shared was too good to give up without a fight. He said a small prayer when the front door opened.

"Come on in, child," Ruth Ladner said, as she opened the door. She led the way back into her new kitchen. She had been expecting him since Simone swept in announcing she was leaving. "You look like a man who could use a cold beer."

"I need Simone, Miss Ruth. Is she here?" He listened for sound of another person.

Ruth Ladner continued to the refrigerator for the beer. The poor boy would need it when he discovered Simone was gone. "Drink that. You look like you could use it." She took a seat at the kitchen table.

Keithen followed her lead. It was apparent to him that things would be done at her pace. He popped the tab on the beer and took a long drink. The cool liquid felt good to his parched throat. He was so worried about Simone he had forgotten how thirsty he had been.

"Tell me about the woman." Ruth didn't waste time.

"She's nobody."

"My granddaughter didn't run away upset over a nobody." She cast a disapproving glare at him.

Keithen dropped his head as he released a deep sigh. "Courtney and I have had an off and on relationship for two years."

"You in love with this woman?"

"No." Keithen looked her directly in the eyes. "Our relationship wasn't about love. It was more about money than anything else. People like the things I have and the places I go."

"That's human nature. People are drawn to what they don't have and some women just want to be close to wealth. This Courtney sounds like the type."

"She is, but I allowed it. I'm responsible for the direction of my life." He looked at the petite dark brown woman and saw compassion and understanding. "Miss Ruth, I've been completely honest with Simone about the life I've led. I'm not proud of who I was. But this storm and the havoc it caused changed me. I saw hard-working, honest people, struggling to survive. I witnessed people from all walks of life trying to help their fellow man. I was moved by it and wanted to be a part of the rebuilding." He took another sip of his beer. "I wasn't prepared for Simone. But there was no forgetting her once I'd laid eyes on her."

"She's beautiful, isn't she?" The older woman smiled with pride.

"Inside and out. I love her," Keithen whispered. "Courtney and my brother, Jay, are trying to force me back to California. He's concerned about the business, and Courtney is trying to protect her interest."

"You're a man carrying a lot of weight on his shoulders."

"I'm a big guy, Miss Ruth, I can handle it. But what I can't handle is a life without your granddaughter."

Soft eyes held his. "She's in New York. Mason called…"

"Mason? Damn it! I'm sorry. Please forgive my language." Keithen looked sheepish.

Ruth chuckled. "Honey, I've heard worse and probably said it. So you don't have to apologize. What do you know about Mason?"

"From the photographs in Simone's albums it's clear the man's in love with her."

Ruth laughed as though she had heard the funniest joke. "You're right, son, but Simone doesn't see it. Give her a day or two, and then go get your woman."

Chapter Twelve

Simone stepped into the restaurant that had once been part hers. Everything looked the same. The table linens were the ones that she had selected, as well as the china. She stood there taking in the sounds of a busy establishment, realizing how badly she had missed being a part of the action. Several diners who were regulars to the restaurant called out a greeting. She stopped and made small talk with several of them, easily falling back into her old habit. When she finally made her way to the kitchen door, her pulse raced with excitement. She heard Toliver, the pastry chef, yelling out an order. How she had missed his strawberry cheesecake tart and big warm smile.

"Are you going in?" Mason Herbert couldn't believe Simone was there with him. He had feared never to see her back in New York again, but here she was. Picking her up at the airport, he promised not to let her leave without telling her how he felt about her.

"In a minute. I want to stand here and take in the sounds."

"You miss it don't you?"

"You have no idea." She looked at her handsome friend and smiled. His clean-shaven head was still a surprise to her, but she liked it. It gave him a maturity that hadn't been there before. Equal to her in height, Mason was stocky in build. His wide, toothy smile seemed extra bright in his dark face.

"You know that you can come back." Mason caressed her arm, unable to refrain from touching her. He noticed the firmness beneath his hand. She looked damn good in the black slacks and sleeveless shirt. He had never thought arms could be so sexy, but Simone's were toned, the muscles defined. She had shed a couple of pounds as well.

Simone shook her head as she pushed open the door to the kitchen. "There's too much to be done back home." She was immediately swept into the loving arms of the staff. For the next hour, she and Mason went over some of the details for the upcoming wedding reception. When they were finally finished, they returned to the active kitchen. "Pass me an apron."

"You think you're ready for this?" Mason knew from experience that Simone was a natural. He waited until she had washed and dried her hands before tossing her an apron. He stood back watching as she jumped right into the thick of things.

Simone found pleasure in the activity of the kitchen, but in the corner of her mind, thoughts of Keithen's betrayal lingered. Despite what she now knew and the pain she was in, she missed him. She missed his smiling eyes and his gentle touch. His loving caress to her hair had become a special gesture that warmed her heart. Swearing under her breath, she told herself to forget him. He had probably forgotten her the moment he climbed into bed with that woman.

"Hey, take it easy with that knife." Mason knew something was going on with Simone but didn't push. He would allow her to settle back into her old lifestyle, and when she was comfortable, he would try to get her to open up. "Let's get out of here. You've had a long flight and before I go under the knife, I'd like to spend some time with you."

"Do you have to say it like that?" Simone removed the apron. "Are you sure this is minor one day surgery?"

"You sound like you care," Mason teased, wrapping an arm around her waist. "Let's go."

"Of course I care about you." She allowed him to lead her out back to his shiny new sports car. She sat quietly in the passenger seat as he pulled out into the flow of traffic. She looked around, taking in the sights and sounds. Although she could appreciate all New York City had to offer, she was a small town girl who enjoyed a slower pace of life. Her thoughts returned to home and the man she'd left behind. A tear slipped down her cheek before she could stop it. God, how he had hurt her.

"You want to talk about it?" Mason had never seen Simone so distraught. He had the sinking feeling that another man was the source of her pain.

"No." She shook her head reinforcing her words. "Tell me what's going with the gang." She listened as Mason began filling her in on their circle of friends. She laughed when he told humorous stories, and asked appropriate questions when they were called for. But never far from her mind were memories of the way the sun reflected off Keithen's hair, or his deep booming laugh. When she closed her eyes, she was assaulted by images of his handsome face. Somehow, though, by the time Mason pulled into his underground garage space, she had managed to lock away her memories and plaster on a smile.

"The place looks good," she commented on entering Mason's loft apartment. She walked over to the large window, taking in the breathtaking view. "I love this city at night."

Mason deposited her luggage just inside the door, before joining her by the window. He slid his arms around Simone's waist, loving the feel of her in his arms. "You know I'm here for you."

"I know, but I'm not ready to talk about it." She moved out of his arms and returned to her luggage by the door. "If you don't mind, I'm going to take a shower and turn in. It's been a long day for me."

"I still can't believe you're roofing houses." He led her to the guest area. He had creatively used bookcases to create a guest bedroom.

"Believe it. I can also install drywall and flooring." She dropped her luggage and marched over to him, holding out her hands. "See, I have the calluses to prove it."

Mason took Simone's hands in his. He could indeed feel the calluses. He caressed her hands lovingly. "You shouldn't be doing manual labor."

"Everyone back home is doing manual labor and thinking nothing of it. It's the only way to rebuild our community. But I have to tell you, I enjoy the physical labor."

It was now or never, Mason thought. He could see some guy had hurt Simone badly. Sure, she was vulnerable, but just maybe she would finally realize that they were perfect for each other. He watched as she sat on the bed then fell backwards. She stared at the ceiling in silence. Then when he thought she had fallen asleep, she began to talk.

"He's a volunteer from California. We are from different walks of life, and as I realize now, there was never a future for us."

Mason joined her on the bed. He too fell back. He stared up at the ceiling, following the industrial pipework with his eyes. "Does this guy have a name?"

"He does, but it's not important. What made you shave your head?"

Mason turned his head to look at her. He followed her profile down to her kissable lips. "I love you, Simone."

"I love you too, Mason," Simone responded automatically.

"No, you don't understand." He rolled over onto his side and leaned over, wanting to cover Simone's mouth with his.

She immediately came out of her relaxed state and turned her head to avoid the unwanted kiss. She pushed at his chest. "Stop it. No, Mason, don't." She wiggled from under him to stand beside the bed. "Oh, my God, Keithen was right about you."

"So that's his name." Mason rolled over onto his back, feeling like a fool. He realized that he had probably ruined their friendship. "I've been in love with you since the weekend we were snowed in together."

"That was over a year ago." How had she missed the signs? She met his anguished eyes as he sat up facing her.

"We could be good together, if you would only give us a chance."

She couldn't believe this. Here was a man who loved her. Unfortunately, he wasn't the right man. "There's someone else."

"Someone who sent you running to New York," he shouted angrily. "Look, I can make you forget about him."

Simone left the guest area and headed back toward the front door. "I think it's best if I stay at a hotel. I'll be in the restaurant by ten so that we can start going over the wedding menu and arrangements. "

"Please don't go. Let's talk about this," he said, rising from the bed.

"There's nothing to talk about. You're my friend, Mason, and I don't want to lose you."

Mason collapsed onto the sofa and sat with his head in his hands. "You're still in love with him, aren't you?"

"Fool that I am, yes. I'll see to the reception but then I'm heading home."

"Back to him?" His tone was harsh from the pain of rejection.

She didn't see that happening unless she lost her pride. "That's not your concern." She opened the door and walked out, leaving Mason to stare after her.

Simone rushed into the restaurant around one o'clock after picking Mason up from the hospital and driving him home. She had stuck around to get him settled into bed after the surgery. Neither had broached the subject that had sent her to a hotel. What little conversation they had managed was strained. As they'd discussed the arrangements for the wedding reception, she had prayed for the survival of their friendship. But by the time she was ready to head to the restaurant, the void was still there between them.

She pushed thoughts of last night to the rear of her mind as she completed the last preparations for tomorrow's wedding. Next she went through the process of checking the restaurant supplies and the reservation list. One name in particular caught her attention and inspired an addition to the menu. Julia and Lance Johnson were an older couple who had come to the restaurant on its opening night. They had returned every Friday night since, promptly at eight. Married sixty years, the couple was still very much in love. It would be wonderful to see them. With that in mind, she quickly got down to work.

By the time eight o'clock rolled around, Simone had been called out to the dinner floor numerous times to receive compliments on the special, Blackened Red Fish. Just as she turned to head back to the kitchen, the Johnsons were seated. Simone stopped a waiter and placed their drink orders. When the young man returned with the tray bearing two dry martinis, she thanked him, taking possession of the tray.

"Two dry martinis." Simone stood smiling, anticipating the couple's response to seeing her.

"Thank you, but we…" Julia Johnson glanced up. Her blue eyes widen at the same time a smile blossomed on her winkled face. "Honey, it's so good to see you." The regal woman rose, giving Simone a hug.

Slightly shorter, with silver hair, she wore a classy little black dinner dress with her trademark string of pearls.

"It's wonderful to see you both." Simone leaned down to embrace Mr. Johnson, who was wheelchair bound. Once an avid skier over six feet tall, Mr. Johnson had been struck by a drunk driver, and left paralyzed from the waist down.

"How are you, young lady? We saw the damage on television," Lance said, shaking his balding head, sympathetically. "We were praying for you." His soft gray eyes reflected his sincerity.

"Thank you. There's a great deal still to be done."

"But you're back now. That's wonderful." Julia beamed.

"And I'm here to take the lady home," a familiar male voice said from behind Simone.

Julia and Lance Johnson looked at the man with great curiosity, then back at Simone. The sudden look of surprise blazing in her eyes told them all they needed to know. The couple glanced at each other, remembering what young love was like, and smiled.

Simone's heart gave a joyous thump at the sound of Keithen's voice. Slowly turning around to face him, she was once again swept away by his handsomeness. His blond hair was a little longer than when they first met and streaked with sun-induced highlights. A whiff of his cologne did strange things to her system, but when the ache of longing reared its head, she reminded herself of his betrayal. But damn, he looked good. "What are you doing here?" she asked, lowering her voice.

"I'm here for you."

Simone made a grand show of looking around the room. "Where's your fiancée? Oh, I guess you've conveniently forgotten her, *again*."

Keithen was aware of the older couple pretending not to listen. "Is there somewhere we can talk in private?"

"I'm working if you haven't noticed. How did you get in here anyway? I know we're pretty much booked."

A sly smile tilted up the corners of his mouth. "I have my ways." His eyes familiarized themselves with her beautiful face. He loved her expressive eyes and that mouth. He fought the urge to steal a kiss.

"You paid off the hostess."

"You were worth it."

Simone rolled her eyes, annoyed, then abruptly turned around and headed for the kitchen. "Are you coming?"

Keithen tagged along, pleased with himself. At least she hadn't kicked him out. He followed her path around white linen draped tables, taking in the details of the restaurant. It really was an elegant establishment. The occupied tables confirmed that business was good, which indicated the food was as well. He could definitely see Simone's influence in the place.

She was keenly aware of him behind her. Not only could she hear his footsteps, but she could also feel his magnetism, drawing her to him. However, there was a fiancée and a humongous lie standing between them. With that in mind, she hit the swinging kitchen door marked *In* with all her might. If she was lucky, it would bounce back and knock some sense into the man behind her. What did he think he could say to make her forgive him?

Keithen barely dodged the swinging door as it ricocheted back in his direction. He knew she had done it deliberately. Well, he guessed he had some fast talking to do. He followed behind her, noticing the speculative glances from the kitchen crew. Everyone seemed to be attuned to Simone's mood and knew he was the source of her aggravation. One male cook in particular wielded a sharp meat cleaver while sneering at him. The resounding thud against the chopping board sent chills down his spine. He suddenly realized that these cooking types were a little dangerous. He followed her into a small office and jumped when she slammed the door shut behind him.

"Say whatever you have to say, then go. I have work to do." Simone folded her arms across her chest, glaring at him. How she missed being free to touch him, to be held by him. She patted her right foot in agitation.

"Mind if I sit down?"

"You won't be here that long."

Keithen's brows rose in response. "All right, here it goes. Courtney Bounds is not my fiancée. I have never claimed to love her, nor have I proposed marriage."

"Please, the woman had a rock the size of a small planet on her hand. It takes deep pockets to purchase something like that."

"It was a family heirloom."

"That really makes me feel better, you jerk," Simone yelled, throwing her arms up. "You gave a woman you didn't love an heirloom?"

"I didn't give Courtney anything. It was her heirloom." He slowly approached her. "I love only you. There is no one else for me.'"

"Obviously there is." She tilted her chin up, fuming. "That woman didn't come all the way to Biloxi for nothing. You must have made some promise to her."

"I made no promises. Look, I've told you about the type of life I led. Courtney was a part of that life. I'm not proud of the fact, but it's true. I have money and she was there for the good time I could offer."

"And you enjoyed the sex." Her eyes flashed with fury. "I've never understood sex without emotional attachment."

This conversation wasn't going the way he had hoped. Keithen collapsed onto the small sofa, holding his head. "It happens, darling, but that's what I love about you. You're a romantic."

"You're right and look where it's gotten me." She desperately wanted to give in to her desire to forgive him. "Tell me this, when you left California, were you still sleeping with the Barbie doll?"

Any other time Keithen would have found humor in those words, but he was still fighting for their love. "We were still attending social functions together, but it had been a couple of months since we had been intimate. I realize now I was already growing tired of the life I was living. I had planned on telling Courtney about us when I returned home in a couple of weeks."

That was news to Simone. "You were planning on leaving?" She sat beside him. "When were you going to tell me?" She looked over at him.

"Right before I asked you to come with me." He reached over, taking her hand, and sighed with relief when she didn't pull away. "I love you, no one else. I was returning for an important meeting, that's all. Jay and Courtney were trying to force me back. I know how my brother operates. He was hoping Courtney would cause a rift between us, just as she has."

"And you would return to California." She looked at their joined hands. His was large and heavily veined. Despite the size it was gentle against hers. "I have to get back to work." She really needed time to think.

"Tell me something," Keithen said softly.

"If I can."

"Are you staying at Mason's?" He looked directly at her. His gut was tied into knots just thinking about the guy being close to her.

She shook her head no. "You were right about him."

"He told you he was in love with you?"

"Yes, he did."

He caressed the back of her hand with his thumb. "What did you tell him?"

"The truth. I love him as a friend and nothing else." She watched as Keithen rose from the sofa and headed to the door. "I'm staying at the Lowell Hotel, Room 1410. I'll be waiting for you."

"It will be around one when I get off, and I have a wedding reception tomorrow evening. Maybe we should do this another time." She chewed her lower lip, uncertain of her next move.

"Stop making excuses. We need to discuss us." He retraced his steps to where she still sat, and securing her hands, he pulled her to stand in front of him. His eyes looked directly into hers. "I love you." He kissed her slow and tender, letting her know what was in his heart. "Be careful." He pulled the door open, walked past the menacing cook, and left the restaurant with the hope of seeing her later.

Keithen paced the floor of his luxurious suite waiting for Simone to arrive. She had to come. He couldn't conceive of losing her over a lie. He wouldn't lose her. Whatever it took, he would make her see the truth. They belonged together. They complemented each other. And he definitely was a better man because of her.

He checked his watch for the third time within the last thirty minutes. Where was she? It was nearing two o'clock in the morning. He didn't like the idea of her being out on the streets by herself, but then the Big Apple never slept. He walked over to the mini bar and poured himself a bourbon. He needed to calm down. When Simone arrived, he would need to be thinking clearly. Taking a sip of his drink, he walked over to the large window overlooking Madison Avenue. He wanted the opportunity to roam the city with Simone on his arm. As he raised the glass once more, a knock came at the door. Quickly returning the glass to the bar, he headed to the door and pulled it open.

Simone fought the desire to rush into his arms. She instead walked calmly past him to stand in the center of the room. "Hi." She admired the cozy deluxe suite with classic dark wood and tradional furnishings. The walls were painted a soothing shade of beige which made the room feel spacious and warm. A romantic fire burned in the majestic white fireplace. The suite was spectacular and all that she had heard about the Lowell. "I was beginning to think you weren't coming." He shoved his hands into his pockets to keep from touching her. She had changed from kitchen whites into a pretty green dress. She looked incredibly sexy.

"I'm here." She placed her purse on the mini bar, noticing his glass. She had never seen him drink anything more than a beer or glass of wine. Maybe the man was as stressed about their relationship as he'd said. "I've done a great deal of thinking," she said, turning around to face him.

"Simone, I love you." Keithen's green eyes were intense. He pulled his hands free of his pockets and closed the space between them.

A smile touched her lips as she looked into his beautiful eyes. She had come to know the man and respected who he was. Despite the personal flaws he had confided in her, she had only seen an honest man struggling to be a better man. He had been good to her. Sometimes you had to trust your instincts or in this case, your heart.

"I love you too. I've decided your brother and the Barbie aren't going to win. If you must go home, then I'm going with you."

Relief flooded Keithen's body. He pulled Simone into his arms. "I was so afraid I was going to lose you. This is the first time in my life I've had the real thing, and I thought I was watching it slip away." He pressed a kiss into her hair.

"I'm right here." She closed her eyes, absorbing the pleasure of being back in his arms. "I didn't think I would ever be here again."

"In my arms is where you're staying." He sandwiched her face between his hands and proceeded to kiss her with a ravenous hunger. She was warm and sweet, responsive in his arms. His lips feasted on hers like there was no tomorrow, while his hands reacquainted themselves with the shape and feel of her body. He finally tore his mouth away, sucking in a much needed breath. He swept Simone into his arms and carried her into the opulent bedroom. The king size bed dominated the room as it was framed by a canopy of flowing drapes. With his right hand, he tore the bedding back, sending decorative pillows tumbling to the floor, and placed his precious cargo in the center of the bed. He kissed her hard before standing back up. "You should get some sleep. You've had a long day and face another one tomorrow." He went to the closet and came back with a T-shirt, handing it to her.

"Sleep? You want me to sleep here?" Simone whispered, uncertain. She tried to ignore how good the plush bed felt, and how exhausted she was.

Keithen knew what she was thinking. "It's too late for you to return to your hotel, and I just need to hold you tonight. To know I'm not dreaming." His smile was boyish. He sat down on the bed and reached out, tracing the shape of her lips with his finger. He loved having her with him. "Marry me."

Simone stared wide-eyed at Keithen, not sure if she had heard him correctly. "What did you say?"

He smiled, so sure of his decision. It wasn't the best setting, but it was definitely the perfect time. He slid from the bed, dropping down onto one knee and took her hand in his. He looked into her stunned gaze. "Simone Ladner, will you do me the honor of becoming my wife?"

Her heart was beating a hundred miles a minute. She couldn't believe this was happening. And never in a million years would she have believed a man would be proposing marriage to her in his suite. But the proposal was sudden. "Are you sure? Now that I know the truth, I'm not going anywhere."

"I'm sure and I know what I'm doing. I want you for my wife, Simone. I love you."

Simone knew she smiled like a fool, but she didn't care. The man loved her. "Yes, I'll marry you." She practically leaped into his arms. She rained kisses down on his face, happy with her decision. "You know everyone will think we're crazy."

"I don't give a damn what other people think." He kissed her eyes and her nose. "I'm so happy right now." He rose, placing her back in bed, but this time he followed her. Reclining on his back he held her against his chest. "Why don't we invite Jasmine and Bobby up here to be our witnesses."

"Our witnesses?" Simone sat up and looked at him. "You want to get married here?"

"Why wait? I love you and you love me. Let's do it." He grinned foolishly, alive with excitement.

It was infectious and she found herself exhilarated by the idea. "Well, when? We can't do it tomorrow because I'll be working."

"We'll do it just as soon as Jasmine and Bobby can get here. I'll take care of everything." He suddenly fell silent looking at her. His hand caressed her hair. "God, I love you," he finally said. He pulled her down and began kissing her luscious mouth once more. When they parted, he reached for the T-shirt. "Change clothes and come to bed."

Simone scrambled off the bed and entered the bathroom. She stood there admiring the elegance. Marble countertops gleamed in the soft lighting of the sconces. Green glass tiles created a soothing environment. The deep soaking bathtub enticed her to try it out. Containers in all designs and colors held an assortment of bath salts and beads. She couldn't resist.

"Do you mind if I take a bath?" she asked, sticking her head through the cracked door.

Keithen rolled over onto his side looking at her. "Of course not." He groaned after the door closed and the water came on. He lay on the bed imagining that green dress sliding off her body, and when he heard her step into the water, every muscle in his body went tight. What he wouldn't give to slide into the tub with her. But he wanted to do things properly with Simone. She would be his wife soon and only then would he make love to her.

Simone returned to the bedroom dressed in Keithen's T-shirt. A lone bedside lamp was on. She smiled into his alert eyes and slipped into bed beside him. Something long, hard, and pulsing with life pressed against her backside.

"Relax, honey." His arm fell across her waist.

"You relax," Simone said, looking back over her shoulder. "How am I to relax with that thing poking me?"

Keithen laughed. "I'm the one having the problem here. Do you know what a turn-on a bath can be?"

Simone giggled as she settled back down. The bedding was deliciously warm from his body heat.

"Enjoy your bath?" He kissed her shoulder as she aligned her body with his.

"That bathtub is wonderful." She snuggled in closer, feeling completely safe with him, despite his current state. A yawn escaped her. "Excuse me."

"Get some sleep, sweetheart." Keithen reached over, turning out the side lamp. He curved his body around Simone's, thanking the big guy up above for the opportunity to love her.

Chapter Thirteen

Three days later, Simone stood before the full length mirror. She wore a beautiful creation in white adorned with fine lace and delicate pearl beads. Her makeup was flawless, and her hair simply stunning. A team of stylists had arrived earlier to prepare her for the special day. And on her feet were designer satin-beaded sandals. Even her undergarments had name tags that she had only dreamed of wearing. Her husband to be had thought of everything to make her feel like a princess. Now as she stood in the heavenly wedding gown, looking as though she'd stepped off the pages of a bridal magazine, she could hardly wait to become his wife.

The pampering had begun yesterday. The wedding reception she had overseen the night before had left her exhausted, so a visit to a day spa was just what she needed. Keithen had accompanied her. They had shared a light breakfast, followed by a wonderful massage.

She giggled to herself recalling how Keithen had refused the male masseur who had arrived to perform her massage. The young man had assured him he was a professional, to which Keithen had assured him that if he touched her, he would pull back a stump. The young man had rushed out the room as if the hounds of hell were behind him. She had laughed and called Keithen a caveman. In response, he had thrown her over his shoulder and swatted her bottom while she tried to hang onto her towel. They'd shared a passionate kiss before the male masseur returned with a female masseuse in tow. Dinner was at a five star restaurant where Keithen presented her with a brilliant diamond engagement ring that left her speechless.

"You look beautiful," Jasmine whispered in awe from behind her. "The man has exquisite taste."

Simone looked at her friend's reflection in the mirror. "Expensive taste. He's spent a mini fortune on this gown and ring."

"This is a ring," Jasmine said holding up her two carat diamond. "That thing is a small continent."

"Stop exaggerating."

"All right. He loves you." Jasmine came to stand beside her. "That man was a nervous wreck when he thought he had lost you. You've found your prince."

"He is wonderful." Simone turned to Jasmine, taking her hands. "I'm so glad you and Bobby could make it. My folks are going to be angry."

"I don't know, they're pretty romantic minded."

"Yeah, right."

There was a knock at the door. The wedding planner announced that it was time. Simone hadn't understood the need for a planner for such a small affair, but Keithen had assured her that he knew what he was doing. The wedding was taking place in a turn of the century bed and breakfast outside the city. As she and Jasmine prepared to leave the dressing room, she wished for a moment her parents could be there. Every girl's dream was to be walked down the aisle by her father. But that wasn't to be the case today.

Another knock came at the door. "Come in," she called, retrieving her bouquet of red and white roses.

"Is my girl ready to get married?"

Simone whipped around to find her father standing off to the side. "Daddy! What are you doing here?"

"Keithen told us there was going to be a wedding, and no way was I going to let my daughter walk down the aisle alone."

"I can't believe he did this." She gushed with happiness. "I'm so glad that you're here," she said, embracing him. "Where's…"

"Move out of the way, Gary," Delores ordered as she and her mother-in-law pushed into the small room. "Oh baby, you look beautiful."

"Like a princess." Ruth hugged her granddaughter. "That man of yours has spent a small fortune on this wedding."

"Isn't he wonderful?" Her eyes sparkled with excitement. Now the day was complete. Her family was there to share this moment with her.

"Are you happy, baby?" Gary asked.

"Yes, Daddy, I am. Very happy. And very much in love," she added. Her brilliant smile reflected her joy.

Ruth reached out taking her granddaughter's hands. "Marriage is a wonderful thing, darling, but there are going to be difficult patches. Just remember that as long as you two are honest with each other, lies can't hurt you. Trust in the Lord and each other."

"Your grandmother's right," Delores added. "But the love of a good man is priceless. And I've come to realize that he is indeed a good man. I wish you both a lifetime of happiness." She looked over at her husband and smiled.

"Thanks Mom."

Gary placed a kiss on his wife's lips, and then turned back to his daughter. "Well then, let's get you married." He gave his daughter his arm and escorted her out the room.

Keithen stood at the altar with Bobby at his side. He looked around the beautiful garden, pleased with the setting. He knew Simone would love it and that was all that mattered to him. He wanted her to remember this day for the rest of her life. That's why he had made arrangements for her family and the volunteer crew that they worked with to come to New York. The wedding march began as the French doors to the garden opened, revealing his stunning bride. His chest swelled with pride as he watched Simone advance down the aisle on her father's arm. She smiled brilliantly under the sheer veil, causing his heart to beat with excitement.

Simone couldn't believe that everyone was there to share in their day. The man waiting at the altar for her was responsible. Dressed in a traditional black tuxedo, his handsomeness stole her breath away. At the altar she kissed her father before placing her hand into Keithen's as they pledged their love and life to each other.

Simone grasped the bathroom doorknob and took a moment to calm her runaway nerves. The moment had finally come when she and Keithen would make love. She was nervous and excited all at the same time. The wedding had been perfect and so she wanted the honeymoon to be as well. They had arrived back at the Roosevelt, this time occupying the honeymoon suite. Roses in every shade had greeted her as she entered. A romantic candlelight dinner had been arranged for them, and afterward, her new husband had presented her with a stunning pair of diamond earrings. She had immediately put them on. She checked her appearance in the mirror one more time. The white peignoir was delicately feminine and flowed gracefully over her body. She felt sexy and desirable as she opened the door.

Keithen turned at the sound of the bathroom door. His pulse quickened at the sight of his lovely wife dressed in a glamorous peignoir. The silky fabric moved sensually against her body as she came to him. She smelled good and looked absolutely breathtaking. He placed his hands on her small waist. Their eyes connected and in the moment that passed between them, he detected complete trust. This would be her first time and she came to him without hesitation. She smiled brilliantly at him and his heart overflowed with love.

"I didn't think you could look more beautiful than you did in your wedding gown, but you steal my breath away," Keithen told her with awe.

"Thank you." Simone took in his appearance, liking the dark merlot robe he wore. His muscled chest was visible through the black trim opening. Realizing she had every right to touch him intimately, she ran her fingers down his chest. Her eyes met his. They were dark and moody with curiosity. But despite the need she saw in his eyes, and the heat of passion burning his flesh, Keithen didn't make a move. He waited for her to take the lead. She appreciated his patience, but wanted to experience being loved by him. "I'm not made of glass, sweetheart. You can touch me."

Keithen released one of his roaring laughs that broke the ice. "Do you know how much I love you?"

"I'm hoping you'll show me." Simone slipped her arms around his neck. "Love me."

"With pleasure." He swept Simone into his arms and carried her to a nearby chair. Taking a seat, he placed his wife across his thighs, and then took her mouth in a scorching kiss. His large hands traced the lines of her body, tantalizing soft curves and hidden places, until the need to be flesh to flesh took over. He removed the sheer robe, and slowly lowered the thin straps holding up the gown. The silky fabric slinked down the swells of her breasts to leave her bare before him. He looked his fill, and followed the path of his wandering hands with his mouth. At her full bosom he licked and sucked the dark nipples until they turned hard and pebbly.

He continued to flick his warm, wet tongue across the berry-like protrusions until he set off a series of soft whimpers in his wife. But he didn't stop there. He followed the path of his hands once more around and under her breasts, all the while the flesh between his legs responding with aching need. And when his wife squirmed across the sensitive organ, he wanted to roar like a primal beast and lay claim to his mate.

Simone had known Keithen was a big guy, but just how big was only now becoming clear. A moment of panic seized her as the stiff flesh stirred beneath her. However, everywhere her husband touched her felt incredibly good. He was gentle with her, attentive to her every response. She concentrated on the delicious things that his mouth was doing to her body and closed her eyes with indescribable pleasure. His fingers traveled under the gown to caress her wet center.

Keithen suddenly stood and carried Simone to the bed. He placed her gently on her feet beside it. Stepping back to appreciate the image of her all kiss-swollen and partially nude, he didn't believe there was a more beautiful woman in the world.

"Step out of the gown, sweetheart." He chewed on his lower lip with the anticipation of finally seeing his wife.

The heat from Keithen's eyes burned her exposed flesh. She felt hot and achy with a sexual hunger that caught her by surprise. Feeling brazen as she hooked her thumbs into the garment suspended at her hips, she flirtatiously wiggled free allowing the material to pool at her feet, then stepping out and kicking it toward her husband. In nothing but the matching white thong, she waited for his next move. She didn't have a long wait. Keithen pulled her slowly into his arms until her breasts flattened against his chest. His mouth swooped down on hers, plundering the soft interior while his hands palmed the cheeks of her rump. But he had reached his limit. He walked Simone back toward the bed and lowered her to the mattress.

Simone sat looking at Keithen when he paused to remove his robe, revealing the silk black boxers beneath. His chest was heavily muscled and tanned from working in the sun. His washboard abs fascinated her as the muscles flexed with each movement that brought him into bed beside her. She ran both hands over the dancing muscles which were powerfully hard, yet warm and velvety smooth. His hips tapered and dipped, disappearing into the boxers. She had always had a thing for men so well defined in that area. Her fingers teased him there. Her lips kissed down the thin line of blond hair of his chest to where it vanished into the boxers.

Keithen groaned in the back of his throat as her sweet lips clamped onto a male nipple. For someone inexperienced, she was blowing his mind with her hot mouth and curious touches. And when she dipped that little pink tongue of hers into his navel, playtime was over. He encouraged her onto her back as he rose above her. He kissed her once more before turning his attention to removing the thong.

The sight of her lying nude before him gave him heart palpitations. He sucked in a deep breath to bring himself under control. Tonight he was making love to his wife, and he wanted to make it a magical moment for them both. He took his time loving her, paying homage to every erogenous zone. With his hands and his mouth, he turned Simone into a body of quivering need. He parted the tender flesh between her legs to bathe it with his flattened tongue. He drew the hard nub between his lips and raked it with his tongue, causing her to jackknife from the mattress. Then with his fingers, he gave her a preview of what was to come. And when sweet nectar flowed over his fingers, he rolled on protection, taking his place between his wife's inviting thighs.

"Sweetheart," he whispered gently to her, while holding her gaze. "If you're uncomfortable with anything I do, let me know. I want you to enjoy our lovemaking as much as I do."

Simone nodded, moved by his concern, but wanting him to get on with it. The gnawing ache inside her cried out to be sated. One look at her husband and she knew that he was quite capable of providing what she craved. She opened wider to him.

"Love me."

Keithen would always remember those two simple words, along with the first heart-stopping moment of entering her body. She was unbelievably hot and so damn tight he thought he would black out from the feel of her clamped around him.

Simone's nails dug into his arms at the initial invasion, the searing pain bringing tears to her eyes. Then he paused, giving her time to adjust. He kissed her deeply with a series of drugging kisses. When he slid out of her, the sensation of the movement took her breath. But before she could absorb the experience, he moved back in and this time she groaned from the exquisite pleasure. Her eyes connected with his to see if he felt what she was feeling. His green eyes had gone dark with desire. The slow back and forth motion continued until she stopped thinking and only felt. Instinctively, she mimicked the rhythm that he created and answered each thrust with a little hip action of her own. And when Keithen closed his eyes and groaned in response, she realized the power she had to give pleasure.

He tried to be gentle with her. But damn, Simone was making that difficult. Each time she threw her hips at him, she gave a subtle squeeze of muscle that made him want to take her hard. If she were any more experienced, he would surely die from the pleasure. He came up on his knees and raised her hips, palming her butt as he increased the tempo. The sight of her bouncing breasts as he thrust into her added to the thrill. Her fingers dug into the bedding, signaling that she was close, but instead of pushing her over the edge, he backed off.

She tried to take control, to encourage him to speed up, but she couldn't in her current position. And so the frustrating slow tempo went on and on until she wept to be set free from the torturous agony.

Keithen soon answered her pleas. He slightly changed his angle so that he was more fully over her as he picked up the pace. Each thrust into her was more powerful than the last. Her intimate walls squeezed, making him swear as he took them both to the mountain top and right over the edge into the dark abyss of ecstasy.

He remained in place for several minutes before he was physically able to shift his weight. He gingerly separated their bodies and leaned forward, kissing her. "Are you all right?" He watched her expressive eyes for the truth.

Simone smiled at him impishly. "Why didn't we do this earlier?"

Keithen expelled an anxious breath as he grinned down on her. "Because you're a precious gift deserving of a proper honor."

"You make me feel precious." She looped her arm around his neck and pulled him down for a kiss. "I love you."

"Not half as much as I love you."

Keithen left the bed for the bathroom and filled the tub with water. It had been Simone's first time and he knew she must be feeling the effects. He returned to the room just in time to see her easing gingerly to the side of the bed. Moving in her direction, he lifted her into his arms and walked toward the bathroom.

"What are you doing now?" She wrapped her arms around him and took his earlobe between her teeth.

"Stop that."

"You're an amazing lover." She traced his ear with her tongue.

"If you don't stop…"

"You'll do what?"

"This." He dumped her into the spa tub, splashing water everywhere.

"I can't believe you did that," she shrieked, watching as he settled at the opposite end. Candlelight bathed his skin in an amber glow. The massaging warm water felt heavenly. She slid further into the water until her head was the only thing sticking out. Her body ached all over. She'd never known so many muscles were involved in making love. She smiled shyly to herself, recalling what they'd done, how shamelessly she had responded. She sat up suddenly, splashing water again. "You did enjoy our lovemaking? I mean, you weren't pretending for my sake, were you?"

Was the woman kidding? "Babycakes, there was no need to pretend. I enjoyed every second of loving you, and I'm eagerly looking forward to the next time." He caressed her leg suggestively.

"Whoa, big fellow, one go round is all you get tonight." Her face was vibrant with love and joy. She sighed with contentment. "This day has been the most amazing of my life."

"I agree, and I have you to thank for that."

"Me? You made everything happen."

He knew that she would see it that way. "Once again you fail to realize what you give to other people."

Simone looked confused. "We gave to each other."

"I'm not just talking about in bed. I'm talking about your family and friends. You've given me a new way to live, and an appreciation for what I have. I didn't have that before meeting you."

"Why didn't you invite your family, or did you?"

"I didn't. I didn't want someone trying to talk me out of my decision."

Simone stiffened. "They wouldn't have approved of your marrying me?"

Keithen looked thoughtful. "It's not the marriage they wouldn't have approved of, but my impulsiveness. It's not normal for me to act so quickly. But what we feel for each other is right. You and I belong together."

"I'm sure your family will be concerned about your money. If you want me to sign anything, I will."

Keithen's eyes sharpened on her face. "You mean a prenuptial agreement?"

"Yes. Isn't that what rich people do? You have to understand their concern."

"I do, but losing you would be more devastating to me than losing money. I have faith in our love. I'm a better man because of you."

"I'm a woman, not a miracle worker." She felt a little uncomfortable with him giving her credit for the many revelations in his life. "I believe a higher power did all the work."

He loved her spiritual nature. "I agree, but you were a very important part of the process. I've just learned so much about myself and the world I thought I knew."

"There's always more to learn." She nudged him with her foot and when he looked at her, she wiggled her brows suggestively.

She was rewarded with one of his laughs. "I'm trying to behave here, but if you keep taunting me, you're going to have to pay the price." He grabbed an ankle, and pulled her toward him. "On second thought, I think I'll collect." He kissed her slowly and passionately, leaving them both breathless. Turning her around in the spacious tub so that her back was to him, he removed a nylon sponge from the small basket sitting near the tub and proceeded to scrub Simone's back. "You have such soft skin."

"Thank you." She blushed, having never had a man to scrub her back. Or having never taken a bath with a man for that matter. Tonight was a night of firsts.

"I can't wait to get you into my shower back in California. There are ten shower heads, all with pulse dials, and one large one in the center that literally rains on you. The back wall is all glass and looks out over the bay. On a clear day you can see downtown San Francisco. "

Simone turned around on that. "Are you telling me that there's a window in the shower."

"Yes, I am."

"Well, I won't be getting in it."

"Yes, you will. No one can see us." He laughed at her look of disbelief. "For one thing it's too high to be seen and for another, the glass is one way, even at night." He pinched her nipple just above the water. "You'll find it a turn-on."

"Right." In actuality, she was already a little turned on at the mere thought of making love to her husband in front of the window.

Chapter Fourteen

The view from the shower was of heavy fog hanging over the bay. Simone and Keithen had spent two more days in New York City before heading out to California. They had arrived only an hour ago, well after nightfall. After depositing their things in the master suite, the shower had been Keithen's next stop. He had quickly disrobed his wife and pushed her toward the lavish bathroom retreat. Water hit them from three directions, the driving pulse inspiring their adventurous love-making.

Simone was more relaxed now and eager to learn what she had been missing out on. She loved exploring his large body with her hands. She stroked and squeezed, then kissed him all over while the fog outside the window shrouded them in intimacy.

Keithen was going out of his mind as her small hand worked him stiff. He pulled her enthusiastic fingers away, afraid that things would be over before they really got started. He had plans for his wife. Picking her up and pinning her to the glass wall, he pushed inside her. This time he didn't go slow and easy, but instead followed her vocal instructions to go faster. Situating her higher so that she took all of him, he closed his eyes, losing himself in her softness, and came like he never had before.

There was definitely something to being in love when having sex. He slowly lowered her to the floor and using his hands, washed her clean. As her soft pants turned into needy whimpers, he shut off the water and carried his bride back into the bedroom. Pushing her forward onto the bed, he thrust inside her.

Simone moaned with pleasure. She hadn't known it would be this way, that *she* would be this way. She enjoyed making love with her husband. Their appetite for each other was insatiable. She glanced in the dresser mirror to the right, realizing she could watch him making love to her. The sight of his body disappearing into hers only heightened the experience. She threw her hips back at him, taking all he had to give.

Keithen couldn't get enough of her. He dug his fingers into her hips. She was soft, hot, and sopping wet as he drove into her. He stroked the sensitive nub in rhythm to his deep hard strokes. The combined stimulation sent Simone spiraling out of control, taking him with her. They collapsed onto the bed in a sated heap. When they were able to move, they made a return trip to the bathroom.

Later, when they were wrapped in their robes, Keithen took Simone to see the rest of the house. It was by far one of his best designs and he was excited to show it to off. The small mansion was a tri-level Mediterranean built into the side of the cliff, full length balconies on each level overlooked bay below.

"We might as well start the tour on this floor," Keithen said to Simone, leaving the master suite. "Because I like to get my workout first thing in the morning, I had the gym placed next door." He opened double doors to showcase the well-equipped room. Painted in bright white because the room contained no distracting windows, he watched as Simone walked through the space checking out the features.

"This is absolutely wonderful. Of course there's never an excuse for not working out." She returned to his side, following him on to the next room.

"Now this is my home office. It's an exact replica of my office at Knight Development."

Simone walked over to the gray wall displaying various awards that Knight Development had been given. There were several from the mayor of the city, two from the governor, and many others from countries around the world. "Wow, this is really impressive. You must be so proud."

"It's great when people appreciate your work."

"Well, if you paid as much attention to detail in those projects as you have in Simone Place, I know they must be wonderful."

"They are pretty nice, but you know what?" He took her hand again, leading the way out.

"What?"

"I more proud of Simone Place than I am of anything else I've done." He surprised himself with the admission.

Simone stopped in the hallway to look at him. "You are? Why? I'm sure other projects are more glamorous, not to mention more profitable."

He nodded as he continued on his way. "They are, but Simone Place is fulfilling a genuine need and I appreciate knowing that." He took her to the library. "This is one of my most favorite rooms in the house."

"It's awesome." She glanced around the traditional room furnished in cognac colored leather with classic nail head upholstering. The sofa and two chairs faced a charming fireplace. "I've always wanted a formal library like this. Somewhere to display the numerous cookbooks I've collected over the years."

Keithen dropped her hand and walked over to the cherry bookcase. He scooped several books into his arms and carried them to the nearby corner, dropping them. "Now you have place for your books. If you need more room, we can get rid of some more books."

Simone giggled, not believing he had done that. "You're crazy, do you know that?" Her eyes held love.

"Crazy about you, sweetheart." He gave her a peck on the lips.

"Sweet talker." Simone decided to bring part of her cookbook collection with her the next time they came west.

The third floor contained three furnished guest bedrooms with baths and a separate entertainment room. They made a quick tour before heading down to the bottom floor. The textured walls of the common areas of the home were all painted and glazed in a honey yellow that accentuated the black wrought iron railing, securing the upstairs landing and staircase. The view from the upstairs landing was breathtaking. Simone was quietly coming to terms with her husband's wealth. The living room alone was the size of three of her rooms put together. Everywhere she looked, she saw extravagance and exquisite beauty. The vibrant red of the dining room caught her attention. Furnished in traditional dark cherry woods with beautiful wrought iron chandelier, she couldn't wait to serve dinner there. A large media room down the hall was equipped with two rows of stadium seating that left her overwhelmed. The pool was just as spectacular because it was actually designed like a private tropical lagoon. But what really got her blood to pumping was the enormous kitchen fit for a chef. She trailed her fingers over the smooth granite countertop with a yellowish hue. Top of the line appliances were strategically placed for ease of use. The restaurant styled refrigerator was a special surprise.

"You have really outdone yourself here. Did you design this?" She looked at Keithen who now sat at the curved bar of the island.

"Yes, with some input from Rita. She got a blast out of picking out the appliances."

"I bet she did. One day I'll have a kitchen like this in my home."

Keithen shook his head laughing. "Sweetheart, this is your home."

Simone looked over at him and blushed, realizing that she had forgotten that fact. "You're right, it is." She suddenly fell quiet.

He was so attuned to her moods that he knew something was bothering her. Getting up from his stool, he pulled her into his arms. "What's the matter?"

She felt foolish. "Nothing."

Keithen grabbed her chin and tilted her face to his. "Simone Knight, I know better than that, so spill it."

She smiled at the sound of her new name, despite her troubling thought. "Where are we going to live?"

He took her hands. "I'm not putting all the property at Simone Place up for sale." He smiled broadly.

"You're not selling my special place?" she asked with mounting excitement.

"How could I when we'll need somewhere to live. I'll keep this place for when we want to get away, or for business, but home is Biloxi."

"Keithen Knight, I love you so much," she said, launching herself into his arms.

"Let's eat and then you can show me how much."

"Deal." Together they prepared a light meal and ate it out on the balcony overlooking the bay as they made plans to see the city. Keithen wasn't telling anyone he was home just yet. He wanted Simone all to himself for a few days more. By the end of the week, he would introduce her to the family. When the meal was gone and the conversation of places to see and things to do no longer held their interest, he led his lovely wife back to their suite.

Over the next three days, Keithen played tour guide, showing Simone the area. On the first day, he showed her around Belvedere Island, then took her to Golden Gate Park where they browsed a museum and tea garden. The second day began with a ride on a world famous cable car, then a trip to Alcatraz. At Pier 39 they played arcade games like children before strolling the outdoor mall hand in hand. Simone purchased several gifts for family and friends.

A part of her felt guilty for enjoying herself while people back home struggled to rebuild their lives. But the bay area was amazing with its mixture of cultures, rolling hills, architecture, and breathtaking bay views, and this was their honeymoon. The third day Keithen took her to some of his favorite eateries and shops. She immensely enjoyed the tour of the unique neighborhoods. A drive through Pacific Heights with its hilltop Victorian mansions like something out of the movies gave her a firsthand view of where Keithen had been reared. As though it were nothing, he pointed out homes owned by world famous people. Simone wondered what she had gotten herself into. She experienced her first moment of doubt.

Keithen could easily read his wife's expression. She had accepted that he was wealthy, but nothing he'd said had prepared her for the level of his wealth. He reached over, threading his fingers through hers. His voice was soft and clear as he spoke, "You see the beauty of these homes and believe the people in them have everything."

Simone looked over at him. "Is that your way of telling me money can't buy happiness?"

"It's true, baby. Behind the gates, men and women are married, yet aren't in love. In my own life, I have friends I don't particularly like, who I just associate with because they're all I know. We share a lifestyle and possess similar business interests. But you know what?"

"What?" She couldn't imagine living like this.

"Ask any one of us about the other and you'll get a recital of that person's net worth, who their parents are and what they own. That person will be able to tell you the value of their home and who they're sleeping with, but nothing of real substance. Isn't that sad?" He looked at her. "We'll visit my parents tomorrow."

"Are your parents in love with each other?" To know him was to get to know his parents.

He kissed the back of hand. "Deeply. I think the depth of their love for each other was my reason for remaining single. I didn't believe I would find that type of love." He squeezed her fingers affectionately. "But it existed for me." He looked at her. "I just had to go to Biloxi to find you."

Simone giggled as the doubt retreated. "I love you, Keithen."

"And I love you."

Keithen made the return drive home and after an early dinner, he and Simone were both exhausted and looking forward to a romantic soak in the bathtub. His housekeeper had been given the week off so that they could enjoy their time together in privacy. Simone went upstairs to run the bath, while Keithen prepared a tray of strawberries, chocolate, and chilled wine.

In the kitchen he surveyed his tray, liking what he saw. But something was missing. Whipped cream. He had just opened the refrigerator, thinking about what he would like to do with the sweet treat, when his brother's voice bellowed from the entryway. He left the tray in an attempt to head him off.

"So you are back?" Jay said, coming into the kitchen. His green eyes zeroed in on the tray. "What do we have here?" he walked around his brother. "Didn't take you long to get back into the swing of things. Is Courtney upstairs? I knew she would bring you home." He snagged a strawberry, biting in to it.

"So you sent Courtney to Biloxi?" Keithen said with understanding.

"Yeah, I had to force you back home."

"Hand over the key and leave. I'll see you tomorrow." Keithen tried to steer his brother out the back door, but the other man turned back around.

"You seem pretty anxious to head upstairs. I guess that little country girl couldn't satisfy your needs, uh?" He grinned like a teenager with a secret.

"I haven't heard any complaints," Simone said from the doorway.

Jay spun around with embarrassment. He stared at the woman dressed in a simple white eyelet sundress that graced soft curves, realizing who she was. A slow look from head to toe and he could definitely understand why his brother was so infatuated. Nice boobs and a pair of beautiful legs that he wouldn't mind getting his hands on, Jay couldn't fault Keithen for being distracted. She was younger than Keithen with a refreshing innocence wrapped in a hot little body made for pleasure. "Now that I've seen you, Simone, I bet you haven't." He licked his lips suggestively.

Keithen pulled Simone to his side. "Simone's my wife, Jay. I expect you to treat her with respect."

Jay looked from one to other with his mouth hanging open. "You're kidding, right?"

"No, he's not. Hi Jay, I'm Simone Knight, your sister-in-law." She smiled to herself as those words settled over her brother-in-law. She instantly saw the resemblance to Keithen. But there was a definite air of immaturity about him.

The flirtatious smile fell from Jay's face. He looked at the woman once again, but this time seeing her as a major complication. "Excuse us Simone," Jay said, grabbing Keithen by the arm. He dragged his brother out the back door, closing it behind them. He turned angry eyes on to Keithen. "What the hell is wrong with you marrying that woman? Please tell me that you made her sign a pre-nup."

"Wish that I could," Keithen replied calmly. "Actually, she offered to sign one, but I'm betting on our marriage."

Jay's face turned red with fury. "You're what?" he bellowed, then began pacing the patio. "I haven't met a woman yet who could make you behave so careless. What the hell did that girl do to you? Is she knocked up?" He paused to receive his brother's answer.

Keithen was furious. "Don't insult my wife."

"I'll take that as a no. So why marry her?" Then his eyes widen as he released a nasty laugh. "You couldn't get into her pants without saying I do first." Hi grin was cocky. "Oh, man I was worried, but hey enjoy your bride this week, but next week, get rid of her. I'm sure our attorneys can dissolve this marriage without paying her a dime."

"You are truly disgusting," Keithen replied angrily. "I married Simone because I love her, and I will not be getting rid of her as you say. My wife is here to stay and if you don't like it, then the hell with you."

"Dammit, Keithen, you sound like a love sick school boy. That woman could ruin your life and our business. What do you think our friends are going to say about your Nubian Princess? And what about our mostly conservative business associates?"

Keithen's eyes narrowed. "Are you upset because I married without a pre-nup, or because I married an African American woman?"

"Both, if you must know, but why a black woman? At least Courtney is one of us."

Keithen was speechless. It was long moment before he could speak. "I never knew you were a racist." He was disappointed. He stood looking at his brother with sadness.

Jay replayed his words realizing how they had sound. No matter how upset he was about his brother's decision, he didn't want him thinking the worst of him. "I meant of our circle. I'm not a racist, but I don't believe in making life more difficult than it has to be. Our friends won't accept her. You know what they're like."

"Then we'll make our own friends, and those conservative business associates that object to my wife can take their business elsewhere."

"You're ready to throw everyone and everything away for this woman. Have you introduced your wife to the folks?"

"I'm taking Simone to meet them tomorrow."

"Have you given any thought to what they'll think? I'm sure when they told us to get married and make them grandparents they never expected those grandchildren to be black. I know I didn't think of brown-faced nieces and nephews."

"You are a racist," Keithen accused. "All you keep spouting about is color."

"I'm not a racist," Jay declared, "but I'm honest. Did you ever consider little brown babies bouncing on your knee?"

Keithen glared at his brother, frustrated and furious, but he couldn't say he had. "Of course not, but it doesn't matter to me as long as they're healthy."

"Oh sure, that's what everyone says, but don't you want to be able to look in your son's face and see yourself. You'll never be able to do that now." Jay smirked because he could see the wheels of doubt turning in Keithen's head. "Look, I know Courtney is shallow and a bore, but she's well connected and won't turn off business associates."

Keith shoved his hands into his pockets, rocking back on his heels. He too had once been concerned only about social status and making money, but things were different now. "I love Simone and I have no doubt the folks will welcome her to the family. Should they not, under-stand, Jay, I will walk away from it all for that woman. Now, if you can't accept my wife or no longer want to work with me, then I suggest you find yourself another job."

"You are a damned fool. No woman is worth throwing away all that you've worked so hard to build. I don't understand you, and I'm the one everyone calls impulsive. Well I want no part of your marriage," Jay yelled. "I care what people think of me and want to continue to be welcomed by *our* friends." He stomped off the patio and around to the side gate leading to the driveway where his car was parked. He stopped long enough to deliver a final parting shot. "We'll see what the folks have to say about your bride."

Simone had watched the heated exchange from the window. Her stomach knotted with tension and the realization that the real world had come crashing in on their happiness. She had known that eventually they would encounter someone opposed to their union, but she had prayed that it wouldn't be Keithen's family. Now faced with the ugly truth, she waited to see what affect it would have on her husband, and their marriage.

Keithen stepped back into the kitchen immediately spotting Simone. One look into her hurt-filled eyes and he knew that she had witnessed the exchange between he and Jay.

"Ignore him."

"Can you?"

Keithen swept his eyes over her, noting that her back was ramrod straight, and that sweet girl that he had fallen in love with was a woman, no stranger to ugly bigotry. "Yes. You're my family and all that matters to me."

Simone let out an anxious breath as her shoulders relaxed. "I was afraid you were rethinking your decision to marry me."

The corners of his mouth tilted up as he walked toward her. "There is no regret in my decision. You are the best thing that's happened to me and I am honored to call you my wife."

Tears suddenly clouded Simone's vision. "It's the second time someone had questioned our desire to be together."

"And I'm sure your mother and Jay won't be the last." He pulled her into the security of his arms. "But they don't possess the power to destroy what we have, only we can do that by not believing in our love."

"That will never happen." She held on tight, listening to the steady beat of his heart.

"That's my girl. Now, how about that bath?"

Simone's stomach was alive with butterflies as Keithen parked in the driveway of his parents' San Francisco home. Her husband assured her his parents were wonderful people who cared about others, who had been the only ones to support his need to volunteer. But could they accept a black woman as their son's wife?. Jay hadn't been able to accept her. She took her husband's hand and stepped from the sports car.

Making their way to the door, she tugged on his hand, halting his advancement.

"What is it, sweetheart?" Keithen stared into Simone's stiff face. The smiling mouth that he loved to kiss was thinned into a strained line. Her eyes held uncertainty.

"What if they don't like me? What if they feel the same as Jay?"

"Simone, they're going to love you," Keithen assured her with a wide smile. He had faith in his parents. Jay on the other hand, he would just have to wait and see. He prayed Jay would one day accept his marriage to Simone. "You're just the type of girl my mother told me to look for." He folded her arm across his as he led them toward the house.

"She did? What type of woman am I?" She tried to relax.

He placed his lips close to her ear. "I'll tell you later and show you, too."

"Show me? That sounds interesting." Simone smiled lovingly at him as the front door opened.

Sandy Knight stared at the African American woman looking so adoringly at her son. She noticed that his expression was equally as affectionate. She smiled to herself. "You're both embarrassing me," she said, getting their attention.

Simone jerked around. She smiled guiltily at the older woman wearing a pair of blue jeans. Her salt and pepper hair was cut into an attractive style which flattered her heart-shaped face and brought out her hazel eyes.

"Oh, please, Mom. I've watched you and Dad making eyes at each other all my life."

"Something tells me you two will be doing the same thing."

Simone and Keithen exchange glances realizing that his parents already knew about their marriage, which meant Jay had informed them.

Sandy smiled at Simone, and pulled her into her arms. "Welcome to the family, Simone. Come with me, Dad's out back by the pool." She walked arm in arm with her daughter-in-law. "My husband and I were in Biloxi a couple of years ago. We loved the area. The resort we visited was simply breathtaking."

"And it will be again. Everyone is working hard to rebuild."

"I'm really proud of Keithen for getting involved. As parents, you worry that your children are so accustomed to having that they don't know how to give."

Simone glanced at the woman, surprised by her words. She relaxed a bit as she walked beside her mother-law. Perhaps she had been worried about their meeting for nothing.

"Jay came by yesterday evening to tell us about your marriage," Sandy said, changing the subject abruptly. She felt Simone immediately stiffen beside her. She patted the young woman's arm as she continued to speak. "He was a little upset and concerned."

Simone glanced behind her to where her husband walked. She could see that his green eyes had darkened, anticipating a confrontation.

"I reminded him that love knows no color, and family was more important than so-called friends," Sandy continued speaking. She looked back at her son and winked. "He'll come around to the idea of your being married."

"I don't think it's the idea," Simone spoke up.

Sandy looked at her shaking her head. "Jay could care less that you're black, Simone. He's worried about his social status. He has yet to realize that those people he calls friends, really aren't, and that true friends celebrate your happiness."

"I hope you're right because Keithen loves him," Simone said, softly.

"Jay loves his brother as well, and I'll tell you something else about Jay. Once he gets over what people think and truly gets to know you, he'll come to love you as well."

Simone had her doubts but as the day progressed and she got to know Sandy and Dawson Knight, she worried less about Jay's reaction. The Knights were a charming couple who never once questioned their decision. They had, like any good parents, given them words of advice.

"Never allow anyone, including family to come between you and Keithen, and always tell each other the truth," Dawson said to Simone as he led the way to the outdoor kitchen area.

She examined her father-in-law and liked what she saw. Big like his son, his hair was silvery gray. He too had green eyes. They were direct, open, and honest. His smile was easy, and the way he looked at his wife with love, made Simone like him even more. He looked the epitome of wealth dressed in expensive clothing with his gentlemanly manners; however, the more she listened to him speak, the more she realized he was a down to earth type of man.

"Life is so much better when you have the person you love beside you," Dawson said, smiling over at his wife. "Now young lady, my son has been telling me about Simone Place."

The women sat by the huge stone fireplace. The San Francisco evening was cool and the large fireplace was perfect for such a night.

"It's a beautiful piece of property, and the homes Knight Development will construct are desperately needed. The entire city is excited about the project." Simone smiled with pride at Keithen. "Your son is doing a wonderful thing for my hometown."

Sandy and Dawson noticed the loving expression cast in their son's direction and nodded at each other proudly.

"I'm told you can practically build a house by yourself." Dawson's eyes twinkled with humor.

Simone chuckled. "I don't know about all that."

"Are volunteers still needed?" Sandy asked with interest. She looked at Dawson for a response.

"Volunteers are very much needed," Keithen replied, sliding onto the lounge beside his wife. "And the people are very appreciative."

"I think I'll come down and help." Sandy was looking forward to joining the rebuilding effort.

"I think it would be good for your brother to get involved," Dawson suggested to Keithen. "Invite him back to Biloxi with you. Allow him to see what you and Simone have been doing."

Keithen jumped up, pacing. "Dad, I don't know if that's a good idea. Jay is upset about our marriage. Besides, he's too hung up on money, things, and having a good time to care about the people down there. Hell, he doesn't even care about my feelings. I don't have time for his foolishness."

Simone understood what Mr. Knight was hoping to accomplish with the suggestion. She was willing to try if it meant making Keithen happy. "There's nothing wrong with fun, sweetheart," Simone said, listening to the exchange. She gathered that Keithen had been saddled with the responsibility of helping his brother to mature. She touched his arm. "Perhaps time spent on the Coast with *us* is exactly what Jay needs. Right now all he knows is making money and the good life. Seeing firsthand what the storm left behind will give him an appreciation for what you're trying to do, and for what he has as well."

Keithen's facial expression softened. His wife made a good point. Hadn't being in Biloxi and getting to know the citizens changed him? "You're right. It and you definitely changed my outlook on life."

"That's not true," Simone responded with a shake of her head. "You were already searching for something meaningful."

"Seems like he found what he was looking for," Dawson chimed in. He liked his daughter-in-law very much. A sensible girl who didn't mind hard work was just what his son needed. The women in his son's social circle were so busy trying to please, they often made themselves boring. He didn't think his son would ever be bored with Simone.

Chapter Fifteen

Keithen didn't think he would ever get enough of his wife. He ran his large hands down to her bottom as he held her in place against the shower window. Warm water hit them from all angles as they made love. The sounds of their pleasure echoed off the walls

"You're going to be late for the meeting," Simone panted out between steady strokes. She and Keithen seemed to get better each time they made love. She tightened her legs around his waist as she rode him hard into another wave of pleasure. The sting of the water on her flesh only heightened the sensation.

"Forget the meeting." Keithen increased the pace, slamming into her. He wanted Simone's mind solely on him. He surged upward, repeatedly hitting the spot that made her purr like a kitten. Over and over he moved deep in the heat of her passion slick body, unable to get enough. He slid his hand to where they were joined and raked back and forth over the sensitive flesh, driving his wife crazy. Instantly, he was all she concentrated on, as she slid her body rapidly along the hard length of him, taking more. When she screamed his name, and then trembled in the afterglow of their lovemaking, he knew he had succeeded. He lowered her legs to the floor when she was able to stand again. They showered quickly, and then Keithen ran to get dressed.

"You look handsome." Simone wrapped her arms around Keithen's waist from behind. "Smell good too."

"I love you, Simone." He touched her face with his right hand. "You're so giving and understanding."

"So are you." She released him to sit upon the bed in her robe.

Keithen turned around. "I have to go, but what about meeting me for a late lunch? I'll send a car for you. Say one o'clock?"

"I'll see you then." She rose from the bed and stepped into his arms. "Be safe."

Keithen smiled all through the meeting as his mind kept replaying those words. No woman had ever worried about his safety, except of course his mother. He had definitely gotten lucky. The meeting finalized with him and Mr. Wong shaking on their deal. Knight Development would be building a gated community for the Wong employees. He left the conference room and returned to his office. He had closed the door before he realized he wasn't alone.

"What are you doing here?"

"Waiting for you." Courtney strutted across the floor to where he stood. She was dressed in Michael Kors clothing, looking every bit the epitome of San Francisco wealth. "How could you marry her and bring her here amongst our friends? Everyone will be laughing at me. Did you for once consider my feelings?"

"I'm really sorry if you're hurt, but Courtney, you and I both know we weren't in love. I'm not even sure you like me."

"Of course I like you."

Keithen noticed she hadn't said love. "Simone loves me, as I do her."

"I don't believe you, but who cares? What she doesn't know won't hurt." She slid a hand up his lapel. "We don't have to stop seeing each other. Men have had mistresses for years."

"I don't plan on being one of them. You really should leave," Keithen stated without emotion. He knew to get upset with Courtney would only serve to make her more desperate. He maneuvered around her, taking the chair behind his desk. He kept his facial expression blank.

"You can't just dismiss me. I'm somebody in this city and people expect to see me with you," she said, stomping a foot. She moved behind the desk to perch on the corner. She hiked her skirt high on her thighs. "We have a history together. I know how to please you."

Keithen hit the intercom. "Erin, will you come in here, please."

"What are you doing?" Courtney asked, alarmed. "Dammit, you were supposed to marry me," she shouted angrily. "She can't make you happy."

"She does make me happy, and I want you to find someone who will make you happy as well. You deserve that, Courtney, for putting up with my bad attitude and selfishness."

"Oh shut up, Keithen. I'll be around when you send her packing back South, but it will cost you."

The door to the office opened and his secretary walked in. She glanced at Courtney, who had her skirt high above her knees.

"Show Ms. Bounds out. She won't be returning," Keithen instructed the older woman.

"Yes, sir."

Courtney was embarrassed and furious. With her head high, she stomped out of the office and right into Simone. She gave Keithen's wife a slow look. Dressed as Simone was today in a stunning teal dress with her thick head of hair down on her shoulders, Courtney saw what Keithen saw. The woman was beautiful. She hated herself for noticing and pushed past Simone to storm out the door.

Keithen spotted Simone and jumped up from his chair. "I can explain," he said, taking his wife's hand. He walked her into his office, closing the door behind them.

"What did Courtney want?" Simone looked around her husband's office. The spacious area had huge windows and was stylishly decoreated. Plush leather furniture was arranged for a cozy sitting area away from the desk and drafting table. Books of the trade lined the shelves of a built-in bookcase. She turned around, taking it all in, including the numerous awards on the wall.

"This *is* like your home office." She glanced out the window and marveled at the Golden Gate Bridge. "Your view is spectacular."

"Courtney is upset about our marriage." Keithen came to stand beside her. He wasn't up to chit-chat.

"Will she be all right?"

Keithen pulled her into his arm. "She'll be fine, but you never cease to amaze me."

"Will you stop it?" Simone pulled out of his arms. "I'm not a saint. Far from it actually. When I saw her leaving your office, I wanted to slap her face and tell her to stay away from you. It makes me sick to know you've made love to her. And another thing, I want the bed in the master suite gone. I tried not to let it bother me, but it does. I refuse to continue sleeping in a bed where you've lain with other women."

Keithen heard what she said and agreed with the change of bed, but something more was going on here. He grabbed Simone's hand and pulled her over to the sofa, positioning her across his thighs. "I never made love to Courtney. If you were more experienced, you would know the difference between sex and making love."

"Is there a difference? That woman wants you and she sure as hell knows how to please you."

He looked at her, finally understanding. "Baby, you can't be jealous of Courtney."

"Don't tell me what I can't be." She jumped up angrily.

"You're my wife. My love." He joined her across the room. "My heart belongs to no one but you, Simone. You're all I want and need."

"You aren't going to grow bored with me?" She swept a wayward strand of hair from her eyes.

He tugged her against him, kissing her hard. "Never."

"She wants you back."

"She's not upset because she loves me. Courtney's embarrassed because everyone will know I married someone else."

Simone wrapped her arms tightly around his waist. "You people are really messed up."

Keithen chuckled. "I believe I already told you that."

"You did, didn't you?" She pulled back to look into his eyes. "Can you be happy in Biloxi?" She had her doubts.

"As long as you're with me, I'm happy."

"That's not an answer. You know we really have to talk about this."

"You're right, so let's get out of here."

Lunch was at a favorite restaurant of Keithen's. He had selected the establishment because the food was good, the atmosphere afforded conversation and the view of the bay was fabulous. The calming picturesque water worked its magic as they relaxed and behaved like newlyweds. Keithen smiled a great deal while holding hands with Simone. After ordering, Simone returned to the topic of Biloxi.

"I know you said we would build our home in Biloxi, but is that what you really want?"

"Yes. I was thinking of opening an office."

"In Biloxi?" Her tone was unbelieving.

"You sound like Jay," Keithen told her with a chuckle. "You of all people should know that the city is about to go through a major growth period. New business of all types will be moving in, and I want to be a part of that growth. And furthermore, I happen to like the slower pace of life the area offers."

Simone sat back looking at him. "You mean that, don't you?"

Keithen nodded. "Yes, I do. I want to make our life there. How many children were you thinking?"

"Two to start, and after that we can reevaluate the situation."

He raised her hand and kissed it. "But in the meantime we can practice."

"Shouldn't we wait for our meals?" Her eyes twinkled at the prospect of taking her husband to bed.

A shadow fell over the table. "I thought that was you," the new arrival addressed Keithen.

"Colton." Keithen rose from the table, shaking the man's hand. "It's good to see you."

"You, too." His eyes strayed to Simone.

The corners of Keithen's mouth curled up with pride as he introduced her. "This beautiful lady is my wife, Simone."

"Your wife?" Colton said with a surprised grin. He quickly stuck out his hand to her. "It's a pleasure to meet you, Simone. I'm Colton Caine, an old friend of your husband's."

Simone accepted the handshake while taking in the man's appearance. He seemed friendly enough. His smile was warm and inviting. Though tall like her husband, the man wasn't nearly as good looking. He was extremely thin with whitish blond hair and pale skin. But his large blue eyes were absolutely mesmerizing. She detected a genuinely nice person.

Keithen was realizing the same thing as his wife. For all the years he and Colton had known each other, he had never really considered Colton his friend. He wondered why. But as he stood there listening as he and Simone talked, he realized Colton was a humble man despite his family's enormous wealth. He didn't carry himself with the sense of entitlement Keithen and the others did. As he thought on it, Keithen realized Colton was always generous, donating his money and time to the underprivileged children of the city. This man would understand the personal journey he had taken. He invited Colton to join them.

"I have to tell you I was surprised when I heard that you had gone South to volunteer," Colton confessed as he sat down.

"I'm sure you were. God, I can't believe how self-involved I was. I guess it took me longer than you to realize we don't live in this world by ourselves." Keithen glanced at Simone to gauge her response to their conversation. When she covered his hand supportively, he knew he would love her forever.

"Doesn't matter how long it took, just that you understand." Colton noticed the private communication between husband and wife. He could feel the love between the two and was sincerely happy for Keithen. Although they hadn't been close friends, he had always known that there was a good man beneath the rich boy image. He had caught flashes of a deep thinking, compassionate man on the rare occasions they had talked. It was only when the others in their circle were around that the decent man took a backseat to the image. "I'm involved with a local group raising money for the hurricane victims. Tell me what's needed and how we can help."

So for the next two hours the three discussed the devastation of the Coast and what it would take to help rebuild lives. Colton asked sincere questions and offered his group's assistance. By the time lunch ended, Colton had invited them to his home for dinner the following evening, an invitation they readily accepted.

"I really like Colton," Simone said on the drive home as she admired the beautiful scenery. "Is he married by chance?"

Keithen glanced at her quickly. She looked so contented in the passenger seat. "No."

"That's a shame. Some woman is really missing out on a good man."

"You know, if I wasn't a confident man, I might be a little jealous." He laughed as she swatted his thigh playfully.

"Maybe you should be. He's rich, kind, and generous, too."

Keithen chuckled. "But can he make you purr like I can?" He looked at her and winked.

Simone laughed. "We're back to sex."

"Baby, my mind has never left the subject, before, during, or after our conversation with Colton. I was merely waiting to get you home."

A wanton tremor zinged down her spine. The now familiar ache for her husband began low in her abdomen. "Well, hurry up and get us there."

Simone stood surrounded by San Francisco's wealthy elite listening to tales of extravagant trips and shopping sprees, and expensive toys. A few whispered about their costly bad habits. Jay sipped on his drink in the corner silently observing her. She and Keithen had arrived at Colton's palatial estate over an hour ago. They had been met at the door by their host and a league of servants who had provided champagne and tasty

morsels. A soaring foyer with a magnificent chandelier and grand staircase screamed wealth. Their steps into the beautifully decorated living
room echoed on gleaming Italian marble floors. Simone was once again
awed by the wealth, but not wanting to behave like the small town girl
she was, she pretended to be immune.

Their arrival in the living room set off a hum of whispers and speculative glances from the milling guests. However, as the evening
progressed, their curiosity about her outweighed their sense of superiority. They all knew the general story of how she and Keithen had met,
thanks to Courtney and Jay, but they wanted to hear the details from the
horse's mouth. By the time they sat down to dinner, she was having an
enjoyable time. The conversation was good and the meal scrumptious.
Course after course of delectable food was set before them. Simone, the
chef, assessed each dish, mindful of aroma, appearance, and taste. She
enjoyed the meal so much she requested Colton to allow her to compliment the cook. When he arrived, the young man immediately recognized her from the New York restaurant.

Keithen sat across from his wife, unable to take his eyes off her. She
looked absolutely stunning in the black Versace dress. Her beautiful face
was smiling and animated as she spoke to the cook. Her joy in speaking
with someone from her line of business was obvious as was her pride in
discovering he had visited The Arbor. When the man continued to talk
while surreptitiously checking out his wife, Keithen suddenly realized he
possessed a jealous streak. That fact actually caught him off guard. Never
before had he cared what a woman did or with whom. It wasn't the same
with Simone. He was territorial and didn't give a damn who knew. He
glanced across the table and down to where his brother sat, and realized
that he had been watching him. He made eye contact briefly then
turning back to his wife.

Jay had never seen his brother so hooked on a woman before. He had
feared Keithen was going to physically shove the cook away from his wife.
He sipped his drink lost in thought.

"Will you be opening a restaurant here in San Francisco?" the cook
asked.

"This is exciting," Tara Farrington, real estate heir, offered. "I'm sure we could find the perfect location for you."

Keithen glanced at Simone, and for the first time saw a flicker of possibility in her eyes. He hoped she would give the idea real consideration. Now that she had his money at her disposal there was no reason for her not to pursue her passion.

Simone entertained the idea of going back into business for herself. She missed the excitement of owning a restaurant. The menu planning, cooking, and meeting diners were all aspects of the business she loved. Being married to Keithen, she shouldn't have any problem obtaining the necessary loan, but Biloxi was her home and where she wanted to open a business. Her city needed the revenue and she needed to be a part of the new growth. Maybe down the road, if the Biloxi restaurant was successful, she would consider San Francisco. She had to admit she liked the vibe of the city.

But first there was the position at the casino restaurant to decline. If she was working as a chef, it would be in her own place.

"My wonderful husband has been encouraging me to open a new restaurant." She looked over at Keithen lovingly. "However, if I do, it will have to be in Biloxi. The city needs the revenue and I have to support the growth."

"You should do it," Colton encouraged her.

"You're a woman of many talents, aren't you?" said a woman down the table.

Petite in stature, Shawna Townsend didn't try to hide her snobbery, or the fact she was friends with Courtney. Her collagen enhanced lips pouted with dislike. "You cook, build houses, and as I was told, don't mind getting dirty. Oh, and you wear one of those tool belts too," she stated with a smirk.

Keithen bristled. He knew Shawna was deliberately trying to embarrass Simone, by reminding everyone that she wasn't one of them. He also knew her actions were driven by her relationship with Courtney. Her sole purpose at the dinner was to be the eyes and ears for her friend.

"My wife can work with my construction crew any day," he boasted proudly. "And you're right, Shawna, she *is* a woman of many talents. But

I have to tell you, fellows, there's nothing sexier than a woman wearing a tool belt. I lost my heart the moment I saw her." He winked at Simone, who sat blushing.

Everyone laughed, except for Shawna. She tossed her brunette hair with displeasure. Red tinged cheeks brightened her unhealthy looking sunbed tanned-face.

"What exactly do you do at these homes?" Charlotte Wilson demurely asked Simone.

Simone dismissed Shawna and her cattiness. "Whatever needs to be done," she said jokingly. "I've learned frame work, drywall, roofing."

"I met her on a roof," Keithen told them.

"You're kidding!" Charlotte exclaimed.

"No. I'm quite good at roofing." Simone was very proud of her newly acquired skills, and no one was going to make her feel ashamed.

"I admire you so much," Charlotte remarked. A quiet, reserved woman, who was the epitome of a lady, longed to break the boundaries of what was expected. In Simone she saw an opportunity. "Do you think I could learn to roof a house?"

Laughter erupted around the table as her friends dismissed her seriousness. Embarrassed, Charlotte lowered her head and withdrew from the conversation.

Simone wanted to smack some sense into each one of them. Couldn't they see the butterfly trying to emerge from its cocoon? Of course not, because they were all so busy trying to feel superior.

"Sure you can learn. Before the storm, I didn't know how to do any of it. You're an intelligent woman who will learn quickly, just as I did. Anytime you want to come to Biloxi and volunteer, give us a call. We would greatly appreciate the extra pair of hands."

Charlotte sat tall in her chair, her blue eyes dancing with excitement. In that single moment, Simone made a friend for life. The woman chatted and expressed opinions she hadn't dared before. She and Simone made a lunch date for the next day.

Jay reluctantly admired the way Simone handled both situations. She hadn't given Shawna the attention she craved chosing to ignore her, but had gone the extra step to be nice to Charlotte. Beautiful Charlotte.

He had always liked the shy woman and had one time thought to ask her out, but knowing what the others thought of her, he hadn't bothered. He acknowledged for the first time that he lacked the courage of his brother to go against the crowd. He looked at his brother through different eyes.

"Your wife is a breath of fresh air," Colton leaned over and whispered to Keithen. "You did well getting away from this lot. Simone is intelligent and beautiful. The change in you looks good." He patted Keithen on the back.

"I like the change as well, and I couldn't agree with you more about my wife. She's inspired me to build a new affordable subdivision in Biloxi called Simone Place."

"I'm really proud of you, my friend."

"And your saying so means a great deal to me, *friend*."

"So what did you think of the gang?"

Simone stuck her head out of the bathroom where she was preparing for bed. She pulled her nightgown over her head and down her hips. It was good for a second or two delay. "Is this a trick question?"

Keithen laughed robustly from his prone position in bed. "Come on, give it to me"

"I'd rather give you something else," she offered, stretching out atop him. "But since you asked, they're not bad. A little spoiled, image conscious, but down deep I think they are decent people."

"What did you make of Jay?"

"I don't know. I noticed him quietly watching you."

"He was doing the same to you," Keithen told her. "I think you made an impression with them all." His large hands caressed her hips.

"I was a little uncomfortable." She stroked his blond head. "But I reminded myself that they were merely people."

"Have I told you how proud of you I am?" He looked at her, realizing her hair was longer than when they first met. It was soft on his chest where it touched him.

"I'm proud of us. We make a great couple."

Keithen tumbled her onto her back. "We also make great lovers."

"Oh, now you want to get back to my offer."

"Don't play hard to get. You know you want me." He pushed the pink short gown over her hips.

Simone framed his face and pulled him down for a kiss. "I want us to have a wonderful life together."

"We will. You have my word on it."

Chapter Sixteen

Simone stepped out of the black Porsche and handed the valet the key. Her bloodstream was pumping with adrenaline. Never before had she driven such an expensive car or one so powerful. But Keithen had convinced her into taking his *baby*, and she was so glad she had. The car was a treat to drive. The only thing better than driving his car, would be to have one of her own.

She headed toward the entrance of the chic restaurant, well aware this was the playground of the wealthy. Cars she had seen only on television or at the car shows rolled into the driveway, one behind the other. And the people who drove them oozed money, from their designer clothes and shoes to their diamond studded jewelry. Even their haircuts had come out of expensive salons. She checked her reflection in the glass doors, liking what she saw. The leopard print wrap dress, a gift from her husband, was beautiful and sexy. A smile touched her lips just thinking about him. Last night he had made love to her so sweetly tears had formed in her eyes. God, how she loved the man.

She entered the restaurant and marveled at the décor. The place was stunning, yet warm and inviting, the lighting perfect for a pleasurable dining experience. And the view looking out on the Golden Gate Bridge was spectacular. She approached the hostess and supplied her name.

"It's a pleasure to finally meet you, Mrs. Knight," the hostess said. "We were delighted by the news of Mr. Knight's marriage. If you'll follow me, please."

Simone did as requested, surprised that the young woman knew of their recent marriage. But as she followed, she realized people were looking at her. It appeared they all knew who she was as well. For a big city, San Francisco was starting to feel very small. She spotted Charlotte at a table up ahead. As she passed a party of six, a woman slid her chair out, blocking the way. She immediately recognized Courtney.

"Gee, look who came down off the roof," Courtney said, loud enough for those dining to hear. "The first time I saw you, you were covered in dirt and grime."

Anger, hot and explosive, set Simone's blood to boiling, but she wouldn't give this woman the satisfaction of knowing she was getting to her.

"*Miss* Bounds, isn't it?" Simone caught sight of Shawna trying not to be seen. Now she understood the comment about the roof. "Shawna, so good to see you again."

"You have some nerve walking in here like you belong." Courtney couldn't believe this woman had been invited to dinner with her friends.

Simone kept her voice low. The last thing she wanted to do was to embarrass her husband by causing a scene. "Say what you have to say because I'm meeting someone for lunch."

Courtney glanced in the direction of the table where Charlotte sat waiting. "It's just Charlotte, she's used to being kept waiting. And as for you." She turned to Simone once more. "Keithen will grow bored and send you back home."

"Like he did you? I don't think so. You see, my home is where my *husband* is. Have a nice lunch, ladies." Simone brushed past the woman without looking back. When she reached the table, she eased herself into the chair, laughing.

"I don't know what you said, but Courtney just stormed out," Charlotte whispered in awe.

"Ignore her. We came here for lunch and to enjoy each other's company."

The waiter appeared to fill their glasses with water and take their lunch orders. Once he stepped away, Charlotte giggled.

"Courtney's not accustomed to losing."

"The woman told me she was Keithen's fiancée when she arrived in Biloxi, and I believed her."

Charlotte shook her head from side to side. "No way. Keithen isn't like the rest of them. I always knew he would eventually outgrow the rich and spoiled phase. Courtney, on the other hand, is rich and spoiled through and through."

Simone chuckled. "And what about you, Charlotte? You hang around them." She sipped on her water.

"Fair question." She glanced around the room before looking directly at her companion. "The honest answer is it's easier staying in my comfort zone than seeing what else is out there. That's why I admire Colton and Keithen so much. They aren't afraid to venture out into the real world."

"Why are you?"

"This is all that I know." Charlotte ran her finger down the frosted water glass. "I know why people are my friends."

"I guess you all have to be extremely careful about who you befriend."

"Yes, we do, and it gets tiresome. That's one reason we all stick together, even though we really don't care for one another. Isn't that pathetic?"

Simone wanted to respond yes. However, who was she to judge these people? She hadn't lived their lives or been weighed down by enormous wealth. "You tell me."

"Of course it is. Courtney has no interest outside of money and trying to marry more. Shawna can't put together a decent conversation without consulting Courtney. And the guys would rather we not use our brain. So why are we friends?"

"Because it's comfortable," Simone answered understandingly.

"I've always liked Colton and Keithen. I knew they were different from the others. They play hard, but work hard as well. They treat me with respect and share meaningful conversations. Colton with his charities and Keithen with his drive for business have demonstrated to me that we can be more than the money."

Simone covered Charlotte's hand. "They're right, you know. My husband is. He arrived in Biloxi like all the other volunteers, working long hours for the simple reward of a humble thank you. When he climbed on top of that roof with me, I had no idea he was wealthy. And when I did, he was completely honest about the life he had led and what he was searching for. He's shown my family and friends kindness. The development he's constructing will provide housing for working class families who lost their homes in the hurricane, and can't rebuild on their property because their neighborhood are now designated flood zones. I know he could have built far more expensive homes on that same land and raked in the money, but he didn't."

"I watched him wrestling with the need to change. He would be with us, but not be a part of us. When the hurricane struck, he needed to get involved. I wasn't surprised when he announced he was headed South."

"Well, I was definitely surprised when this handsome man from California climbed on top of that roof with me. I had no idea I was looking at the man that I would love forever."

"He's head over heels in love with you as well," Charlotte told her. "I've never seen the man smile so much. And proud...that guy of yours can't stop talking about you."

Simone blushed. "We are foolishly happy."

"Will you wipe that damn silly grin off your face," Jay ordered from across the conference table. They had gathered to look over the development plans for the Wong project.

Keithen sat up straight in his chair and glanced at his brother. But the grin remained in place. "I'm sorry, Jay. Now where were we?"

Jay unleashed a string of expletives. "I guess I don't have to ask where your mind is."

Keithen rose from his chair. "Guilty as charged. I was thinking about my wife."

"You really love her, don't you?"

"Very much. So much so that...I've made a decision about the company."

Jay rose from his chair to join his brother by the small refrigerator. Things had been strained between them since that day on the patio. He yanked the refrigerator open and grabbed two bottles of water. He passed one to Keithen, then quickly opened his. "What decision have you made?"

"I was thinking I would open an office in Biloxi and work the Gulf Coast region, especially during the rebuilding period. You, as my partner, would take over this office, unless you still believe my marriage will ruin the business"

Jay couldn't believe what he was hearing. He slapped the bottle of water down on the nearest surface. "You're going to make me a partner after what I said?"

"Look, your response to my wife and marriage hurt, but we have a business to run. I'm hoping we can still work together.

"I wasn't trying to hurt you, Keithen, but make you think about what you were doing." He paused, thinking about Colton's dinner party. "They seemed to like Simone."

"What?" Keithen asked not following his line of conversation.

"The gang...the other night at Colton's party, they seemed to like Simone."

"Not Shawna," Keithen reminded him.

"Shawna doesn't like anybody unless Courtney tells her to." Jay frowned. "I may have been wrong. You and Simone seem to really love each other. I admire that you don't care what others think."

"I care, Jay, but following my heart and doing what I believe is right, is more important than what my so-called friends think." He left his brother with something to think about. "About the partnership, Dad left the business to you. You both think I'm a money hungry, hotheaded jet-setter."

Keithen nodded because everything his brother said was true. "You're young and I understand that, Jay. However, when it comes to your job performance, I couldn't ask for better. Your people skills could use a little work, which is why I'm asking you to return to Biloxi with me. I think seeing the destruction firsthand will help you to understand that there are more important things than having a good time and making money."

"I don't believe it, but I'll admit I've been leading the life of a spoiled rich boy." He looked his brother in the eyes.

"Hey, we both have." Keithen patted his brother's shoulder. "But it's time you step up to the plate and assume the responsibility of being a Knight."

Jay thought about his wild lifestyle. It had gotten out of hand this last year. "I'm not sure this is a good idea, but I'm willing to try."

"So you want the partnership?" Keithen punched his brother good-naturedly in the shoulder.

"You know that I do. I was a little hurt when Dad cut me out of the business." Jay shoved his hands into his pockets and he dropped his head. He thought about how he had retaliated. "I ran wild to get back at Dad. I knew he hated it, but I hated being left out."

"Well, now you have the opportunity to show him he was wrong about you."

"You're just trying to butter me up so you can run back to Biloxi with that pretty wife of yours."

Keithen looked at him surprised by the compliment. He returned to his chair and downed the remainder of his water. Tossing the empty bottle like a basketball into the trash can, he turned to his brother with another big grin on his face. "Is it working?"

Simone busied herself in the kitchen. She was planning a special meal for her husband and wanted everything to be perfect. She rummaged in what she had come to know as the junk drawer and located matches. A smile stole across her face as she realized that no matter the economic level, there was always a junk drawer. Taking the matches into the dining room, she lit the candles, and then stood back admiring the table. China, crystal and fine linens adorned the elegant table. She checked her watch for the time. Keithen should be home any minute. Heading back to the kitchen, she heard the key slip into the front lock.

Mouthwatering aroma greeted Keithen the moment he opened the door. Inhaling deeply, he dropped his briefcase by the door and followed the delicious smell into the kitchen. Simone stood waiting with a glass of

Cabernet. But the glass held no interest for him as he took in his wife's appearance. She wore a sexy lounge ensemble in the softest shade of pink. Cut in a deep vee, the silk T-shirt was slightly oversized and fell off her shoulders in a seductive fashion. Every time she moved, the shirt moved with her, making him believe he would eventually catch a glimpse of her breasts beneath. He realized as he watched her he was actually willing the damn thing to fall completely off. He finally accepted the offered glass and quickly downed the contents. Wine wasn't what he wanted.

"That's a two hundred dollar Cabernet, Keithen. You don't gulp it."

"You do if you want to get to the good stuff." He slid the glass onto the countertop and focused his attention on his wife.

"I have dinner ready." Simone knew that look. She smiled girlishly.

"I want you for dinner." He took a step in her direction.

"I've prepared a special meal."

"You are a special meal." He grabbed her hand and slowly pulled her against him. He kissed her lips. "You're sweet like sugar." A lick behind her ear. "Spicy like cinnamon." Love bite to the neck. "Delectable as chocolate."

"You've described dessert," Simone managed to say, ignoring the yearning of her body. She pushed against his chest. "Dinner first, then dessert." Her breathing was labored and her body temperature rising.

Keithen licked his lips as his eyes took in the changes in her body, smoldering eyes, flushed skin, and swollen breasts, all signs that his wife was as turned on as he. "All right, have it your way. I'm going to wash my hands. I'll be right back." Keithen laughed all the way to the bathroom. By the time they finished dinner, his sweet little wife would be ready for dessert as well.

Simone's eyes tracked Keithen's mouth as he licked butter from an ear of corn. Swift little flicks of his tongue danced along the slippery surface. And when his tongue circled his lips, licking away the buttery residue, she nearly screamed, *I'm next*. She sighed with relief when he moved on to the asparagus. But the mouthful of apricot-glazed lamb that she had forked into her mouth lost all taste as he began dipping the long stem into the cavern of his baked potato. The plunging motion took on a seductive rhythm that had her squirming in her seat. She dropped her head, unable to watch any longer. Maybe they *should* have had dessert before dinner.

"This is really good," Keithen complimented, trying not to laugh. Poor Simone was all worked up. She avoided looking at him, opting to steal quick glimpses. The color of her eyes had changed to a warm amber, and she was swinging a beautiful leg with barely contained energy.

"Yeah, I can tell."

"What?" he asked innocently, then proceeded to lick his fork suggestively.

Simone dropped her fork and rolled her eyes in his direction. "Now I know you're doing it on purpose. Your manners are better than that."

A smile played around his mouth. "Doing what, babycakes?"

Her response was to send her napkin sailing across the table. "All that nasty eating. My grandmother would swat your backside for being so vulgar." She struggled not to smile.

"I don't know what you're talking about. I was just enjoying my meal." Keithen laughed as a dinner roll hit him in the chest.

"Liar. You were trying to get to dessert."

"I think someone else is ready for dessert," he said, coming out of his chair.

Simone jumped up running. "I married a dirty old man." She ran into the kitchen.

Keithen stopped just in the doorway. "What the hell are you doing in the kitchen? I thought we were headed upstairs?"

"We are, but what's dessert without whipped cream?"

In the bedroom, Keithen made love to his wife with a ravenous hunger. His lovemaking had started off playful with liberal use of the whipped cream. However, as the evening progressed, so did the intensity of his lovemaking. He rolled onto his back and stared into Simone's surprised face when she realized he was allowing her to take the lead. He had to admit he was a little old-fashioned and loved being the dominant lover, but once in a while, a man liked to lean back and leave the work to someone else.

Simone didn't have a problem with that, liking the idea. She was more confident in the bedroom now and was ready to spread her wings. Flashing a flirtatious smile, she reached over, snagging the whipped cream.

"What are you going to do with that?"

"Have my way with you," she replied, squeezing it onto chest. But she didn't stop there. She continued to lay a line of cream, following along his treasure trail, until she had topped off the jewels.

Keithen's eyes flared with heat as he watched his wife working on that trail with her wet little tongue. She circled his nipples, and then pulled hard with a sucking motion that tightened his gut. His fingers tangled in her hair as she made love to him with her mouth. Between the warm wet licks, the pulling sucks, she added a few stinging love bites that made him groan from the surprising pleasure. And when her head went even lower, still eating away whipped cream, he nearly came up off the bed. He couldn't believe this was happening. She was a little tentative at first, but reading his response, she grew more daring.

Simone was surprised and pleased by her husband's response. She had never done this before and wasn't quite sure of what she was doing. But from his reaction, she surmised she must be doing it right. Emboldened, she took him into her body. She set a slow pace that drove Keithen crazy. He placed his hands on her hips trying to increase the tempo, but she wasn't having it. She removed his hands and placed them beside his head. She threaded her fingers with his as she sped up her strokes. Leaning forward, she kissed him deep while her breasts stroked his chest. Her tongue tangled with his while she continued to ride him, an up and down motion that was slowly increasing with each stroke. Releasing his mouth, she reached behind her to find him swollen and hard. Using her nails, she trailed them lightly over the heavy sacks, adding a new sensation.

Keithen released the F word because that's exactly what Simone was doing to him. She was showing him that the innocent girl was now a woman more than capable of pleasing her man. When he could think, he would ask where she had learned that trick, but as for now, he wanted some more of his wife's good loving.

Simone wanted more of him. Her body demanded all that he had to give. She rode him harder, faster with abandon, throwing her head back.

Keithen tried to stop the free fall, but it was too late. A final plunge into Simone's giving body and the world dropped away. He pulled her mouth to his thrusting his tongue into her mouth the way he had into her body, possessed by the hunger that she had created. His lips left her mouth to rain kisses over her face and neck. He pulled her down to his chest and held her tight. His heart beat rapidly with a love that ran deep.

"That was incredible," he said. His chest heaved for oxygen. "Where the hell did you learn the nail thing?"

Simone giggled. "I'll never tell."

"I love you so much, Simone." He pressed a kiss to the top of her head.

"I love you, too, big guy." She caressed his chest with soft fingers. "I'm so happy. You've shown me a world I could only imagine." She suddenly grew quiet.

He waited for her to continue. "Are you all right?" He rubbed her back.

"Wonderful. I was only thinking how much I've come to love this house. I've fallen in love with the Bay area. Everything is so clean and fresh. There's no destruction and debris." Once again she fell silent.

But Keithen heard what she wasn't saying. "You're feeling guilty because you're tempted to stay here instead of going back."

"Does that make me awful?"

He pressed another kiss into her hair. "Of course not, sweetheart, it makes you human. You and the people of the Biloxi have been dealing with so much. I'm not sure how you all have survived this long without having a breakdown."

"Sometimes I think it would be best if people simply walked away from the devastation. Just picked up and started life somewhere else."

He peered down into her face. "Is that what you want? You want to make our life here?"

After a long period of silence, he felt the first tremor in her body. The next thing he knew, tears ran down her face. He held on tight, not saying a word. He would bet this was the first time she had allowed herself to really feel the loss of the city she loved. The months of being strong for friends and family hadn't provided her with the opportunity to grieve for her loss. He lay there listening to her anguished cry, trying to imagine how he would handle coming back to his home city only to discover everything was damaged or gone, washed away in a matter of hours.

He recalled the last big earthquake San Francisco area had experienced. The destruction had been extensive with a double-decker freeway collapsing. There had been numerous casualties and people left homeless, and yet the entire Bay Area wasn't affected. In the smaller Gulf Coast cities, nearly everyone had been affected by the hurricane. In every direction there was a blue tarp, affectionately referred to as a blue roof, or no roof, he recalled, thinking of his first day in the area. Traffic was horrendous because the main bridges had been washed out. Grocery stores, which had fed the community, were no more. The few remaining stores were forever crowded with people despite the shelves being half empty due to slow deliveries and people stockpiling food. The minute a delivery was made, people rushed in taking it all. Everywhere one went you were forced to wait.

Eventually the tears quieted but Simone continued to lie where she was.

"You can stay here while I get the subdivision underway," Keithen said softly. He stroked her hair lovingly.

"No, I can't." Simone raised her head to look at him. "My family and friends didn't run away from the problem and neither will I. It's a weak moment for me."

"Weak is something you're not, baby." Keithen leaned forward capturing her mouth. But before the passion could evolve into another round of lovemaking, the telephone rang. They both groaned as he reached over to answer it.

"Noah? What's going on?"

Simone sat up at the mention of the project budget manager's name. She watched her husband's face closely, reading that something was definitely wrong. "What is it?"

Keithen looked at her, but didn't respond as he continued to listen to his manager. He didn't like what he was hearing. "Sit tight. Simone and I will be headed your way just as soon as the jet is fueled. I'll get to the bottom of this." He hung up and made another quick call to his pilot. Satisfied that they could leave in a couple of hours, he slammed the telephone down on the nightstand, swinging his feet to the floor. He grabbed Simone by the hand and pulled her from bed. "We have to get back to Biloxi. Someone has bought up the property surrounding Simone Place and will not allow us to bring the utilities across the property. My pilot will be ready to take us back in a couple of hours."

"You have a pilot?"

"We have a pilot. When I left for Biloxi I thought I wouldn't be requiring his services. How was I to know I would be getting married? I hope you didn't mind flying commercial."

"Sweetheart, that's all I know, but I am looking forward to seeing *our* plane. As for someone halting the utilities, it makes no sense," Simone said, stepping into the shower. Her mind was processing this new development. "Why wouldn't you allow someone to pay for the installation of utilities on your property? It's a valuable saving that makes your property more profitable."

Standing under the showerhead at the opposite end, Keithen agreed in silence. He was too angry to speak at the moment. Something bigger was going on here, but before he could make a plan of attack, he had to know who he was dealing with. He left Simone in the bathroom and returned to the telephone. He would need all the help he could get with this sneak attack.

"Jay, I've got trouble in Biloxi and will be requiring your help. We're getting dressed now. The plane will be ready for takeoff in two hours. Round up Tristan. I think his services are going to be required." Next he placed a call to Bobby alerting him to their arrival. The man had agreed to meet them at the airport.

Simone slipped into her undergarments while watching and listening to her husband. She was seeing yet another side to Keithen Knight. Tonight she was witnessing a shrewd businessman who didn't mind a fight. He was focused and his mind calculating on and off the telephone. She didn't bother him with questions as she could sense his mood was dark and in combat mode. Her heart swelled with love because he was fighting this battle not for himself, but for the people of her city. She felt truly ashamed for her moment of weakness.

On the jet, Simone couldn't take her eyes off Keithen. He, Jay, and the Latino private detective introduced to her as Tristan Cardenas had their heads together. They were all very intense men and she was thankful that she wasn't up against them. Dark and extremely sexy, Tristan ran down a list of contacts that he had already put on the trail of uncovering this new player. Jay read over Biloxi building laws online in an attempt to find a way around this roadblock. Keithen sat disturbingly quiet while both men spoke. Through the intensity of his eyes, she knew he was analyzing every aspect of the situation. She had faith he would defeat this enemy.

Chapter Seventeen

Bobby and Noah met them at the Biloxi-Gulfport airport early the next morning and quickly filled them in on the latest developments. Simone sat in the rear seat of the three-row van Bobby usually used to transport his work crew. Outside the window Simone saw that progress was still being made, but there was much yet to be done. The weight of the depressed city descended upon her. She glanced at Jay, who had elected to ride in the rear with her. On the plane he had taken a moment to apologize for his rude behavior and welcomed her to the family. She had accepted the apology, leaving the incident behind. He now sat stoically surveying the miles of damage as they rode along the coastline. His usually high energy personality was dulled by what he saw. His softly spoken comments indicated surprise at the magnitude of it all. He turned, looking at her. Taking her hand, he-in that single moment-became a true Knight man.

Simone smiled, having once again been a witness to the wonders of Katrina. In the midst of ugliness, a man had been born. That old saying of her grandmother's about God moving in mysterious ways sure fit the moment.

"Bobby, will you drop me off at my grandmother's?" Simone suddenly needed the comfort of her arms.

"Are you all right?" Keithen asked, turning around to look at her. Her crying last night had left him concerned, and now this mess was no doubt adding to her stress.

"Stop worrying. I had one moment of weakness, but today I'm back in fighting mode."

"That's my girl." He looked at her for several moments more before turning back around. He was more determined than ever to get to the bottom of the situation. Whoever was blocking the progress of this project was causing his wife anxiety, and he vowed to make them pay.

When Bobby pulled up in front of Miss. Ruth's house, he listened with pride as Simone informed Jay they had worked to rebuild her grandmother's home and the one next door.

"I met your brother up on that roof." She wore a silly grin as she looked over at her husband.

"Really romantic, you two," Jay joked. However, after seeing the state of the city, he was quite inspired by their work. He definitely wanted to be a part of the rebirth. "There's a great deal to be done here, and Knight Development isn't going to let some jerk stand in our way. We'll get this project back on track, Simone. You have my word on it."

Simone gave her brother-in-law a big hug. She looked at her husband once more and winked. She saw pride shining in his eyes. "You guys get going, but be back here around five for dinner."

"Ah, does that include me?" Bobby asked with a grin.

"Of course, I'll give Jaz a call and tell her to bring the kids."

Keithen slid the side door of the van open and hopped out into the stifling August heat. He helped Simone step from the van and pulled her into his arms. "Enjoy your time with your grandmother and try not to worry."

"Easier said than done, but I have faith in all of you." She kissed him.

"Stop entertaining the workers and come on in here," Ruth Ladner yelled from the front porch. "I've got breakfast on the table."

The sound of building welcomed them back. Several men called a good morning to Keithen and Simone as they made their way up the sidewalk.

"Hey, Carlos. How's it going?" Keithen yelled casually.

Jay watched and listened as more men and women greeted his brother warmly. They shared a story or two and a laugh before finally allowing him to proceed to the house. Jay found himself envious.

"How did you know that we were back?" Simone asked her grandmother.

"Bobby told Jasmine that you were headed back and…"

"And of course she told you," Simone concluded.

"And I knew *you* would come directly to me," Ruth responded with confidence. Whenever her granddaughter was trouble, she was Simone's source of wisdom or comfort.

Simone and Keithen looked at each other and shared a smile. They waved the others on into the house. Once inside, Simone made quick introductions. She assisted her grandmother with serving breakfast before taking a seat beside her husband. Ruth asked they all take hands, then motioned for Bobby to give the blessing. Afterward the conversation turned immediately to the current crisis.

"So what's the plan?" Ruth asked. "Jasmine told me everything. I can't believe someone would try to stop this project." Her dark features showed her ire.

"They have stopped it," Keithen replied. "The drainage and sewer lines are being laid, but the electrical, water, and cable can't be installed without crossing that land."

"But we're going to find out who's responsible and make them see things our way," Jay promised. He stirred the bowl of white creamy mixture beside his place with curiosity. Then he watched his brother add butter, salt and pepper into his bowl. Bobby dashed hot sauce into his. His sister-in-law added jelly to hers. He glanced at Tristan and realized that he, too, was trying to figure out what to do with the bowl.

"They're called grits, Jay, and they're really good. Here, add a little butter and salt," Keithen offered.

Simone laughed. She, too, had noticed Jay dubiously eyeing the bowl of grits. "They've become your brother's favorite."

"You try yours first," Jay said to Tristan, and received a round of laughter.

All eyes were now on the handsome detective as he took his first bite. "Mmm. That is good." He nudged Jay to encourage him to try them.

"All right, here goes nothing." Jay took his first bite and smiled. He quickly took another. "Miss Ruth, do you think you could teach me how to make these?"

The room erupted into laughter as everyone sat back to enjoy their meal. The only downside was the knowledge there was a crisis that had to be addressed.

Keithen looked around the table and laid his fork down. It was time to get down to business. "I hate to ruin the moment, but we have a project to get back on track."

"What do we do?" Simone had no idea how they were going to make the owner of that property give them the green light to come onto his property.

"Tristan is going to do what he does best. Make contact with a few local private detectives and elicit their assistance in unmasking our new neighbor," Jay stated.

"Bobby, has there been any rumbling about someone building in that area?" Keithen was trying to think of every angle.

"No. The news has all been about Simone Place. The community is excited, and hoping Knight Development will build other neighborhoods."

Noah, who had been sitting quietly at the table, suddenly spoke up. "We know one thing for sure about this new player, he has money to spare."

"Good point." Keithen's mind was working overtime. "We can't continue to sit idle. Noah, see if you can find us a storage facility close to our site. If not, purchase a couple of trailers and we can use them for storing building materials. I want to be able to hit the ground running when we get the green light."

"Good idea," Jay agreed.

Ruth Ladner sat listening to everything being discussed. They had a good plan, but in her estimation they weren't looking at the big picture. "I know I'm an old woman," Ruth said, drawing everyone's attention.

"Miss Ruth, you're the smartest woman I know. I mean next to my wife, that is," Keithen added, cutting a glance in Simone's direction.

"Oh, please. Go ahead, Grandma."

"I think you young people are missing the big picture."

"What?" Keithen asked.

"Whoever this is has your kind of money, Keithen."

"Agreed." Keithen didn't know where she was headed, but he was listening closely.

"Therefore you have to ask who your enemies are." Ruth held Keithen's gaze.

"You're saying this move is personal?" He suddenly pushed back his chair to pace the room. "I guess it could be possible."

Simone rose from her chair and began clearing the table. She couldn't believe someone would jeopardize the lives of others for something like revenge. "Who could you have angered here in Biloxi?"

"Another developer?" Tristan asked. "I'll sniff around and see if someone else had their eye on the property."

Ruth gathered dishes and carried them over to Simone. "I didn't know something like this could be done."

"Stopping a city project would be extremely difficult. However, this is a private development, and with the right amount of money, it's possible," Jay told her.

Simone tossed the dishcloth into the sink angrily and turned to face the others. "If someone has that type of money, you would think they would be putting it to good use, like trying to rebuild the area. Don't they realize innocent people are going to be deprived of homes?"

Keithen pulled his wife into his arms. "I promise you Simone Place will happen." He looked back at his brother and Tristan. Both men nodded in agreement, and he knew that they wouldn't stop digging until they unmasked the person behind the money.

"So how was California?" Jasmine had come over to help Simone and Miss Ruth with dinner preparations.

"California is wonderful. I absolutely loved San Francisco."

"And the honeymoon?" Jasmine wiggled her brows suggestively. "Was it good?"

Simone giggled as she checked the back door for her grandmother. "The man is incredible. He was patient and loving. He made me feel cherished." She flashed a radiant smile.

"You're happy."

"Unbelievably so." Simone picked up another apple and began peeling. "He has this huge window in a shower that overlooks the bay and downtown San Francisco."

"A shower, did you say?" Jasmine began to giggle. "Don't tell me the man had you naked in the window?"

Simone sliced apples without responding. Only the telling smile gave her away.

"Simone Ladner, you freak. You and that man did the nasty in the window," Jasmine squealed.

"Be quiet before my grandmother hears you." Simone laughed with joy. "I think it's become my favorite place to make out."

"Shameful. Simply shameful." Jasmine couldn't be happier for her friend. She deserved the love of a good man. "So tell me about his home. Any place with a window in the shower has to be fabulous." She took the string beans to the sink."

Simone stopped peeling apples. "His house is on Belvedere Island across the bay from San Francisco, and it's huge. Three levels with balconies on each level overlooking the bay and city. The master suite is the size of my entire house. And the kitchen is to die for." She suddenly grew quiet. "I don't know how he's going to be able to live in my little place. The man is used to the finer things in life, Jaz. How can he live here with me and be happy?"

"The man is in love with you, Simone. He'll live under a bridge just to be with you."

The women laughed as they continued dinner preparations. The back door suddenly opened as Miss Ruth and Miss Lorna came rushing into the kitchen. Miss Lorna was waving a piece of paper in her hand.

"Look at this, child." Miss Lorna collapsed into a chair, fanning herself.

Simone read over the letter given to her and felt her blood boil. A development company by the name of Highpoint was trying to buy up the hurricane-damaged neighborhood. With the community so financially desperate, their monetary offer would be snapped up without thought to tomorrow or their neighbors.

"This can't be happening," Simone whispered as she sat staring at the letter. "Right when the neighborhood is trying to come back, these vultures show up. Surely people in the community realize it can be rebuilt. We've already completed five homes." She felt anxious. She also knew at the pace they were going, people would be without homes for months to come.

"Baby, at our age, losing everything was real hard to take. Without you and the volunteers, Lorna and I wouldn't have been able to rebuild. People want to get back to normalcy." She walked to the front door and looked out over the neighborhood that she loved so much. She and her late husband, Leon, had moved into the neighborhood right after getting married. She missed him dearly, but was thankful he wasn't around to see what was going on.

"Are you all right, Grandma?" Simone placed her arms around the smaller woman. She had caught the look of sadness in her eyes as she left the room.

"I'll be fine. I just don't like people trying to take advantage of us."

"Neither do I. Come on, let's go join the others."

Miss Lorna, too, had a heavy heart, but she was spitting fire. "Probably some of those folk who want to build condominiums. Well, they can build around me because I'm not selling."

Jasmine glanced at Simone and smiled. She knew this developer was in for a fight. "Let's organize a neighborhood meeting to get a feel for the community on the subject."

"That's a good idea, Jasmine, the sooner the better." Simone picked up the telephone. "We should tell Keithen and Jimmy our idea since he's the councilman for this area."

Keithen escorted the councilman into the office where he had gathered his team. "Jimmy, I really appreciate your trying to help us." He quickly introduced the new arrival to everyone.

"I'll do whatever I can."

"Is there some way around this stoppage?" Jay asked. "I'm not above bribing somebody."

"Jay, please," Keithen warned. "The man doesn't know you and might believe you're serious."

Jimmy laughed. "Man, as bad as this city needs housing, I'm not above bribing the right person myself."

"I say let's identify this guy and give him an old fashioned butt whipping," Bobby said, laughing.

"That would definitely make me feel better." Noah pushed his glasses up on his nose. This delay was costing the company money and time, two things he didn't believe in wasting.

All eyes swung in the direction of the conservative budget manager. Mild-mannered Noah looked as if he could rip the mystery guy apart. Keithen knew how he felt. Not only were they losing money, but good people were still in trailers, waiting for homes. He couldn't allow this new player to hurt so many with his selfishness. But first he needed a name.

A knock sounded at the door. Keithen watched as Jay opened it. When he saw Tristan stride in, he prayed that he possessed the name of the owner.

"The name on the records downtown is Highpoint Development, which leads me to believe our mystery man wants to remain in the shadows," Tristan told them. He went over to the bar and removed a cold bottle of water from the refrigerator. "How do you people survive in this humidity?" He removed his sport coat and rolled up his sleeves. Cracking open the bottle, he downed the cold liquid in one long swallow.

Keithen turned to Jimmy. "Does the development company sound familiar? Are they local?"

"I don't believe so." Jimmy sat on the sofa next to Bobby. "There are about six major developers in the city and we see them all in front of the council when they're planning each new site. This one hasn't approached the council yet. Bobby, have you heard of them? I know you pick up jobs in Alabama and Florida."

Bobby shook his head no. "I'll call some of my contacts in both states and see if they know anything about this developer."

Keithen paced the room, pondering what little they had. A new developer with enough money to stop a major project and remain anonymous was in town. Since he wasn't interested in having city utilities on the land, he wasn't interested in developing. That in itself raised the question of what he had in mind for the property. And the matter of the owner being anonymous gave Keithen further cause to be concern.

"Jimmy, can you check downtown and see if there is a major casino player looking at property in the area? Possibly Highpoint has knowledge of someone wanting to keep the area commercial property. There could be plans for a casino golf course or something along those lines."

"Do you think this move was designed to force you to sell your property to them?" Jay asked.

Jimmy suddenly stood up. "This type of deal happens with golf courses. I have a few people who owe me a favor. Let me see what I can find out." He headed to the door as Keithen's cell phone rang.

"Wait a moment, Jimmy," Keithen said, reaching for his phone. "It's Simone," he announced to the room. "Hi baby, what's going on?" Keithen listened with interest to the news his wife was delivering. He walked to the desk and pulled out a notepad, writing down the return address as Simone read it off the letterhead. "Don't worry, sweetheart, we'll come up with a plan to stop them. Arrange a meeting with the neighborhood for tomorrow evening. Hopefully we'll get a sense of which way the community is leaning."

By now all eyes in the room were riveted on Keithen as those present tried to piece together the conversation. From the expression on his face, they all knew that it wasn't good news that Simone was delivering. They braced themselves for the latest as he disconnected.

"What's going on?" Jay asked the moment Keithen pocketed his phone.

"Highpoint Development is trying to buy up the neighborhood. Letters of interest were mailed to everyone. According to Simone, the money offered is just enough to lure those with so little into accepting the offer."

Bobby swore, striking the arm of the sofa with a closed fist. "Haven't we been through enough? We don't need people throwing around money, trying to buy us out."

Jimmy didn't like it either. "What they're doing is taking advantage of vulnerable people who aren't thinking clearly. And what exactly does Highpoint have in mind for the neighborhood? It's not in the designated gambling area so that can only mean one thing."

"Condos," everyone said in unison.

"Outsiders who don't care about our way of life are trying to turn us into a Miami for profit. We can't allow this to happen. We have to stop this guy before he ruins an historic neighborhood," Jimmy said in desperation.

"What we have to do is unmask this developer and discover his weak spot, then hit him where it hurts."

Chapter Eighteen

Ruth Ladner's home was a buzz with conversation about the phantom developer. Although the meal had been wonderful, and everyone had eaten their fill, the main focus was how to deal with the threat. A community meeting was to be held the next evening at the church to gauge the neighborhood's mood about the buyout. Simone hated to think about the neighborhood no longer existing. And what did a buyout mean for the church? She looked at her grandmother sitting quietly in the living room. Deep frown lines hinted at her troubled thoughts.

"Are you all right?"

Simone smiled at the sound of her husband's voice, and the feel of his strong arms around her waist. They stood in the open kitchen, looking into the living area. "I'm fine, sweetheart, but I'm worried about my grandmother."

"I noticed how quiet she was through dinner. I missed her feistiness." Keithen pressed a kiss into Simone's hair.

"She has the same forlorn expression on her face as when I came home after the hurricane. I can't bear to see her in pain again."

"I promise you that I'll stop this guy," Keithen whispered into her ear.

Simone loved him for saying so, but she feared that this developer might be more powerful than her husband knew.

Simone lay in her husband's arms discussing the current situation. They had left her grandmother's home and returned to her place. After being in Keithen's spacious house, hers felt especially small. And boy did she ever miss the shower at his place. But this was home, and her heart was with the people of Biloxi. That was why it was so important to stop Highpoint Development.

"I'm afraid people who can no longer wait for the insurance companies or volunteers to rebuild their houses are going to sell their property. They're tired of living in trailers and just want some semblance of normalcy. Highpoint is playing on their emotions."

Keithen lightly stroked Simone's hair. "It's understandable people want to get on with their lives."

"I know, but there's so much history in the neighborhood I would hate to see it reduced to a memory."

"What really angers me is that this company isn't offering top dollar for the land. Despite the physical destruction to the homes, the value of the land has doubled."

"They're preying on people who have lost everything."

"Jay and I are trying to figure out what more we could do."

Simone raised her head to look at him. "You're doing so much as it is. I'm proud of you."

Keithen leaned forward, covering her mouth. "To preserve the neighborhood we could buy out those that want to move. However, doing so could give the wrong appearance."

"You mean people would think we were making a land grab as well." Simone sighed with frustration. "Let's face it, you can't stop those who want to sell from doing so. But maybe we can tell them why they shouldn't."

There wasn't an available seat left in the church at the neighborhood meeting. People stood around the walls and in the rear. .

"People, please don't be fooled by this developer," Councilman Jimmy Archer told the gathering. "This company isn't out to help us."

"I don't know about y'all, but that money will help me," a woman to the rear of the church shouted out.

There were several muffed grunts and words of agreement.

"How far do you think that money will go?" Keithen spoke up. "Everything has gone up in price. Land, houses, furniture, appliances, and oh, let's not forget insurance."

"And let's not forget you're trying to sell houses," the same woman yelled. "I bet you won't be complaining about this money when some of us purchase your homes." The woman's tone was rude and insolent.

Simone had stood on the sidelines listening to the ongoing discussion in silence, but this woman was attacking her husband, and she wasn't having it. "If Highpoint Development has its way, you won't be able to purchase one of my husband's homes."

"What do you care?" the woman continued in the same tone.

"Obviously you moved into the neighborhood after I left," Simone replied. "I'm Simone Ladner-Knight. Miss Ruth, as you all call her, is my grandmother. I was baptized in this church. This is my neighborhood and most of you know me." She reached back, grabbing Keithen's hand, and pulled him beside her. This is my husband Keithen and you're right, he is wealthy...." She gestured for the woman to identify herself.

"LaTasha Williams."

"LaTasha, my husband could be buying up land for condominiums like the rest of the developers. Better yet, he could buy this entire neighborhood and turn Simone Place into an exclusive gated community none of you could afford. He isn't doing that. He came to the Coast after the storm wearing blue jeans and work boots. He pulled on his gloves and climbed onto rooftop after rooftop making repairs. He's worked tirelessly in this very neighborhood helping to rebuild lives. He slept in a trailer and ate the same food as all the other volunteers. Now tell me, what has the owner of Highpoint done for this community?"

"He's going to buy our property so we can move." LaTasha wasn't backing down.

"So you can move where? What homes survived the storm have been bought up. New home construction has doubled and in some cases tripled in price. Apartment owners are kicking renters out so they can cash in on the condominium craze. Highpoint knows this. They also know the majority of the homes in the neighborhood have been handed down through the generations, so the resale value isn't much. It's the land Highpoint wants and it's extremely valuable, but they know they don't have to pay top dollar to get it. We're living in tents, and in trailers, so they dangle this appetizing carrot before starving people counting on us to grab it." Simone walked toward LaTasha, holding her gaze. "And the one place your money could have gotten you into a new home isn't going to be built, because Highpoint has purchased the surrounding land and stopped the city from laying the necessary utilities, thereby halting construction. So you see, Highpoint doesn't care about where you live, just as long as they get what they want."

The level of noise rose inside the church as people expressed outrage.

"Look, I know everyone here is exhausted and desperate to be out of the FEMA trailers. And no one can stop you from selling your land, but before you make a deal with the devil, please reconsider and remember that a neighborhood is its people. Who'll make sure Mrs. Gilmore takes her medication each day if Mrs. Thompson moves away? And what about little Derek Simmons?" Simone pointed to the seven year old on the front pew. "Who'll watch out for Derek when he gets off the school bus if Mr. Duncan sells his property? And this church that has nourished our souls as well as many bellies, what's to become of it?" She fell silent before speaking once more. "There's history within these walls. This is where our parents and grandparents met and planned civil rights marches. The night before they marched down to the beach in defiance of the law, they prayed here for safety." Simone glanced at her grand-mother before facing the gathering. "If you are determined to sell to Highpoint, then at least demand more money, because I can assure you this company will be making a fortune when they put up high rise condominiums. The snowbirds will be flocking in to buy units and enjoy the beauty of the area you have come to take for granted."

Keithen watched his wife with admiration and a proud heart. The sometimes shy and insecure girl was a woman set for battle tonight. She moved through the room holding the gazes of neighbors and friends. She challenged those who were ready to throw in the towel and run to stay and rebuild by reminding them of their ancestors and the difficult times they'd had to overcome simply to own a piece a land. By the time Simone fell silent, there wasn't a dry eye in the building.

Suddenly a thunderous round of applause went up. People stood on their feet and began echoing her sentiment to stay and rebuild. Ruth Ladner rushed to her granddaughter with her heart overflowing.

"Young lady, when I looked at you up there in front of everyone, it was like looking at myself all those many years ago when we were fighting just to go to the beach," Ruth told her. "Your granddaddy, rest his soul, would be so proud of you."

Tears spilled from Simone's eyes. She knew how much her grandmother had loved and admired her husband, so those words were especially meaningful to her. "I learned from the best."

"And you learned well, child," Ruth said, framing Simone's face in her aging hands. "That husband of yours is pretty proud of you as well. I don't think his chest can expand any further."

Simone laughed as she kissed her grandmother's cheek, then spotted her husband smiling at her. She released her grandmother and rushed into his arms.

"I think Jimmy better watch his councilman seat, because there's a new voice in town," Keithen whispered into her ear. "I'm so proud of you, baby."

"I'm proud of me too, but, you know, no matter how much I love the Bay area and your beautiful house, Biloxi is home for me."

Keithen chuckled and pulled her against his chest, stroking her back. "It's home to me as well."

"You could really be happy here?"

"I've told you repeatedly I can be. As long as you're with me, babycakes, I'm happy."

"So what now? What more can we do?" Simone stepped out of his arms to accept his hand. She followed him back into the church kitchen, where their small group was gathering.

"I think we've done all we can here. It's in the hands of the community now," Keithen told her as they entered the kitchen.

Jay stood quietly observing the people in the room. Jasmine and Bobby began clapping when Simone and Keithen walked in. Ms. Ruth still beamed with pride and Jimmy gave them a thumbs-up. He had come to respect them all. He admired the love and respect they showed each other. There was no selfishness or backstabbing. They did all they could to help one another, and when one stumbled, the others were there to dust them off and lead the way. He finally understood what had attracted his brother to this city and its people. He could also see what had attracted him to Simone. Undeniably, she was a beautiful woman, but it was her inner beauty that was the appeal. "Simone, you were great. I believe you really gave them something to think about."

"Thanks, Jay." Simone walked over to him, taking his hand. "Thank you for being here. It means a great deal to me and your brother. He's very proud of you." She met his gaze.

"You know, I'm proud of me too. For once in my life I really care about something other than money and having a good time. Being here and seeing the aftermath of Hurricane Katrina really humbles a person."

"That it does, little brother." Keithen hooked an arm around his brother's neck. It felt good to have him by his side.

Jimmy walked over to join the threesome. He pointed at Simone. "I think I better watch my back. That little speech you gave sounded like a councilwoman in the making."

"Not me. I don't like public speaking."

Simone relaxed in the bathtub, enjoying the heat and bubbles. Candles burned around the bathroom as she soaked and thought over the meeting. She hadn't planned on speaking tonight. That was Jimmy and Keithen's job, but there she had been, defending her man and the community she loved. She smiled to herself just thinking about her handsome husband. She loved his beautiful eyes and the way they came to life when he laughed. And that booming laugh was infectious. His gentle touch and caring nature made her feel secure in his arms.

The door to the bathroom suddenly opened as the man of her thoughts walked in carrying a tray.

"What's this?"

"Oh, a little something for my warrior princess." Keithen winked at her as he set the tray beside the tub. "We've been so busy over the last several days with the Highpoint situation we haven't had much time for us. So tonight, I intend to add a little romance."

"Well now, what did you have in mind?" She checked out the tray's contents. Cheese and crackers, a bowl of strawberries, wine and two glasses.

Keithen left briefly and returned with an iPod and speakers. He placed them on the vanity and turned it on. Loud rhythmic music filled the small space.

"Not very romantic," she commented, pointing to the iPod.

"You're right, but it's perfect for a striptease."

Simone sat straight up. "Did you say striptease?" She chewed on her lower lip as her husband smiled flirtatiously. Leaning back, she sank into the warm water to enjoy the show. His shirt hit the floor while he perform a bump and grind that had her fighting back a laugh. Her husband wasn't the most rhythmic, but damn if he wasn't gorgeous. "Come on, baby, take it off," she screamed, getting into the mood.

Keithen began to laugh, missing a step of his raunchy dance. He knew that he was making a fool of himself. His moves weren't the smoothest, but to have his wife looking at him with so much desire was worth it. He worked his slacks off his hips, and then turned, wiggling his backside.

"Show mama what you got." Simone swung her hands over her head, snapping her fingers to the beat of the music.

"Be patient, woman." He stepped completely out of his slacks.

"I want to see the goods, big boy," Simone continued to scream. By this time she was laughing as well.

Keithen made quick work of the black briefs. Standing completely nude, he allowed his wife to get a good look.

Simone licked her lips as she slowly perused his tall form. She beckoned him forward. "Get in."

"There's no room for me."

"Sure there is," she purred, spreading her legs wide. "Get in."

"Yes, ma'am." Keithen stepped into the spacious old fashioned bathtub and settled between his wife's sprawled legs, sighing with pleasure as she drew him back against her.

"See, you fit."

He released a rumbling laugh. "You're being quite suggestive, sweetheart." He stroked her leg, leisurely.

Simone nipped his ear as she wrapped her arms around his neck. "You started it with that striptease." Her fingers raked his chest.

"Did you enjoy it?"

"What do you think?" She rubbed her nipples against his back.

"I think we should do this more often."

"I agree." She passed him a glass of wine before reaching for her own.

They sat in the glow of the candlelight enjoying the music and feeding each other. It was a special moment neither would forget. As the water began to cool, Keithen used his foot to turn the faucet, adding more hot water.

"We'll definitely have to include a large bathtub in our home design," he said, breaking the silence. "I thought the shower was fun, but a nice tub has greater possibilities."

"Will you get your mind off sex?"

"How can I when I'm positioned where I am?" He rubbed himself against her.

Simone laughed. "Can we have a window?"

"Babycakes, I'll make the whole damn wall a window."

Keithen stood and pulled Simone up. Together they stepped out of the cooling water and reached for towels. He attended to the bathroom while Simone retrieved the tray and carried it to the bed. He joined her in the bedroom. Dropping the towel, he slid under the covers with his wife, pulling her into his arms and kissed her head.

"The quiet around here still surprises me," he whispered softly, afraid to disturb the silence.

"That's small town living." Simone turned, looking up at him. "Sometimes it's too quiet."

"Is that what you thought, growing up here?"

"God, yes. It seemed nothing exciting ever happened." She munched on a cracker. "Now I pray for the return of boredom."

Keithen caressed her hair. "Every day it gets better around here."

"You're right, but with each tropical wave, the Gulf Coast collectively holds its breath." She laid her head back onto his chest. "I want to get back to cruising the Coast with the top down on the car, sunglasses on, and as little clothing as possible." She smiled, remembering what life before the storm had been like. "Just about every restaurant and club had an outdoor area. It was wonderful to dine on the beach. I've been thinking."

Keithen glanced at her. "About?"

"About opening a restaurant." She sat up, draping the sheet across her, and then faced him. She could see his pleasure with her decision. "Well, say something." She beamed happily.

"Tell me what you have in mind." He caressed her knee. He loved touching her.

"I want to bring that old Biloxi feel back to town. I would like to find a spot on the beach. Possibly rent space from a casino or beach condo."

"Would it be casual dining or elegant?"

"Ooh, listen at you talking my language," she teased, getting excited about the decision. "Elegant, with mood lighting and the option to dine on a veranda. But the Gulf view would be the main attraction."

"Sounds like you know what you want. Do your proposal and budget so we know what we're doing. Then we'll get in touch with a realtor and start looking at properties.

"Are you sure now is a good time?"

"It's perfect. We're on hold until we find a way around the stoppage, or Tristan uncovers the identity of the owner of Highpoint. Noah and Jay can see to the site, which leaves me to you."

"Thank you."

"You don't have to thank me, honey. I live to make you happy."

"Yeah?" Simone removed the tray from the bed, then climbed on top of her husband. "How about making me happy right now?"

"With pleasure, baby."

Chapter Nineteen

Simone and Keith hit the ground running a week later. They drove out to Simone Place to check in with Jay and Noah and to await a call from Tristan. While waiting, Simone made contact with the realtor they were scheduled to meet at ten o'clock that morning. She made herself at home in the outer office and went over her plans for the restaurant, compiling a list of everything she was looking for in a property. She vacillated between locating it in a condominium, casino, or a commercial site. By the time she had made her decision, Tristan was on the telephone. She wrapped up what she was working on and rushed to join the others.

"Go ahead, Tristan, everyone's here now," Keithen said over the speaker phone.

"For starters I'm in Atlanta. Highpoint Development is owned by a corporation called The Advantage Group. Since several names are listed on the records, it's going to take me a while to find the true owner."

"Read the names to me Tristian," Keithen requested. When the final name was read and he and Jay didn't recognized one, he instructed the private detective to keep digging.

"Will do, but I can tell you, whoever it is has money and connections."

"Are you being stonewalled?" Jay asked.

"You know it. I went to the address listed for the group and found an unflappable receptionist and a cagey guy in the office."

"Do what you need to do," Keithen told him. "I want to take this guy down and get on with the development."

"Be safe, Tristan," Simone called over her husband's shoulder.

Keithen glanced at her with a smile on his lips. That was so like Simone. She worried about everybody. "Take care."

"Will do."

Keithen pushed the button ending the call and leaned back in his chair, thinking over the conversation. Whoever owned Highpoint Development didn't want to be discovered. Why? And why the land adjacent to his? He was beginning to think Simone's grandmother was on to something. He had an enemy out to make his life difficult.

"You're processing," Jay said from his chair across the room. He had been watching his brother and knew that something was going on behind those piercing eyes. "Usually when you're quiet like this, it means you're plotting something."

Simone looked at Keithen closely. He did appear rather annoyed. She leaned down, wrapping her arms around his neck, cheek against his. "Am I going to need bail money?"

Keithen chuckled, reaching up to touch her cheek. "It won't come to that, although when I'm finished with this guy, he's going to regret crossing me." There was a tone to his voice that sent shivers down his wife's spine.

"Do you think we've stumbled into mob activity?" Jay asked.

Those words got Simone's attention. "We should forget about Simone Place. Sell the land," she blurted. "It's possible Highpoint wanted the property and we beat them to it." If the mob was involved, it wasn't worth the danger. She wouldn't have Keithen placing himself in jeopardy. "Possibly Highpoint will go away and leave everyone alone, if they get what they want. We'll look for another building site."

"Like hell we will," Keithen practically growled as he pulled free of her arms to stand. He looked back at her. "Your grandmother is right. This is personal."

Jay and Noah sat upright. They listened as Keithen began talking out loud, reviewing the timeline of events. They too came to the same conclusion.

"The only thing I can't figure out is who? I haven't been here long enough to offend anyone."

"We're not rolling over," Noah spoke up. He looked mild mannered, but when it came to dollars and cents, he was downright cunning. "Let's turn the tables on them and disrupt one of their developments. Something painfully expensive, preferably."

196

Jay liked the sound of that. "We could buy up supplies in the area. Or…recruit their subcontractors for some of our projects."

Simone was becoming increasingly uneasy. Business was one thing, but personal could lead to someone being hurt. "You think this is a personal attack. Isn't that all the more reason to let Highpoint have the property? Sell it to them." She came from behind the desk chair. Fear was visible in her eyes. "Let them have it and end this."

Keithen turned, hearing the fear in her voice. He motioned for the others to leave them alone. "Simone, this is what I do for a living. There are times when you cross paths with another developer."

"This is more than crossing paths, Keithen." She stomped around the room. "Don't play me stupid. This thing, whatever it is, has gone beyond business. You're talking about organized crime possibly. People get killed messing with those people. I don't want you hurt."

"Come here," he demanded, pulling her down into a chair. "Look at me." He squatted down in front of her. His stomach knotted just looking into her anxious gaze. "I don't believe this is organized crime. I've come across a few of those players before, and believe me, they have no problem letting you know you've waded into their swimming hole."

"Is this supposed to make me feel better?"

Keithen smiled. "I'm asking you to trust that I know what I'm doing. This is someone I know."

"Well, if it's not someone local, who has that kind of far-reaching power?" She stroked his face.

"Who has the money is the question." He rose and began pacing the office. Who had he crossed in the last year? He glanced at his watch, noting the time. "We have to meet the realtor."

Simone gawked at him in disbelief. "Who cares about the realtor? Forget the restaurant and the damn development. Sell it and let's go back to San Francisco." Tears swam in her eyes.

"Sweetheart, if I cut and run now, I may as well get out of the business." He squatted back before her.

"So get out." She suddenly dropped her head with shame against his shoulder. Her arms wrapped tightly around him. "I trust you to do what's best." She raised her head, looking into his eyes. "Let's go keep that appointment with the realtor."

Keithen sighed heavily with relief. He needed Simone strong. "Lead the way."

The eager realtor showed Simone and Keithen around the new condominium property. It was the last stop. The designated restaurant site was perfect for what Simone had in mind. Standing in the middle of what would be the dining room floor, she could imagine the linen-draped tables and the hum of diners. The corner location would afford the opportunity to have an outdoor eating area. She wandered into the kitchen, surprised that all the necessary appliances were already installed.

"So what do you think?" Keithen asked, coming up behind her. He placed his hands onto her shoulders and rubbed his chin against her hair.

"I can't believe no one has snapped up this property." She continued to look around the spacious preparation area. She could see the staff that she would hire, busy at work. "I want the location, but we need to go over the proposal." She turned in his arms. "I'm applying for a loan."

"A loan? Simone, that doesn't make sense. I can help you."

"You will. Being married to you will guarantee me a loan."

"You are so frustrating." He gave her a good shake. "You'll borrow the money from me. For your sense of pride, we'll have an attorney draw up an agreement between us."

Simone pondered the offer. "Deal." She stuck out her hand, but was pulled into her husband's arms for a kiss. They walked arm in arm back into the dining room.

"Will you be making an offer on the space?" The realtor's hopeful gaze swung between them.

Simone looked over at Keithen. "Yes, we will."

After the necessary papers were signed, Keithen whipped out a tape measure and got down to taking measurements. Simone shared her ideas with him. She pointed to where the dining tables would be set and the corner where the piano player would sit. She talked of color schemes and lighting. Keithen learned more than he ever thought possible about the restaurant industry. The only thing Simone didn't discuss with him was the name for the establishment.

"Have you thought about a name?" He shoved the tape measure back into his pocket.

"I'm tossing around a few ideas." She reached for his hand as they headed to the front door. "I'll let you know when I've decided."

"This is the new family room," Jasmine said, giving a tour of their home. It was still in the building stage, but her excitement couldn't be contained. "We've taken the opportunity to change those things we didn't like about the old house."

"You must be so happy, Jaz. It's going to be beautiful." Simone trailed behind her friend. She and Keithen had received a call from their friends to come see the rebuilding of their home. Framed, roofed, and dry walled, the house was taking shape. Bobby and Keithen were outside looking at the brickwork, while Jasmine showed off the interior of the home.

"I am happy, girl. It will be wonderful to be out of Mama's house. The kids are looking forward to having their own rooms again."

"And you and Bobby are looking forward to a little privacy," Simone sang in her friend's ear as they came to the master suite. She walked into the master bath and burst out laughing. "You hussy." Simone pointed to the large window in the shower.

"Girl, please, I'm trying to put a little spice back into the marriage."

"Watch out or you'll be having baby number four."

"Oh no, three is enough. What about you?" She looked at Simone, grinning.

"What about *me*?" Simone pretended ignorance.

Keithen and Bobby stopped outside the window at that very moment. From their animated expressions, and back slapping, it was obvious what they were discussing. The women turned to each other, laughing.

"Want to guess what those two are discussing?" Simone asked.

"The same thing we are," Jasmine said laughing. She lead Simone back through the house and around back to where their husbands stood.

"Simone, Keithen tells me you've located a space for a restaurant," Bobby commented.

Jasmine reacted with surprise. "You didn't tell me that you were going back into the business."

Simone blushed, because she hadn't planned on telling them. This was their moment to show off their house and she didn't want to rain on their parade.

Keithen read his wife's expression and realized he had let the cat out of the bag. He wondered why she would keep the news a secret.

"I would have told you about it later." She waved it off as nothing.

Keithen's cell phone rang. He announced it was the realtor as he answered. He held Simone's excited gaze. But as the conversation progressed, his head dropped as his anger rose. He slapped the cell phone closed, then stood facing the three people staring at him. "The bastard has someone watching us."

Simone didn't understand what he was talking about. "I thought it was the realtor."

"It was," he said looking at her. "Highpoint bought the property right out from under us."

"That makes no sense. Why would a developer want a restaurant property?" Then it hit her. "This *is* personal. Someone's following us."

Keithen unleashed a string of obscenities as he ran to the front of the property. He scanned up and down the street. Next he ran to his truck and began checking underneath it. Bobby joined him, knowing what he was searching for.

"Got it," Bobby shouted from the front of the truck. He pointed to a tracking device. "God, I thought this only happened in the movies."

Keithen crawled in beside him and swore. "Surveillance like this costs money."

"Are you going to remove it?" Simone asked, bending down.

"No. I don't want this guy to know we're on to him," he answered. "But I want him found. It was one thing to stop my project, but the neighborhood and Simone's dream are something else. I'm going to blow this guy out the water."

Keithen and Bobby crawled from under the truck and the couples said their good-byes. Keithen opened the door for Simone and helped her inside. "Bobby, I'll be in touch."

"Take care. Let me know if there's anything that I can do to help."

"Watch my back," Keithen called as he pulled from the curb.

Simone kept looking out the back window, trying to spot someone following them. She didn't like the idea one bit. "This is scary, Keithen. Are you sure this isn't organized crime?" It sure did seem like mobster activity to her. Of course, her knowledge of crime families came from books and movies.

Keithen reached over to take her hand and bring it to his lips. "I assure you this isn't organized crime. "This is someone striking back at me. I told you we were a ruthless bunch."

Simone was starting to agree with him. But the idea that someone he knew would go to such lengths for revenge was horrifying.

Keithen stormed into the site office fuming. Simone dragged in behind him and sat in the corner seat listening as Keithen brought Jay and Noah up to speed. Feeling as though their life had turned into a never-ending nightmare, she longed for the quiet days in California.

"Jimmy called while you both were out," Jay said, filling his brother in on the latest development. "The city is considering invoking eminent domain on Highpoint's property because they haven't made their plans for the property known, and our project is for the betterment of the city."

"I never thought eminent domain was a good thing until now." Simone looked toward her husband for a response. "Keithen?"

Brooding eyes swung in her direction. "The only thing that's going to stop Highpoint is to discover who's behind it and bring him down."

Tristan burst into the office. He had come directly from the airport and was energized with excitement. He quickly took stock of everyone in the room, before tossing a folder onto the desk. Leaning forward, he announced, "I've got your man." His dark eyes sparkled from the thrill of the hunt.

"Who is it?" the room chorused.

Tristan held up a calming hand as he gave them the background details. "I decided to track the money Highpoint Development has been throwing around, while my staff checked the names listed on the Advantage Group's records. The money traced backed to San Francisco."

"San Francisco?" the three men parroted.

"You heard me," Tristan continued."

"Why haven't we heard of Highpoint?" Keithen asked, puzzled.

"Because they're a rather small company that until recently has remained in the shadows," Tristan explained.

"Well, they're not in the shadows anymore," Simone offered.

"I don't see the significance," Noah commented.

Tristan beamed. "That's because I haven't told you the Advantage Group is owned by someone that you know quite well."

Keithen's brain was processing the information and when all the pieces fell into place his eyes went nearly black with outrage. "Andy Haywood."

"Who is Andy Haywood?" Simone asked.

"Keithen's nemesis," Jay told her. "From childhood it was always a competition between the two, with Keithen usually being the victor."

"It doesn't make sense," Keithen said, leaning back in his chair. "Andy is into commercial development and this is residential property."

"Listen to the rest of what I discovered." Tristan straightened. "In San Francisco, Haywood Construction placed bids on five city contracts and lost each one to Highpoint Development."

"But you said he owned the Advantage Group, thus owning Highpoint," Jay said, then fell silent.

"That low-life has two companies placing bids on San Francisco contracts." Keithen released a thunderous burst of laughter as he rose from his chair. "That scheming snake."

"I don't understand," Simone said. "Why would he have his companies bidding against each other? Wouldn't he just place the lowest bid?"

Keithen turned to his wife. "When a city is planning to build a new building they issue a public release welcoming bids from local and sometimes national contractors. The city establishes a budget, and then waits to see which company comes close to that magic number. The company who says they can construct the building for the lowest amount of money and least amount of time, wins the bid. There was talk a year ago when Andy's company, Haywood Construction won several city contracts. The rumor mill said he had someone inside city hall supplying him with the magic number. So, to throw suspicion off Haywood Construction, he established another company in Atlanta to submit that magic number, thus winning the San Francisco contracts."

"Is that illegal?" Simone inquired.

"Damn right it is, under several laws, not to mention failure to disclose this information," Noah answered.

"I hope your people are digging further," Keithen spun around, thoughtful. "I want the bastard followed. I want to know every move that he makes."

Tristan nodded. "I'm going to fly back home tomorrow. My guys are already tailing him."

"Can't we just go to the police now?" Simone inquired.

"We could, but then the Simone Place property would get tangled in legal matters," Keithen explained.

Simone nodded. "So what next?"

Keithen pulled her up from the chair and slid an arm around her waist. "For starters we find Andy's guy here in Biloxi and see what he can tell us. Then we get the dirt on Andy and make him an offer he can't refuse."

"Sounds like blackmail," Simone commented.

"Whatever works, baby." Keithen kissed the top of her head thoughtful.

Simone pulled on jeans, then sat down on the bed to tie up her work boots. She went to the mirror and brushed her hair into a ponytail. She smiled into the mirror as her husband's reflection appeared behind her.

"Where are you off to?" Keithen asked, placing a kiss on her exposed neck. He wrapped his arms around her middle, loving it when she gave him her weight.

"I need something physical to do while we wait, so I signed on to a crew in the neighborhood."

"I don't want you worrying, honey."

"I'm a natural worrier."

"That I do know," he said softly, looking at her by way of the mirror. "I fell in love with your caring nature."

"I fell in love with your great body."

Keithen chuckled with amusement. "Stick around and I'll share it with you."

Simone turned in his arms, looking up at him. She placed a kiss on his lips. "I'd love to, but I promised to work. I've been slacking since marrying you."

"Oh, blaming me, are you?"

"I'm foolishly happy in love." She wore a dreamy expression. "I want Highpoint or Andy gone from our lives."

"He will be."

Simone nodded and turned back to the mirror. She removed her wedding rings, placing them in the jewelry box. "Did you know Jay is joining me today?"

"No, I didn't. It will do him good to get involved." He sat down on the bed. "He's come a long way since arriving here. I think my father would be proud of him."

Simone turned back to him. "I believe someone else is proud of him."

"You're right, I am." He pulled her to him. "His interest in the community is genuine. He's been doing all he can to make sure the land is ready when we get the green light. He's discussed building more afford-able housing in the area."

"That's wonderful." She grabbed the keys to her truck and with one last kiss, dashed out the door.

Simone used the claw end of the hammer to pry loose the moldy drywall. Pulling vigorously, she was rewarded when a large section pulled free. A cloud of dust rose into the air as it crashed to the floor. The work was filthy and exhausting, but had to be done before the new drywall could go up. Breathing through the protective mask made the work difficult, but was quite necessary.

Tearing the last of the drywall out with her hands was a good workout. She managed to take her frustration over the Highpoint situa-tion out through the physical labor. Swiping her brow with a sleeve, she looked over at her brother-in-law who was also busy tearing out the wall. Jay had pulled on his gloves and jumped right in. He had left his wealthy lifestyle behind without complaint. She was actually quite proud of him.

She turned her attention to hauling out some of the debris. Locating a wheelbarrow, she shoveled up broken drywall, and then hauled it outside to the large metal dumpster. Then she went over to her truck and reached into the cooler in the bed of the truck. She grabbed two bottles of water and went in search of Jay. He was headed outside with another load of debris.

"Here, have a bottle of water and I'll go dump this stuff." Simone tossed her brother-in-law the container and made a return trip to the dumpster.

"Demolishing the inside of your home must be extremely heartbreaking," Jay said when Simone sat down beside him. They leaned against an aged oak. "I had no idea things were still so bad."

"It's getting better," she reassured him. "But it's people like yourself who are helping us to recover." She went to the truck, bringing back sandwiches, and retook her place under the tree, passing Jay a couple of sandwiches. "Keithen tells me he couldn't do what he does without you."

Jay laughed as he took a bite of his sandwich. "He probably told you I'm a hothead who needs to take life more seriously."

Simone nodded. "He mentioned it. He felt your father leaving him the business had something to do with your behavior." She pinched off the toasted bun.

"I'm thirty-years-old, and my father complains about my behavior, but you know what?" He looked directly into her eyes.

"You can tell me anything."

"I apologize for sending Courtney here. I didn't know my brother was serious about you." Realizing what he was saying, he fell quiet.

Simone nudged him in the ribs. "Your brother has been completely honest about his life. Why did you send her here? I guess you were hoping she would become your sister-in-law."

He picked up her hand while looking at her. "No, I wasn't. I was hoping she would bring him back so he could take charge of his business, and I could get back to mine."

"What is your business?"

"Having a good time, haven't you heard?" Jay frowned, losing the attitude. "I love what we do, and Keithen and I are a great team."

Simone detected a small hitch in his voice and a look of hurt in his eyes. "You behave the way your father expects you to."

Jay nodded. "I didn't see any point to becoming stuffy and mature. What was in it for me? He gave the family business to Keithen. It was always about Keithen. Giving the family business to Keithen told me what my father thought of me."

"That's between you and your father. Your brother has told me on several occasions you're a savvy businessman. He misses the closeness you once shared."

"He does?"

"Of course he does. He's also extremely happy to have you by his side now. I'm very proud of you as well."

He looked at her curiously. "I haven't done anything for you."

"But you have. Your support of my city and the people here means a great deal to me. And I've taken notice of the man my brother-in-law has turned into. I think it's the man his father always knew he could be." She squeezed his hand affectionately.

Jay chuckled self-consciously, letting her hand go. He took another bite out of his sandwich, proud of himself.

Keithen tossed the cordless telephone onto the desk top after speaking with Tristan. The investigator had spent the past three days in San Francisco running down leads and shadowing Andy Haywood. Unfortunately, there was nothing to show for the man's efforts, and the Simone Place project was still at a standstill. They needed a break in the investigation soon. The people of the Coast needed affordable housing and he intended to give it to them.

"Hey, Keithen, get out here."

Recognizing the urgency in Noah's voice, Keithen pushed away from the desk and dashed to the door. Shielding his eyes, he spotted Noah and three of his crew members and another man. The stranger was being manhandled by the crew as they marched him in the direction of the trailer.

"Who do we have here?" Keithen asked when the small party came to a stop before him. The man standing in the circle of his employees was young and nerdy looking, and obviously frightened.

"I was returning from seeing Jimmy when I spotted an abandoned vehicle on the side of the road. I got a little suspicious because it was a newer model car and didn't appear to be broken down. You know, no hazard lights, raised hood, or flat tire," Noah informed Keithen. "I called the guys and told them to head back my way and to be on the lookout for someone spying. Evidently, this guy heard the crew in the bushes and came tearing through the trees."

Keithen laughed. "And you were waiting at his vehicle."

"You know it, and on the backseat I found a sports bag containing expensive surveillance equipment. Another tracking device like the one you found under your truck was inside."

Keithen looked at the thin dark-haired young man with interest. He wasn't exactly what he had been expecting, but the man was obviously good at his job. He had fed key information back to Andy in San Francisco, halting the building of Simone Place and the purchase of the restaurant site. "You know what I want to know so let's not waste time. If you haven't noticed, the people around here are living in desperate conditions and your boss is standing in the way of progress."

The young man lowered his eyes to the ground, pondering those words. Deciding that this wasn't his fight, he spoke up. "All I know is that Mr. Haywood wanted me to perform surveillance on you and report back.

"You know more than that." Keithen's piercing gaze held the man's attention.

"I don't know anything else. Mr. Haywood said he was seizing an opportunity to stick it to you." The man stood nervous, awaiting his response.

"He would take advantage of a dire situation just for revenge?" Keithen glared at the man before looking at Noah. "God, was I that heartless?"

Noah shook his head no. "Your being here is proof you weren't. So what do we do about him?" he asked, nodding to indicate Andy's employee.

Keithen's attention focused once more on the young man. "What can you tell me about Andy? I'm sure a surveillance guy like you has something on the man to use at a later date."

The man blushed with guilt. He shifted from one foot to the other with nervousness. "I know he has a secret lover that he doesn't trust. He asked me for an audio surveillance system about a year ago."

Noah looked at Keithen with hope in his eyes. "He's bugging his lover? Who is it?"

"I don't know. He paid me well and I didn't get into his business. But I can tell you he's really into this woman. I heard him on the telephone confirming an out of town rendezvous and the tone of his voice completely changed."

Keithen chuckled. "The adulterer is afraid of being cheated on. You have to love it." He turned to the young man. "Kid, you have nothing. Andy's wife already knows about the other women and she's not planning on divorcing him."

Chapter Twenty

Tristan stayed two car lengths behind Andy Haywood. After a week of surveillance in San Francisco, he felt that his luck was about to change. He made the next right, mindful not to be seen. When Haywood made a sudden stop in front of a Nob Hill home, Tristan quickly whipped in behind a parked van and slid down in the driver's seat to avoid being spotted. In a couple of minutes it would be dark, affording him the ability to move in closer.

As Haywood stepped out of the Mercedes, the door to the house was eagerly thrown open. Tristan snapped several pictures of the house before making his way closer. When Haywood was inside the house, he crept onto the small porch. The numerous plants gave him protection from being detected. The blinds of the room were open and the lights on. He could clearly make out Haywood, but the mystery woman had her back to him. It soon became obvious she was doing a little dance for her man. She was a quite talented, from the look on Haywood's face. He took more compromising photographs. Then the woman turned around, and it all became clear. He quickly retraced his steps. He would sit tight and phone his information into the office while he waited.

Haywood was on the move again around midnight. From the direction he was driving, it was obvious that he wasn't headed home. It appeared the man did his prowling on Friday night like everyone else. They took to the highway. As sign after sign went by, it became clear Haywood was headed to Napa. When Haywood exited, Tristan followed at a safe distance until the car turned into a private drive. Pulling over, Tristan left his vehicle and jogged down the long drive, holding up behind a large oleander. He spotted Haywood using a key to let himself inside. A moving shadow in another window caught his attention. He needed to get closer. Taking off running, he stopped behind Haywood's car, moving to the shrubbery. The large front window was covered with drapes. He moved further around the house, checking each window, hoping for a view inside. He couldn't find one, so he retraced his steps to the bush to play a waiting game.

As the sun came up and there was still no sign of Haywood and the mystery person in the house, Tristan made his way back to the car. He needed to download those pictures and check in with his staff.

Back in Biloxi, Keithen waited for the photographs to download. He had read Tristan's account of previous evening with interest. However, the one thing the private detective had omitted from his report was the identity of the woman. An odd omission, but to be honest, he really didn't care about Andy's extracurricular activity. The man was known for his affairs. Why his wife stayed with him was beyond Keithen. Wealthy in her own right, she didn't need Andy's money. Something powerful kept her in their loveless marriage. He glanced over at the wedding photograph of himself and Simone. He ran a finger down her image, thankful for her love.

He picked up the printout of Tristan's report. The house in Napa was interesting, raising several questions, such as who Andy was visiting, and why they needed to meet out of town. But there was nothing here about his shady business practice. He had been hoping something would turn up in that area. The photograph continued to download. He could make out the top of a woman's head. Most likely knowing the woman's identity wouldn't be of much use in getting Andy to back off. He needed something the man didn't want exposed to hold over him. Correction, something to blackmail him into going away. It was out there. He read the passage about the house in Napa once more. It was possible that he was looking at the key. He leaned back in his chair watching the monitor as more of the photograph appeared. He suddenly sat upright as an image of Courtney came into focus. He now understood why Tristan had omitted the woman's identity.

A smile suddenly spread across his face. He was looking at the key to getting Andy to back off. He tossed the report onto the desk and hit the print button on the computer. Grabbing the pictures from the printer, he left his office and jumped in the truck. He reached for his cell phone and called Tristan while he drove. He needed him to keep digging.

"Tristan, thanks for the information," he said the moment the telephone was answered.

"Just doing my job."

"I need you to keep digging. We cornered Andy's surveillance guy who was shadowing us here in Biloxi. He told us Andy suspected his lover of cheating on him and asked for audio surveillance equipment. This lover may be the same person in Napa."

"I'll keep searching for information. I'm trying to find out who owns the house," Tristan told him. "We're still following Haywood. Ah, about…"

"Don't worry about it." Keithen turned at the next corner and pulled over. "I'll be in San Francisco later this evening. I'll be in touch."

"Are you going to see the woman?"

"You better believe it."

Simone spotted her husband's truck from the second floor window where she was working. She wondered if he had heard from Tristan. She took to the stairs, trying to brush away some of the dirt and dust. As she cleared the doorway, she saw Jay come from the side yard. He too was heading toward Keithen. They reached him just as he was putting away the cell phone.

"Hi. Didn't expect to see you out here," Simone said before giving him a kiss.

Keithen removed his dark sunglasses, sticking them into his shirt pocket. "I thought you both would be interested in this." He held up the picture of the woman. "The reason behind Andy's actions."

"That witch," Simone snapped angrily.

Jay scoffed. "Witch is too nice a word for Courtney. This was pure bitchiness. Keithen didn't want her and she used his enemy to strike out at him. I feel responsible because I sent her here."

"Don't. It was over between us before I came to Biloxi. Courtney was going to be angry no matter what. But there's more going on here," Keithen told them.

"Like what, sweetheart?"

"Andy wouldn't spend that kind of money and go to so much trouble for a woman."

"Perhaps he's married and doesn't want his wife to know about Courtney," Simone suggested.

Jay laughed. "He *is* married. Has been for several years now, and Courtney is not his first affair."

Keithen stared at his brother, happy with the transformation in him. He knew Simone was responsible. He pulled her against him and placed a kiss in her hair.

"So if he isn't afraid of being exposed, why did he help her?" Simone glanced up at her husband for the answer. "You think she knows about his shady business dealings?"

"He's afraid of being exposed, just not about an affair." Keithen puckered his lips in thought. "We have to find out what Courtney knows."

Jay nodded. "More like what Courtney is blackmailing him with."

Simone looked surprised. "You think she's blackmailing him into helping her?"

"I know that she is. Courtney wants what she wants, and will do anything to get it." Keithen spoke from experience.

"She wants you." Simone glared at him.

Keithen's features softened and the corners of his mouth turned up. "Well, she can't have me."

"Damn right she can't," Simone swore, pulling him down for a kiss.

"Okay you two," Jay warned, reminding them that he was present. "What are we going to do?"

Keithen kissed his wife one more time, then straightened and looked over at his brother. "I'm going to San Francisco to confront her. Possibly I can get her to call him off. If not, I've got Tristan following Andy. It seems Andy drove to a home in Napa after leaving Courtney. Apparently another woman was inside waiting for him, but Tristan couldn't get a look at her. He spent the night there hoping for an opportunity to see her."

"The man has another lover?" Simone couldn't believe the audacity of the guy. All she could think about was his poor wife.

Jay chuckled. "The secret is in that house in Napa." He tapped his fingers against his lips in thought. "Whoever he's meeting must be well known for them to go to such lengths to hide."

"That's exactly what I was thinking," Keithen replied. "Also according to his surveillance tech, he's been bugging the Napa house. Andy suspects his lover of cheating on him."

"Serves him right," Simone commented.

"So are you coming with me?" Keithen asked his brother.

"Try to stop me," Jay responded.

Keithen turned to Simone. "Sweetheart…"

"Don't sweetheart me, because I'm going with you." Simone stomped off toward his truck. She turned and tossed Jay her keys. "You can drive my truck. Your brother and I have something to discuss." She cast her husband a warning stare.

Laughing, Jay plucked the keys out the air. He was still laughing when he pulled off with a wave.

Simone and Keithen followed in his truck. As promised, Simone had plenty to say to him.

"There is no way you're going to see that woman without me."

Keithen shook his head, knowing that he wasn't going to win this argument. "Your presence is going to anger her."

"And your being alone with her is going to anger me. Now which one of us is more important to you?"

He just kept driving. This was one of those female traps that foolish men fell into and cowards like him ignored.

Keithen opened the door to their California home and stepped aside to allow Simone to enter. Following behind her, he acknowledged the place no longer felt like home. It was comfortable and familiar, but it wasn't where he longed to be. He looked at his wife climbing the stairs and acknowledged that home was back in Biloxi, the city she had taught him to love. It was in the house where she had made room for him. It was in her arms at the end of the day. He smiled to himself because he was starting to sound like a greeting card. Catching up to his wife, he placed a kiss onto her shoulder and hurriedly ushered her into the shower.

Later he and Tristan met in his home office to discuss the case. He wanted the situation resolved like yesterday. He wanted to get back to Biloxi and begin building Simone Place. The people in FEMA trailers and living with relatives deserved proper homes, and he intended to provide them.

"Where is Courtney now?" he asked the detective. They sipped on the cold beers Simone had placed on the lunch tray with delicious sandwiches.

"My guy reported that she's home alone."

"Good, then let's finish up here and head over to her place. I want to see if I can shake her up into giving something away." Keithen downed the remainder of his beer.

Tristan followed his actions. "What about Simone? Is she going to be upset if you go without her?"

"No. We discussed it and she understands that her presence will only cause Courtney to become defensive."

"You say that as though it were an easy matter. I've seen your wife's determined side, and I'm sure she had plenty to say." Tristan grinned, knowing that he was right.

Keithen laughed. "Oh, she said a great deal, most of which can't be repeated. However, in the end she trusts me to handle it."

"Well, let's get to it then."

Courtney glowered at the men standing in her doorway. She had known Keithen wouldn't take too long to realize she was behind his current troubles. She stepped back into the living room and allowed them to follow. She took notice of Keithen's tanned features and great body, recalling what it was like in bed with him. She missed that. Andy took the edge off, but only Keithen could quench the fire that burned. Oh, she wasn't in love with him, but she sure as hell wanted him, not to mention the lifestyle he could give her.

She slid into the white Queen Anne chair and stared at them. "Where's your little wife? Up on another roof?" She crossed her long bare legs flirtatiously, sneering at them.

"I didn't come here to discuss my wife," Keithen snapped, sitting on the sofa. He made himself comfortable. "You know why I'm here."

A peal of satisfied laughter filled the room. "You bet that fine ass of yours I do."

Tristan raised a brow in response to those words. He studied the woman appreciatively. If a man were into hot and sexy, Courtney Bounds was the right woman.

She noticed the gorgeous detective's response. She trailed her blue eyes down his hard physique. Her lips pursed with curiosity. "Mr. Cardenas, are you as good in bed as you look?"

"Are you as vulgar as your words suggest?" Tristan shot back.

"You know why I'm here," Keithen interrupted. "So why did you do it?"

"To punish you for humiliating me with that construction worker. Oh, correction, cook," she sneered angrily. "How could you dump me for her? Everyone expected us to get married."

"Married?" Keithen sighed. "Come on, Courtney, you and I had no intention of getting married. We weren't in love."

"Who gives a damn about love?" Courtney flew out of the chair. "It was about getting ahead. What we could accomplish together."

"I'm sorry if I hurt you, but enough is enough. Call Andy off."

"Why should I? I'm still without you." She folded her arms defiantly.

"You have Andy, be happy."

"You didn't think I had it in me, did you?" She walked the floor in front of him. "I learned from you."

Keithen raised a brow. "Know your opponent's weakness?"

"And his enemies." She laughed, reclaiming the chair. "What are you going to do, tell his wife?"

"She already knows about you and every other woman he's ever slept with. Karen is there to stay, but you know that." This time Keithen was the one to stand. He walked slowly to her chair, placing his hands on the arms of it. He leaned forward so that they were nose to nose. "Andy didn't do your bidding because of the sex."

"You did."

Keithen smiled sexily down on her. "You're blackmailing him."

There was a tiny flutter of her lashes before she controlled the action. "I don't know what you're talking about."

"Yes, you do." He whispered into her ear. "I know about the house in Napa and I'm going to tell Andy you gave up his secret."

"Keithen, you can't," Courtney pleaded, dropping the attitude. "If he thinks I told you, he'll be out for revenge."

"What do you think I'm after?"

Courtney's eyes flew wide as she followed Keithen and Tristan out the door. Her heart raced with fear. She hadn't planned for this response. She had thought he would scream and yell, but he had been controlled and quiet. There had been only one other time she had seen him that way, and the person who had crossed him had paid dearly for the mistake.

Keithen stepped onto the patio undetected. He spotted Simone in the pool swimming laps. She took his breath away with her beauty. Her gracefulness in the water didn't surprise him because she did everything with grace. He quickly shed his clothing and slid into the water, giving chase.

Simone swam over to the waterfall to await her husband. She had spotted him while making the turn.

"How did things go with Courtney?"

"Is that any way to greet your husband?" He pulled her to him, claiming her mouth in a kiss that had them both heating up.

Simone licked her lips when they came up for air. She held her husband's seductive gaze while sending her hand beneath the water. "Is this a better greeting?"

Keithen sucked in a breath as warm fingers encircled him. "Oh, yeah, baby."

"Now, how was Courtney?" She tightened her grip and gave him a smug smile.

"Sweetheart," Keithen squeaked with alarm. "She was cooperative."

"Was she?" She tightened a little more.

"Baby, it was strictly business." He gave him his best charismatic smile as he pushed aside the bikini top and covered her left breast with his hand. He began to tease the hardening nipple.

"Don't try to distract me."

"Is that distracting? I thought you were rather enjoying it." He kissed her.

"And what made you think that?"

"Oh, that little sound in the back of your throat you're trying desperately not to make." He lowered his head to her breast and clamped on to the nipple with his lips. Simone squirmed against him, but continued to squeeze, this time to excite. Keithen groaned deep with pleasure.

"Now who's making noise?"

He swam toward the shallow end where the stairs were, and pulled Simone along with him. He laid her on the steps and made quick work of stripping her bare. He wrapped her legs around his waist, leaned forward, and eased inside. The heat of her body clamped around his chilled flesh, sent goose bumps racing down his spine. He couldn't get enough of her.

Simone clung to him, using her legs for leverage. Her fingers squeezed his biceps, fighting off the climax that was threatening.

Throwing her head back, she gave herself up to exquisite pleasure as the world around her fell away.

"So what did Courtney have to say about Andy?" Simone curled up next to him on the sofa. They had left the pool for a quick shower and were now wrapped in their robes, sharing a bowl of fruit.

"It's not so much what she said, as what she didn't." He kissed her head. "She was blackmailing him with the identity of the person in Napa." He fed her a slice of apple.

"So she *was* responsible for what Andy did?"

"She knew how to hurt me and used my enemy to do it."

Simone looked at him. "So how does that make you feel?"

His eyes met hers briefly before glancing off into space. "Well, it doesn't feel good to know she would deliberately set out to hurt me. But like I've told you, we're a selfish bunch, only concerned about ourselves."

"You're not one of them any more." She took his hand and kissed his knuckles. "You found your humanity and care very deeply about others. That's how all of this got started."

"You're right, but we still have to stop Andy. I could bluff Courtney into giving away the significance of the Napa house, but…"

"But Andy isn't going to be so easy to bluff."

"No. When I face him, I'd better have the goods."

Chapter Twenty-One

Simone browsed the upscale jewelry store searching for the perfect gift. She was planning a birthday celebration for her grandmother when she returned home. Last night Keithen had suggested a pair of diamond earrings. She wasn't sure because her grandmother was a conservative woman, who only wore delicate pearls. However, the more she thought about it, the more she liked the idea. She could imagine her grandmother showing off a pair of diamond earrings to her friends. Simone giggled to herself as she spotted the perfect pair.

"Care to share the joke?"

Simone turned around to discover Keithen's friend Colton standing behind her. They hadn't seen each other since the dinner at his home. She smiled up at him, once again drawn to his friendly personality. "It was nothing. I was actually thinking about my grandmother, and her response to a gift of diamonds."

"Keithen tells me she's a pistol."

"He would be correct." She shared a laugh with him. "What are you doing here?"

"I'm here to pick up a gift as well."

The saleswoman approached Simone, offering her assistance. Excusing herself to Colton, Simone went about examining the diamond studs. She listened to the knowledgeable salesperson and made her selection. While waiting for her present to be gift wrapped, she continued to look around. She went to the watches where Colton was examining his purchase. Peeping over his shoulder, she admired the elegant gold watch with the woven diamond pattern in the band.

"It's beautiful."

"Thank you. It's one of a kind, designed by me," he told her proudly. He too waited while his gift was wrapped. "So what are you doing for lunch?"

"Actually I don't have plans. My husband is at the office and I'm on my own today."

"How about having lunch with me?"

"I'd love to." Her smile reflected her delight at the invitation. When the saleswoman returned with her gift- wrapped purchase, she moved over by the door and waited for Colton to conclude his transaction.

The two walked several blocks to one of Colton's favorite restaurants, stopping twice along the way to do a little window shopping. At the restaurant they were escorted promptly to a table and their drink orders taken. Simone glanced around, admiring the décor. The colors were cheerful, yet not overly bright. The patrons all seemed to be enjoying themselves and the food. She picked up the menu, studying it closely.

"I bet you check out every restaurant where you dine."

She glanced across the table. "I really should try being more discreet, but it's a hazard of the business. Another reason for my looking around is that I've decided to open another restaurant."

"Here?" His eyes danced with interest.

"No, back home."

Their drinks arrived and they gave their lunch orders. Alone once more, they returned to the conversation.

"I want to be a part of the economic revitalization," Simone explained, then sipped her water with lemon. "I've decided on fine dining. However, as I look around, I'm starting to rethink that decision."

"Well, whatever you decide, I'm sure it will be successful." He picked up his glass and made a toast. "To your success."

The waitress returned with the shrimp salad for Simone and the steak for Colton. The food was good and so was the company. They talked and laughed themselves right into dessert.

"You haven't said how Simone Place is going."

Simone looked across the table, not sure how much to say. "The project has come to a halt due to a conflict with another developer."

"The vultures are circling, I bet. Whenever there is a disaster, you have developers bumping into each other trying to buy up land for as little as possible."

"And the skies over Biloxi are dark with them." She prayed Keithen would be able to stop Andy Haywood.

Keithen shifted in his seat. He was growing hungry, and not for the cold sandwiches he and Tristan had been eating for a week. He wanted one of his wife's wonderful meals. He wanted to be in bed beside her now instead of sitting outside Courtney's home waiting for her and Andy to finish whatever they were doing. Hopefully, tonight would produce what he needed to get Andy to back off. It was out there, he just had to find it.

As he attempted to straighten his long legs, he glanced over at Tristan, wondering how he could look so comfortable after hours of sitting in a car.

"Waiting is what I do for a living," Tristan said in response to his curious stare. "It shouldn't be much longer."

"Hey, I appreciate what you do." Keithen settled back to wait.

Tristan knew Keithen had to be uncomfortable. Waiting was an art that not many people could master. "I admire what you're doing in Biloxi. For a man of your wealth, it would be easy for you to let the project go."

Keithen chuckled. "And go home to my wife? You have got to be kidding. Simone loves that city and to tell you the truth, I love it too. This project is important to both of us."

"The people there are gracious, and Miss Ruth is a joy to be around. She's a wealth of history and wisdom."

Keithen nodded. His grandmother-in-law was all that and so much more. "I see a great deal of her in my wife."

Tristan thought about that for a while. "They're both dedicated to the community. You don't meet people like them everyday."

"No you don't." He turned his attention back to the house. "You know, I'm really surprised Courtney is still seeing this guy. She knows we're on to them. She seemed really frightened the other day. I was sure she would run for the hills."

Tristan studied Keithen closely, searching for a hint of jealousy. He was pleased when he didn't find it. Keithen's remarks were mere curiosity. "It's possible she's trying to help you get the dirt on the guy. She no doubt knows his routine and therefore stuck to their usual arrangement."

There was movement in the house. He and Tristan sat up straight, alert and ready to go. It wasn't long before Andy rushed out the door and into his car. He placed a call on his cell phone while pulling away from the curb, then headed toward the highway.

Keithen and Tristian glanced at each other with excitement, sensing that tonight was the night for a drive to Napa. After driving for several miles it became obvious they were right.

"Do you think the mystery woman will be there?" Keithen asked as Tristan changed lanes two cars behind Andy.

"The way this guy is speeding to get there, you better believe it. But where the hell does he get the energy for two women?"

Keithen laughed deeply, thinking the same thing. He sat back, trying to contain his excitement. He glanced at Tristan, understanding why he enjoyed this line of work so much. Adrenaline was an addictive drug, and at the present moment, he was just as high as Tristan on the stuff. They continued to follow behind Andy until he reached his destination and eventually parked in the driveway. Tristan left the car on the road as he and Keithen ran to hide behind the large oleander. He pulled out the camera and snapped two quick pictures when Andy stepped onto the porch of the house. He snapped one more of him placing the key in the door. There was no other car in the driveway, so they assumed he was waiting for the lady to arrive. Their excitement mounted with every minute that past. But as one hour turned into two and two into three, they were beginning to lose hope. By one o'clock in the morning they decided to call it an night. The mystery lady wasn't coming.

"What do you think could have happened?" Tristan asked once they were back inside the car. He made a quick U-turn, switching on his headlights as they sped away into the early morning hour.

Keithen leaned back in his seat and closed his eyes, suddenly exhausted. "I don't know. Perhaps her husband didn't visit his mistress."

Tristan howled with laughter. "Man, you rich people are crazy."

"You're right, that's why I married up."

Tristan laughed, but his respect for Keithen grew with that one remark. The man had definitely changed over the last year. He had always been pleasant and respectful in their business dealings, but there had still been an air of superiority surrounding him. However, since going to Biloxi to volunteer and subsequently marrying Simone, he'd fast become just one of the guys.

"Changing subjects, are your people chasing down his city hall connection here?" Keithen wanted something, anything so he and Simone could get on with their lives. He wanted to come home to his wife every evening from work and crawl into bed beside her at night. Possibly they would have a child or two in a few years. Yeah, that's the life he wanted.

"My team is the best, and they're working every avenue to uncover the connection." He drove into Keithen's driveway and turned to face him. "I made Miss Ruth a promise I would get this guy, and I intend to keep that promise."

Keithen shook Tristan's hand. "Come by tomorrow. We'll put our heads together, and decide what to do next."

Simone was still awake when her husband slid into bed beside her. She rolled over, snuggling next to him.

"Why aren't you asleep?"

"I couldn't sleep without you." She placed her head on his chest. "Have any luck tonight?"

Keithen didn't answer right away. He instead placed a kiss into her hair. "The mystery woman didn't show."

"Oh no," she groaned.

"How was your day?" He stroked her hair, enjoying the quiet moment.

"Actually it was quite nice. I purchased the earrings for my grandmother. Oh, and I had lunch with Colton."

"How did you manage that?"

"He came into the jewelry store while I was there. We talked a bit, and he invited me to lunch. He really is a nice man."

"You're not still trying to marry him off, are you?" Keithen laughed when she swatted him on the stomach.

"I'm not trying to marry him off. I just think he would make some woman a wonderful husband." She raised up, looking at him. "Aren't you happy to be married?"

Deep rumbling laughter filled the darkness. Keithen knew there was only one answer to that question. "Of course, sweetheart." He pulled her down to claim her lips in a kiss. "I'm extremely happy to be married to you."

The next day around noon, Simone and Keithen welcomed Tristan into their home. A fabulous lunch was waiting to be served. Keithen escorted their guest to the deck while Simone went for the food. A cool breeze made the patio the perfect place for lunch. The men settled around the table relaxing and enjoying the view of the city. They discussed the events of the night before until the mouthwatering aroma of food captured their attention. When Simone walked through the French doors carrying a tray with their meals, Keithen rushed to relieve her of the heavy tray and held it while she removed each plate. She returned for the beverages, then joined the men around the table. While they ate, Keithen and Tristan filled her in on the previous night's stakeout.

"We waited for our mystery lady to appear until one in the morning," Keithen complained.

"And this is all we have to show for it." Tristan tossed an envelope onto the table.

Simone reached for the envelope. "What's this?"

"Are those the pictures you took?" Keithen asked, pointing to the envelope.

Tristan nodded, taking another bite of his muffalata. "This is wonderful, Simone. I've never had this before. Is there mozzarella cheese in here?"

"Yes and provolone." She smiled, pleased that he was enjoying a little taste of the Coast. She opened the envelope and removed the photographs. There was one of a house. The next one showed a man being greeted by a woman. Courtney. She glanced at Keithen, wondering how he felt seeing his ex with his enemy. "So this is Andy Haywood." She studied the photograph of the dark-haired man.

"That's the S.O.B," Keithen replied dryly.

The next photograph was of Andy Haywood stepping out of the car at another location.

"Is this the Napa home?" she asked, holding up the image.

"That's it. Unfortunately for Andy and me, he was alone last night." Keithen pulled the picture from her hand to stare at it. "Why couldn't the woman have shown?"

Simone didn't respond because she was examining the next photograph. She was surprised by the clarity despite the time of evening. "Your camera is awesome, Tristan."

"In my business you need the best," the investigator responded. "It turns night into day."

Simone could see that as she flipped to the next photograph. It was a shot of Andy letting himself into the Napa house.

"We have absolutely nothing." Keithen flicked a picture onto the table, agitated.

Simone retrieved the print from the table and placed it behind the others that she held. She started to slide them into the envelope, but suddenly stopped. Her heart began to pound with excitement. She snatched the top photograph from the stack and held it up for closer examination. She couldn't believe it. Surely she was foolish to think what she was thinking. But the truth was staring her right in the eyes. "Does Colton have ties to city hall?"

Keithen frowned. "Why are we discussing Colton? You aren't back on trying to marry him off?" He looked at her and noticed the attention that she was giving the photograph. He leaned over, examining it. "Why the question about Colton?"

"Just answer the question," she snapped.

"Okay." Keithen threw up his hands defensively and looked over at Tristan. "Sure he does. His uncle is Mayor Cates, but what does that have to do with anything?"

"This." Simone slapped the picture down on the table top. "I recognize this watch." She pointed to the enlarged photograph of Andy Haywood letting himself into the Napa house.

Keithen and Tristan both leaned over the image. It was Tristan who spoke. "Where do you recognize the watch from?"

She studied the photograph closely. The woven diamond pattern of the band was quite distinctive. "Colton purchased this watch yesterday as a gift. See the pattern on the watchband? It's a woven diamond pattern. I thought it was for a male family member."

"What are you saying?" Keithen asked, taking his seat. "I'm sure there are other watches with that same pattern. It's just a coincidence."

Simone shook her head no. "It's a one of a kind. Colton was proud to tell me he designed it."

"Are you sure?" He continued to look at her while his mind processed the new information. Of all the people in his social circle, Colton was the most honest and upstanding.

"You know what this means?" Tristan commented. He could see that Keithen was having a difficult time accepting the truth. He watched as he rose from the chair to stand overlooking the city.

"There's no mystery woman. Andy's having an affair with a man." Keithen looked back at Simone and Tristan. "It all makes sense now."

"Andy has been listening in on Colton's private conversations with his uncle, the mayor," Tristan spoke up, putting the pieces together.

"Colton is the son Cates never had. The two are extremely close and I'm willing to wager that Cates consults with Colton on city business." Keithen looked from Simone to Tristan.

"You've known Colton a long time. You never suspected he was gay?" Simone joined her husband and placed her hand on top of his.

"No," Keithen replied dryly. He threaded his fingers through his wife's. "I don't give a damn whether he's gay or straight, but I do care that he's being used."

"We have to speak with Colton," Tristan replied. He rose, approaching Simone. "Lunch was fantastic. At a later date you'll have to tell me how to make a muffalata."

Simone smiled at the handsome detective. "I'll write the instructions down for you."

"Thank you." Tristan turned to Keithen. "Want to come with me?"

"Just try and stop us."

Colton entered his bedroom and retrieved his overnight bag from the bed. Grabbing his car keys he left the room, excited to finally be on his way. A late evening problem at work had prevented him from making the Friday evening drive to Napa. He checked the kitchen one last time, making sure everything was turned off. Comfortable that all was in order, he headed to the front door and pulled it open only to come to an immediate halt. Keithen, Simone, and a man he didn't know were standing on the front porch.

"Hi. I was headed out of town," Colton told them as he stepped out onto the porch.

"By chance is your destination Napa?" Simone asked praying she was wrong about her suspicion, but knew that she wasn't. He was a nice man and she hated to see him hurt.

Colton stared at Simone with curiosity. "How did you know where I was headed?" He stepped back inside the house, waving them in. "We can talk in the living room."

The threesome followed him into a cozy sage-colored room. They sat side by side on the sofa, across from the overstuffed chair that Colton took. Keithen introduced Tristan.

Learning that Tristan was a detective, Colton was on pins and needles, sensing bad news. "What's this about, Keithen?"

Keithen removed the photograph of Andy entering their Napa getaway and passed it to Colton. "See anything familiar?"

Colton stared at the photograph, immediately recognizing Andy and the Napa house. Although his pulse had increased dramatically, he tried to remain calm. "It's a picture of Andy Haywood."

"Is that all that you're going to say?" Keithen challenged his friend with a pointed stare.

Colton exhaled heavily. He stood from his chair, still carrying the photograph, and strolled over to the fireplace. "What do you want to know and why?" he asked, turning to face them.

Keithen started to speak, but Simone's hand on his arm stopped him. Her eyes connected with his, begging to do the talking. He nodded, agreeing that Colton would feel less threatened by her.

Simone rose from the sofa and joined Colton at the fireplace. Her voice was soft and non-threatening. "Andy Haywood has been working behind another company named Highpoint Development. As a favor to Courtney to strike back at Keithen for marrying me, he has purchased land adjacent to Simone Place and halted the laying of utilities across the property. Without water and electricity, the project can't go forward. He has also been trying to buy up the homes in my neighborhood, for no other reason than to be a thorn in our side."

"I don't know anything about it," Colton said quietly. "I don't understand why he would do such a favor for Courtney."

"She's blackmailing him," Keithen told him.

"Blackmail? With what…" Colton suddenly fell quiet as everything fell into place. "She knows about us."

"Yes, she does. I recognized the watch in the photograph and knew it was the gift you purchased. We really need your help."

Intense blue eyes connected with Simone's and held her immobile. "Am I being blackmailed?"

"No. We're friends asking another friend for help. But there is something else that you should know."

"What?" He walked around the room, unable to sit. They had been so discreet and yet Andy was being blackmailed. He was waiting for the other shoe to drop.

Keithen took over the conversation. "Highpoint Development has also done business right here in San Francisco. They have received five contracts from the city." He waited for Colton to look at him, which didn't take long.

"I'm familiar with the name. What contracts?"

"The new museum and entertainment center. Highpoint Development recently won the contract on the new courthouse."

Colton was thinking now. He and his uncle met religiously every Sunday for brunch at the Napa house after Andy left. His uncle didn't know about their relationship, only that he was keeping an eye on the place for a friend living out of the country. He had been made welcome to use the place as his own. During brunch his uncle often discussed what was going on at city hall, and asked his advice. They often discussed the city's building projects and now that he thought about it, the price the city was looking to pay.

"That would mean Andy placed a bid against his other company, Haywood Construction. Is that what you're telling me?"

"That's exactly what I'm telling you." Keithen met his gaze across the room. He spelled it out to his friend. "Andy's surveillance guy provided him with listening equipment to bug his lover's place. He led the guy to think he suspected the woman of cheating on him. It's my belief he started this other company to squash speculation about inside information, after Haywood Construction won several city contracts."

"But that's illegal."

"Right again." Keithen could see that his friend was taking the news hard.

Colton's pale skin went impossibly white, almost translucent. It was obvious to all that he was stressed by the news. His eyes searched Keithen's. "He's been spying on me."

"I'm afraid so," Keithen responded.

Tristan stated the facts plainly. "You're gay lovers and Courtney was threatening to expose your affair to Haywood's wife, so he did her bidding."

"Karen doesn't care that Andy has heterosexual affairs. They didn't marry for love, but money and position. However, if she knew he was gay, she would sue him for everything. His business would also be ruined. Your common construction worker is as straight as they come." Colton suddenly felt exhausted. "He used me. I thought he loved me."

Simone felt badly for him. "I'm sure he loves you. The opportunity to gather information was just too good to ignore."

"What do you need me to do?" Colton collapsed into the nearest chair, his eyes dark and angry.

Simone unzipped her purse and removed an envelope. She passed it to Colton as her husband began speaking.

"I want Andy out of my life and out of Biloxi. The people there are hurting and don't have time for his games. You'll find legal documents selling the property he recently purchased to us. There's also a clause stating he will no longer pursue business in my grandmother's neighborhood, and any property he has purchased will revert back to the owner."

"And for doing this, you'll keep our affair a secret?" Colton took the papers, looking them over.

"Yes, I will, but if he refuses, I'll notify the authorities of his illegal dealings which will place him under an intense microscope. You'll be an innocent friend who was taken advantage of. Andy will never confess you two are lovers."

Colton smirked. "You're right, he won't. We've been together for two years. I've asked him twice to file for divorce so that we can live together, but he refuses. I've stopped asking because I know image and money are more important to him." He slapped the papers against his palm, then passed them back to Keithen. "I don't believe I should be the one delivering the papers. Do what you have to do to get that project back on track. The people need housing. I'll deal with Andy on my own."

Chapter Twenty-Two

Simone left the car at a run to keep up with her husband. He cut a path for the side gate as suggested by Colton. He had assured them they would find Andy around back lounging on the patio. Despite her running, Keithen's long stride still maintained a distance between them. Focused on removing Andy from blocking the way of the housing project, each of his steps ate up distance. He had tried to convince her to go home, but she had refused. She knew her presence would be needed to keep him out of trouble. His anger was on behalf of the people of Biloxi and Colton.

Finally catching up with her husband, she felt her heart beating wildly inside her chest. Not from the exertion, but from the look of outrage on his face. She feared that if Andy Haywood said the wrong thing, Keithen would lose all control and beat him within an inch of his life. She glanced behind her at Tristan dressed in all black. He looked lethal and capable of handling any situation. From his bulging muscles she knew that he would be able to stop Keithen physically, but she wasn't so sure that he would. He had learned a great deal about Andy, none of it good during his investigation. He too had expressed a desire for a piece of the man's hide. It would be left up to her to keep all parties as calm as possible.

Rounding the corner of the house, they entered the side gate. Just as Colton had predicted, Andy Haywood was lounging on a chaise as though he didn't have a care in the world. She glanced around, admiring the property. It was really a beautiful place with an infinity swimming pool. Tropical palms and plants created a private oasis.

The sound of the side gate closing caught Andy's attention. He turned with anticipation of being in his lover's arms. Seeing them instead, he slowly stood. The sight of Keithen Knight on the property set his blood to boiling. How the hell had he found this place? And where was Colton? He had phoned earlier saying he was on the way. How would he explain his arrival? They weren't actually known as friends.

He watched the threesome approach. The woman with Keithen was obviously his bride. The khaki shorts she wore showed off her fantastic legs. He had to admit the man had great taste in women. Her body wasn't as willowy as Courtney's, but curvy and fit. His attention switched to the man with them. He didn't recognize him, but from his laid back attitude and body language, he would guess cop or private investigator.

"What the hell are you doing here and who is that?" Andy asked, meeting Keithen across the Spanish tiled patio.

"This is Private Detective Cardenas, and he's uncovered some interesting things about you." Keithen smirked, enjoying the flicker of panic in Andy's eyes. He walked around the grounds admiring the landscaping. "Nice place."

Andy held firm to his nastiness while concentrating on giving nothing away. "Take your wife and flunky and leave the way you came. Make an appointment at the office if you want to see me."

Keithen shrugged nonchalantly. "I could, but then I would have to invite the press."

Brown eyes connected with green ones as they took measure of each other. "You're bluffing. If you had something it would already be in the headlines," Andy replied. He looked over at Simone. "I don't believe we've had the pleasure." He reached for her hand.

"Don't even think about touching my wife," Keithen warned. His lethal tone sliced through the air, halting the man's next move.

"Oh well." He lowered his hand. "I've had Courtney." He grinned, proud of himself. "And we both know what a sex kitten she is in the sack. Did she ever do that thing…"

"Okay, so you've slept with Courtney." Simone spoke up, not allowing him to taunt her with tales of Courtney's exploits.

Andy released a lascivious laugh. "There you're wrong, darling. A man doesn't sleep when Courtney is in his bed. Ask your husband." His barb struck its target. Simone flinched.

Keithen charged Andy from across the patio and pushed him up against the side of the house, planting his beefy forearm firmly against his windpipe. "I've allowed you to play your game too long. Now let me tell you the rules to *my* game."

Andy struggled, clawing at the arm cutting off his breath. His eyes grew large as he thought he would die from a lack of oxygen.

Simone grew alarmed and rushed to her husband's side. "Let him go, Keithen," she tried to persuade him. However, when he continued to apply pressure, she looked to Tristan for assistance, but the damn man merely shrugged his massive shoulders, then proceeded to stretch out on the chaise. Dismissing him as useless, she moved back to her husband. "Keithen, please. You're hurting him."

Angry eyes clouded with hatred swung in her direction. "Stay out of this, Simone."

"No. I won't. I'm not going to allow you to do this." She grabbed his arm and pulled. The man didn't budge. She utilized both hands, pulling against solid muscle, accomplishing nothing.

Keithen looked at his wife struggling to remove his arm and nearly laughed. The damn woman was determined to save Andy's worthless behind. He applied a little more pressure before finally releasing the coward.

Andy collapsed to the floor. He clutched his throat while coughing and sucking in air. When he was able to speak, he hurled more threats. "I'll have you locked up for this." His voice was low and raspy. "I'll buy up that whole damn city."

"Oh, I don't think so," Keithen replied. His expression was cunning as he leaned against a pergola pole. He placed his hands in his pockets, presenting the image of a man holding all the cards.

Simone watched her husband with new eyes. She had made love to the man and knew that he had an incredible body, but just now tugging on his bicep had been like trying to uproot one of the live oak trees back home. He had been immoveable. His arm had felt like a mountain of steel, and yet she knew no matter how angry he might get with her, he would never use his size or his strength against her.

Keithen was aware of Simone watching him. He had noticed her stunned surprise at his strength. He pushed away from the pole. "Tristan, please inform Mr. Haywood of what we discovered."

"With pleasure." Tristan unfolded himself from the chaise and walked in Andy's direction, holding up copies of the city contracts awarded to Highpoint Development. "We know you are Highpoint Development."

Andy briefly looked at the documents. Slowly regaining his footing, he glared defiantly. "Who the hell talked? I bet it was that floozy Courtney. What did you do to make her talk, take her to bed?" He hurled the insulting words in Keithen's direction. "You hear that, sweetheart? Your old man has been doing his ex."

"Do you want another forearm against your windpipe?" Simone asked, shooting him a menacing stare. She moved as far away as possible from the man. His disgusting comments were getting on her nerves. For the life of her, she couldn't see what Colton was attracted to.

Keithen looked at Tristan and grinned proudly. Reaching for the legal documents in his back pocket, he approached Andy and shoved the papers against his chest. "I'm putting an end to your roadblock of my Biloxi project. You're going to sign these and forget you know me."

Andy unfolded the documents and read. "Like hell I will. That property has increased in value since the time I purchased it."

Keithen leaned close so that they were eye to eye. "Let me spell this out for you because I can see you don't really understand the rules. Not only do I know about your illegal bids and your failure to disclose ownership of Highpoint Development, but I also know this place is where you and Colton come to be alone, if you know what I mean. Tristan over there," he pointed to the detective, "has been earning his money. I have several compromising photographs of the two of you."

Andy's face suddenly went ghost white. Beads of sweats dotted his brow as he stood there without a comeback.

Simone giggled to herself. She knew Keithen was bluffing, but old Andy had no idea and was now sweating bullets.

"How can you do this? Colton's a friend of yours."

"But he's a better friend of yours." Tristan waved the envelope of useless photographs.

Keithen jabbed a finger into Andy's chest. "You've made Colton your dirty little secret, running out here to be with him. And he is my friend, but Simone is the woman I love and I will not allow you to cause her heartache."

"I don't give a damn about those people down there or that property. I did it to keep Courtney's mouth shut. I don't know how the hell she found out about us." Then his attitude changed. "Look, Keithen, I care about Colton."

"Then sign the papers."

The next morning Colton followed through on his declaration to take care of Andy Haywood. In bold lettering, the newspaper detailed their two year affair and how Andy had bugged their lovers' nest to acquire information leading to city building contracts. The FBI had moved in to investigate his business dealings. The reporter had even provided a statement from Karen Haywood, who promised a swift divorce. The only person not mentioned in the scandal was Courtney. Simone tossed the newspaper onto the floor beside her, disgusted with the entire mess. She sat staring out the window. The city was coming awake and very soon everyone would be talking about the headline.

Keithen had phoned Jay last night after receiving Andy's signature and instructed him that the project was back on. He faxed the legal documents to Jimmy, who would present them to the city. It seemed everything was finally falling into place.

She sipped her cup of coffee, savoring the warmth against the cool morning. She didn't think she would ever get accustomed to fickle weather there. She longed for the heat of late September on the Gulf Coast. She picked up the newspaper again, thinking about Colton and how hurt he had looked when he learned of Andy's deception. She guessed in a way he had evened the score.

Keithen scooted in behind her, wrapping a warm blanket around her shoulders. His arms held her lovingly and securely. He didn't say a word.

"Did I wake you?" she asked, leaning back against him. She loved times like this.

"I missed you beside me."

"I'm sorry, but I couldn't stop thinking about Colton." She held the newspaper up for his inspection.

Keithen whistled, reading the headline. "Colton is stronger than he looks. He takes care of business in a big way."

"Yeah, and Andy deserved it, but I hate that Colton has been so publicly exposed."

"It was his doing, sweetheart." He reached for her cup of coffee taking a sip. "What Andy did was unforgivable."

"You know, what I don't understand is why he and Courtney slept together? She knew that he was having a gay relationship."

Keithen kissed her temple, loving her innocence. "People look at sexuality differently. Courtney didn't care that he was gay; she was after the power he wielded to hurt us, and who knows, Andy might have left Colton for her."

Simone shook her head. "God, you people are messed up."

Keithen unleashed a deep rumble of laughter. He held his wife tightly in his arms as he rocked her from side to side. "I told you that when we first met, but you still married me."

"And I would do it again, in a heartbeat."

Epilogue

The mayor said a few words of praise and encouragement to the gathering. Then reaching for the ceremonial oversized scissors, he joined Keithen in cutting the silk red ribbon. A round of applause followed. The first family to move into Simone Place received the key to their home. Simone, Keithen, and Jay joined them as they opened the front door and stepped in.

Simone looked around with pride. Her husband and brother-in-law had done a wonderful job of creating quality living with an affordable price tag. Bobby's brickwork added to the excellence of the home. There were minor detail elements inside that made the home grand. The floor plans were open and ceilings high and spacious. She smiled through her tears as the family laughed with excitement, moving from room to room.

Keithen's chest swelled with pride at their accomplishment. Of all the neighborhoods he had created, Simone Place would always be special to him. The people were so genuinely happy and appreciative that he was humbled.

As he looked around taking in the amenities, he was more than pleased with the finished product. His crew had worked non-stop from the day they received the go-ahead from the city. He had Jay to thank for staying on top of the details. His attention had been focused on his surprise for his wife. It hadn't been easy keeping her away from the site, but the planning and opening of her new restaurant had kept her busy.

Knights on the Beach had opened a month ago to rave reviews. The fine dining eatery was the place to be seen, and Chef Knight was the talk of the town. The family friendly Simone's Kitchen would be open in a couple of months in the subdivision. Miss Ruth and Jasmine would be managing the place. Simone had decided to bounce back and forth to keep the integrity of both restaurants. At that moment Keithen spotted Jay and received the nod that his surprise was ready for revealing.

"Where are you taking me?" Simone asked, holding tightly to her husband's hand. She was blindfolded and being led to places unknown.

"Just a little further." Keithen could barely contain his excitement. He led Simone into the center of the room and removed her blindfold. "Welcome home."

Simone opened her eyes and her mouth fell open. She turned in a slow circle, taking in her surroundings, her heart racing with excitement and love. Tears clouded her vision. She walked to the double French doors and spotted Simone Place across the field of grass. Keithen had duplicated the Belvedere home, minus the mountains, and given her another spectacular view to enjoy.

"I thought you'd like to decorate this one yourself."

"I would," she sniffed, fighting back a good crying spell. "I can't believe you did this for me."

"I know how much you love the Belvedere house."

"I do and I have it right here." She began wandering from room to room checking for accuracy.

"Come with me." Keithen grabbed her by the hand and took to the stairs. They entered the master suite and went into the bathroom. Simone burst out laughing when she spotted the large bathtub for two.

"Is that for me or you?" She smiled brilliantly at the man that she loved.

"Definitely for me, but if I'm happy, you're guaranteed to be happy."

Simone laughed because she was happy, and blessed beyond measure. Hurricane Katrina had caused immeasurable damage and ruined lives, but in its aftermath, she'd found love in the arms of a stranger.

About the Author

Giselle Carmichael was born into a military family. Now married to a career military man, she has lived from coast to coast, and several places in between. Two years of living in England afforded her the opportunity to travel extensively throughout Europe. Her experiences as a military spouse have given her a perspective on love and relationships that is reflected in her writing. Finalists in the 2005 Gayle Wilson Award of Excellence Contest with *Lace*, her works include *Magnolia Sunset*, *Life Goes On*, a novella, and *I'll Be Your Shelter*. Native of Birmingham, Alabama she now calls the Hurricane Katrina battered city of Biloxi home.

AUTHOR WEBSITE: Giselle loves to hear from her fans. Visit her at www.gisellecarmichael.com.

Parker Publishing, LLC

Celebrating Black
Love Life Literature

Mail or fax orders to:

12523 Limonite Avenue
Suite #440-438
Mira Loma, CA 91752
(866) 205-7902
(951) 685-8036 fax

or order from our Web site:

www.parker-publishing.com
orders@parker-publishing.com

Ship to:

Name: _____

Address: _____

_____

City: _____

State: _____ Zip:_____

Phone: _____

Qty	Title	Price	Total

Shipping and handling is $3.50, Priority Mail shipping is $6.00
FREE standard shipping for orders over $30 — Add S&H

Alaska, Hawaii, and international orders – call for rates — CA residents add 7.75% sales tax

See Website for special discounts and promotions — Total

Payment methods: We accept Visa, MasterCard, Discovery, or money orders. **NO PERSONAL CHECKS.**

Payment Method: (circle one):   VISA   MC   DISC   Money Order

Name on Card: _____

Card Number: _____ Exp Date: _____

Billing Address: _____

_____

City: _____

State: _____ Zip:_____